ONE AT A TIME, BOYS

SHIRLEY F'N LYLE, 2

CLAYTON LINDEMUTH

Edited by
GAIL LAMBERT

SHIRLEY F'N LYLE

ONE AT A TIME, BOYS

Clayton Lindemuth
Hardgrave Enterprises
SAINT CHARLES, MISSOURI

SHIRLEY F'N LYLE: ONE at a TIME, BOYS/Clayton Lindemuth

ISBN: 9781706218104

✾ Created with Vellum

ALSO BY CLAYTON LINDEMUTH

TREAD

SOLOMON BULL

COLD QUIET COUNTRY

SOMETIMES BONE

NOTHING SAVE THE BONES INSIDE HER

MY BROTHER'S DESTROYER

THE MUNDANE WORK OF VENGEANCE

PRETTY LIKE AN UGLY GIRL

THE OUTLAW STINKY JOE

STRONG AT THE BROKEN PLACES

SHIRLEY F'N LYLE

FOR: KATHRYN PYNCH

FOREWORD

I don't like chic lit at all and I'm also less likely to read books with female protagonists written by men. It seems like men really don't know how women think or feel.

This book isn't chic lit; it's everybody lit.

This is Shirley's story but there are quite a few male characters that are fleshed out and often oily.

Shirley's reaction to them are spot on.

Also spot on is Shirley herself, right down to how difficult it can be to be a heavy woman. It's wonderful to read about a very real character with this kind of challenge that doesn't have any fat shaming or ridiculing humor involved.

I like Shirley.

I like the fact that she's also liked.

Somehow Clayton took this out of the chic lit genre and carved a place of his own: Every day American people dealing with other-side-of-the-tracks problems and taking care of business head on.

This life needs living and shit happens every day. Let's get it done. I'll be reading on eagerly to see where we go next.

— Kathryn Pynch

1

*A*mericans couldn't be this stupid, could they?

As Burian Tkach suspected, the big nosed government man in the black sedan followed Lester turn for turn.

Burian's primary target drove a black Dodge Durango and didn't seem to mind the caravan following her. Lester trailed the Durango at a distance that suggested skills in the art. But the black sedan stayed close on him, as if they worked in tandem but got confused as to which car should be on, and which should be waiting.

Riding a BMW motorcycle Burian kept his distance, only closing in to ensure he never lost them on a turn.

Lester was his third priority, after Shirley Lyle and the blond girl, Ulyana. Women usually offered scant resistance. Killing them was like killing children: simple, but sometimes distasteful. If Lester was available afterward, Burian might conclude his work quickly. Otherwise, he would wait until night and shoot the old man while he slept. Either way, his master, Vanko Demyan, had suggested his quick success would be rewarded with a return to Mother Russia.

They neared the house where police had arrived earlier and his target — Shirley Lyle — left with a man. After following each other to the strip club, everyone scattered and then re-formed on the same road, ostensibly returning to the same house they'd just left. The next right turn would tell.

Far ahead and visible as splashes of black between the trees, the Durango turned right.

Burian slowed.

Why would Shirley return to the same house?

Vanko had told him that Shirley was searching for his other target, Ulyana, who had gone missing. If Shirley believed her to be at this house, but the police had quickly cleared it, perhaps she had gone to the strip club to waste time before returning. Or maybe the woman at the house gave her a story she had to check out.

Burian arrived at the right turn and slowed. Almost out of sight, the Durango swerved hard left onto the lawn of the house where Shirley had spoken to the woman before.

It looked like an attack.

Burian drove beyond the final right turn to the house and studied the woods for a way through to the house. The ditch abutting the road was too deep for the front wheel to negotiate but other than that, the woods appeared passable. Burian gassed the BWM, cut a three-quarter turn and popped the wheel over the ditch. The back wheel bounced him over. He swerved left to avoid a tree and weaving, braking and gassing he wended a path through the forest behind the houses.

Excellent. He would park behind the house, approach and enter through a back door, put a quick bullet in Shirley's head and interrogate the residents about Ulyana.

Everyone talks when they see what a bullet does to a woman's face.

Burian Tkach's first job out of secondary school was Spetznaz, the Soviet special forces. Afterward he picked up skills with the KGB. He thought in simple terms. Am I capable of effecting an outcome, or not? Life was black and white. Many things were susceptible to his influence; others — the rotation of the earth, gravity — were not. The things he could change with action, he did. Everything else was landscape.

Burian's genius rested in his absolute belief that morals were ephemeral and their consideration beyond his pay grade. His discipline and ability to follow orders transferred responsibility for his acts to the issuer of the commands he followed. He operated in a world of thought and action free of dissonance.

Wide-ranging strategies held no interest. Not that he couldn't see big pictures or have views on how to best create new realities. He'd learned not to care because all outcomes were the same. Unseen forces compelled situations to turn. His superiors, for all their mid-level scheming, never knew the few who cast their fates.

The West believed in unseen gods. To Burian, the concept was the same except oligarchs pulled the strings. They remained hidden but truth always matched their desires. Concealed, no coup would ever touch them.

They didn't want the kind of power that was seen — the grandiose bellowing of the pawn — because that power was always subject to the ire of the people. With invisibility came impunity. Burian had no interest in being a mid-level power, convinced he was moving the figures on the board, only to learn his master pulled his elbow. Why bother? The system wasn't corrupt: corruption was the system.

It was good to have a simple life. His skills were always in demand. The people who employed him would never kill their way to peace.

Burian glanced forward and saw the ground rising sharply and the black Durango racing through the trees. There must be a path ahead. Burian toed the rear brake and slid to the bottom of the vale. He reached below the motorcycle's headlight and toggled a switch he'd installed that morning, killing the lamp beam.

The bank ahead of him was steep and his rear wheel was designed for traction on pavement. Burian turned left and ascended at an angle.

Again on flat ground he angled perpendicular to the path the Durango had taken. He followed in first gear, his engine barely at an idle as he scanned the terrain.

He stopped at a fork.

There had been no rainfall in the four days he had been in Arizona, but the ground remained moist from melted snow and the Durango's tracks were easy to follow.

He turned left and quickly spotted a break in the tree cover ahead. He slowed and observed the hard edge of the right side of a building. The image called to mind a familiar sight from Russia: once-stately houses that now looked old.

This must be where Shirley Lyle believed Ulyana might be hidden.

Burian drove the BMW off the trail. He swung a semi circle and stopped where he could observe both the house and the road back to civilization. Knowing his kick stand would sink in the dirt and not wanting to take the time to find a flat rock, he positioned the motorcycle against a tree, facing away from the house.

He dismounted, removed his helmet, dragged a mask over his face and withdrew a 9mm given to him by Vanko.

. . .

*L*ester Toungate followed Shirley Lyle to the Memmelsdorf house, to the Pink Panther and back to the house. FBI man Joe Smith followed in a black sedan behind him. Through all the back and forth, a black motorcycle tracked every turn but the last. Lester couldn't be sure, but since Vanko Demyan sent Mykhaltso to assassinate him, Lester's first inclination was to suspect Vanko sent another killer. That this would redound to Shirley Lyle's benefit made as much sense as anything else over the last couple of weeks.

Lester paused, alert to the realization he hadn't felt so glad to be alive as he was in this moment for a long time. As with any hunt, proximity to game quickened his pulse.

There was something else, also. Familiarity with Shirley... and something bordering respect. She must have been pretending to be an overwrought emotional nitwit when he trashed her trailer—because it didn't seem possible that a woman would grow a steel spine in a matter of days.

Lester half-grinned, transfixed by a thought: If either of his sons, Paul or El Jay, had half of Shirley Lyle's moxie and wit...

Shirley Lyle approached the same house she'd already visited, but this time instead of cutting onto the driveway, she angled off the road without braking and bounced across the driveway into the yard.

Lester pulled to the side of the road and government-man Smith kept rolling. Probably keeping tabs to make sure Lester completed his dirty task. Everything about Smith smacked of cowardice — but that made him dangerous. A coward felt cornered on an open plain.

The Durango roared from around the back of the house

and charged into the woods. Must be a trail he couldn't see from the distance.

Lester checked his side view mirror and resumed the road. He followed Shirley Lyle's wheel prints across the lawn. The border with the woods cut like an arch into a dark hallway. Weeds at bottom and on the sides rendered the passage undetectable from the road.

About to push the gas pedal, Lester hesitated. The woods changed the dynamics. Shirley would have fewer turns available and therefore less opportunities to lose him. At the same time, there would be no other traffic. He'd be very easy to spot. Lester counted to twenty —

Straight ahead — close — the black motorcycle that had been following agent Smith flashed onto the trail. Rear tire spinning, it sprayed dirt and followed in the direction of the now-out-of-sight Durango.

Lester pushed the gas pedal and wondered how well the Prius would handle off-road terrain. Front wheel drive and light, it ought to survive.

The motorcycle's tail light blinked and Lester held back, keeping the bike barely within sight. After the undergrowth at yard's edge, the woods reduced to boulders and trees with very few evergreens or brush.

Far ahead, he caught a glimpse of the Durango — stopped.

The motorcycle veered behind a boulder and halted. The helmeted rider leaned for vantage around the rock.

Lester reversed the Prius and swung into a clearing beside the trail. He advanced on foot from cover to cover, reducing the motorcycle rider's opportunity to spot him. He stopped at a place that afforded a clean line of sight to the Durango. Shirley exited and walked forward. She returned and her male passenger led her off the trail, around a fallen tree.

The motorcycle resumed the trail.

Should Lester return to the Prius?

He'd spent all his life in the parts around Flagstaff. Trails were liable to go on forever but he had an inkling this one wouldn't.

The faint hum of motorcycle engine stilled too quickly to indicate he had passed out of hearing range: the rider had killed the engine.

Lester advanced with his hand on his .357 as if stalking a deer he knew was nearby... but out of sight and armed.

The rider from the black motorcycle was a wild card. Lester's first assumption that he was sent by Vanko to make another attempt at killing him didn't make sense, unless the man leapfrogged Lester to set up an ambush. Another possibility: he existed to protect Shirley from Lester and was positioning himself between them. If that was the case, however, the rest of his behavior betrayed him. He hid from Shirley... and acted more like a man stalking a kill.

A complication: regardless of whether he was there to kill Shirley first and Lester second, or Shirley and not Lester at all, or Lester and not Shirley, his plans would likely change if he spotted sunlight off the Prius windshield.

Lester squeezed his pistol grip. To hell with it.

He veered left and glided on damp leaves. He felt young — as if he hadn't nearly died of a brain injury in the last week — and been shot in the arm and ribs. His fingertips tingled. He smelled pine trees and exhaust. Freckles of sunlight wiggled on the ground. Moths hid on tree bark. As he advanced his head began to ache from excitement. He followed to a dry stream bed, came up low on the other side, unsure what he would see. He stopped and eased erect, feeling naked as a man in gun sights.

After a hundred yards of hurry and wait advances, Lester discovered a clearing to his far right — the direction the Durango and motorcycle had been traveling.

He crouched, his old knees popping, and searched the terrain.

Gunshot! — muffled, from inside the house.

Lester placed his hands on the ground and shifted onto his knees. An ache reminded him of Shirley Lyle hurling a chair at him.

Her remaining minutes were down to double digits. Maybe single.

Another gunshot —

Lester stood, stepped forward. He halted. This gunplay could be an opportunity to move — maybe. Whoever had fired would be juiced with adrenaline and fear. But with the wild card?

Better to wait.

Motion...

A shadow moved where one had not before existed. Lester discerned shoulders and arms. Motorcycle man stalking Shirley Lyle.

Lester could allow the man on the motorcycle to kill her and then kill him on his way out. But there were two problems. First, even with Shirley's paranormal ability to stay alive, Lester still considered her an easier mark than anyone Vanko would send.

Second, you're soft on Shirley.

Lester crinkled his eyelids tight until the skin pulled on the side of his head. He opened his eyes.

Shirley or Ulyana had the thumb drive. Assuming the motorcycle man had been tasked by Vanko, allowing him the opportunity to take possession of the drive's contents could be as bad as having the information fall into the hands of the police.

Lester moved forward, his eyes seeking the unnatural linear pattern signaling twigs hidden under damp leaves. A misstep would sound like a tiny howitzer. He split his attention: the ground, the man, the house, the clearing and the space behind him.

Minutes passed.

The motorcycle man halted his slow advance behind a boulder positioned in the woods, but close to the clearing perimeter. He seemed hesitant to advance any nearer the house. Maybe he debated the final steps of his approach, or waited for his quarry to emerge for a clean shot from afar.

Lester glanced at his watch. Lots of time. Whoever had been shooting — by now the situation was resolved.

The man scrambled twenty feet, ducked, spun around.

Too late.

Lester stood behind a fat juniper with bark so jagged he eyeballed the man while the man stared right past him.

Motorcycle-man peered toward Lester a long time, close enough Lester saw his eyes shift left and right.

Lester's heart raced. Sometimes he liked to toy with a kill — ask stupid questions and delight in stupid answers before sending a man to his end.

Not this guy.

He finally turned.

Lester lifted his .357. Finger on the trigger, he chose a tree nine feet forward and advanced. He selected another and progressed five feet left.

Behind the tree, Lester rested his gun barrel in a handy Y-fork. The slot's natural aim was six inches right of where he wanted the bullet to go. He wiggled higher in the slot and shifted left. Didn't feel right, like he was too clever by half.

He lifted the .357 and stepped from behind the tree. Planted his feet and gripped with two hands. His pulse bounded. He waited for the grand punishing irony of someone shooting him in the back...

Aiming between the man's shoulder blades, Lester pulled back the hammer.

It clicked.

The man dropped and rolled. Lester tracked but the barrel never aligned well enough to justify a trigger pull.

The man popped to his feet, pistol in the air.

Lester fired.

Leaves danced on the slope.

His vision tunneled and the motorcycle man stood in the center. Lester fired again. The other man fired. A bullet cracked past his head — hematoma side. Lester squeezed another shot. The man's shoulder spun.

Righting himself, the man shifted leftward and Lester paralleled. The man swung his arm and his pistol burst orange. The sound was different.

Dead-on different. Lester looked straight down the other man's gun barrel.

He flinched. Good as dead. God lied. Or not. How to tell? Leaves rustled above, like a quick burst of rain that ended in the same instant it began.

Stunned to be standing, Lester blasted off one more shot and the motorcycle man fell.

The other man's final bullet didn't sound right. His barrel was right on Lester.

Lester's touched the side of his head. He patted his chest. Adjusted his sack. Everything was sound — except with the shootout victory his nuts were like the Grinch's heart — three sizes bigger.

Lester reveled.

All of life was taking life. Eating meant killing. You cut open a bell pepper, the plant has guts like any animal. Everything kills to live. How human beings twisted themselves to the notion that killing was bad defied sense. It was impossible. It was nihilism. Killing enabled life and until man could synthesize food out of a bag of carbon, life was impossible without it. Killing was life. It was glee. Being against killing was as suicidal a belief as a man could hold. The hypocrisy was perfect.

Lester rubbed the back of his neck. Grinned.

The man lay sprawled with his shooting arm outstretched, gun in hand. The shoulder shot had gone through him but there were no other blood spots visible.

Lester glanced toward the house.

No one approached to investigate the ruckus.

Holding his .357 on the fallen man, Lester stepped forward and stopped.

Stunned.

His vision had tunneled so tightly on the man, he didn't see the two inch birch between them.

The sapling was splintered neck high.

Lester turned and saw chipped bark on the tree with the Y-slot he'd hidden behind.

The birch tree had slowed the bullet and deflected it from Lester.

God?

Or the devil?

How the hell do you ever know?

2

---

*E*lvita Marín glanced left. Traffic. She placed her paper Starbucks cup in the Mercedes-Benz E-350 center console and noticed the smear of lipstick on the rim. She hadn't slept well and needed an afternoon pick-me-up. She needed a treat.

She was compensating.

Where was Chico?

She assumed who he was with, but not where.

A truck passed, then a white SUV. A Honda Civic was coming next, with a gap between it and the following vehicle. She put both hands on the steering wheel and timed it. With the Civic's trunk in front of her, Elvita gunned the Mercedes. She turned hard right and the car jolted. Coffee splashed on her white skirt.

Her right rear tire hissed and a light flashed on the dash.

Elvita grimaced. She glanced at the rearview mirror — at least she was a comfortable distance ahead of the next vehicle. She searched left and right for an easy turn off the road.

The car wobbled. Had somebody placed a knife or something on the road? Metal sticking out of the curb, somehow?

She lifted her foot off the gas and glanced at both side view mirrors and the rearview again. Her chest tightened and she felt wetness in her eyes. She'd been in dark places before with the world spinning out of control and the corners closing in. She'd survived. She'd built a business. No matter what happened, she'd find a way through this.

Elvita Marín was a survivor. She blinked her eyes clear.

The first turn on her right opened to a small shopping plaza: florist, dentist, hair salon and CPA. She drove by the plaza every day.

The next road on the left led to a series of automotive-type businesses. Two maintenance garages, a tire dealership and an AutoZone. But they were too far. Driving there would ruin her rim, and except for her Starbucks habit, this wasn't the time to be wasting money.

With Chico nowhere to be found and the markets poised to crash every other day, or surge, with no rhyme or reason to the Federal Reserve, and all the rules and all the wisdom gleaned by studying the last hundred years of economics thrown out the window by transcendent policies that ignored the tried-and-true in favor of ivory tower academic theories, and a recent flood of client defections, and having to run all the meetings herself with an assistant who, bless her heart, was smart and worked hard but whose lack of experience rendered her utterly incompetent...

This wasn't the time for a blowout.

Elvita cut the wheel right, hit another curb and probably ruined her rim. She let the Mercedes crawl a dozen yards into the lot before stopping. She pulled the parking brake and popped the trunk. The door pocket held a cloth she kept to wipe dust from the dashboard. She used it to press the spilled coffee deeper into her skirt.

She glanced at her watch.

"Dammit!"

She knew better than to run out for coffee before a client meeting but she'd felt too run down to function.

She checked the window while pressing buttons on her phone. A man in a flannel shirt with cutoff sleeves and a perma-tan to his shoulders was studying her rear wheel.

"Mendi. I have a flat tire and I spilled coffee all over myself. We need to reschedule Salvatore and Estebanita."

"They're already here." Static, as if Mendi changed the phone's position. "Salvatore is pacing and Estebanita keeps huffing."

"Wonderful."

Salvatore and Estebanita were gold clients, top-tier in assets under management and fees generated. In the last few weeks, without knowing why, Elvita and Chico had lost most of their gold clients.

"The S&P is down twenty-five now and Salvatore heard rumors about the Fed adopting negative interest rates."

"I'll be at least fifteen minutes late and I look like hell. Tell them I'll be there as soon as I can."

The man in flannel who had been staring at her tire approached while she spoke on the phone. She studied his face through the window. He wore a dumb smile that seemed more dumb-rotten than dumb-good. He was kind of round. Caucasian. Fuzzy hair on his arms. Ring on his finger. Filthy ball cap on his head.

Elvita rolled down her window. The man circled the front of her car and showed her his hands before standing several feet from her door.

"You split a side wall. You got somebody coming or do you need a hand?"

Elvita flashed a smile. Through the windshield smog boiled out of Phoenix. Late April, and yesterday was already the first hundred-degree day of the year. She didn't notice the polluted air when she was in it, but looking down on the city from a mountain in the north, the gray air made her wonder what petrochemicals lodged in her lungs. Three million people. Three million cars. Like any city, Phoenix had its share of everything. Her grandfather came from Mexico. Her father moved the family from Tucson to Phoenix, and Elvita grew up hard: she knew the rough spots and rough people, spent time with spray paint and Mary Jane. But she got her act together when her father died at thirty-eight and she realized life only gave her one shot. Not to make it big. Just one shot. One go-round. One experience. She worked zealously, got some grants, some loans and three years of a business degree. She quit school to launch her dream... and failed. She built another business with pearls sifted from the ashes and polished them to profit. Fifty-four million under management, generating five hundred thousand dollars a year of gross fees from assets under management. Adding the annuities and life sales, she grossed seven-fifty.

After paying the wages, the rent, the electric and benefits, then splitting the rest even-steven with Uncle Sam, she was lucky to clear a hundred fifty.

Then the crash, the Great Recession. Chico doing what Chico did, probably off with Bubbles somewhere.

Elvita blinked. Half smiled and met the man's gaze.

"My husband is on his way. Thank you, though."

"Is he far? Because I could knock this out in five minutes. Save him the trouble."

She hesitated.

"Ma'am, I do this for a living. I work three blocks that-away at Ferguson's Tire. I'll have you on your way in no time. No need to get your hands grimy, when mine will be in ten minutes anyway.

She closed her mouth. Blew it full with her cheeks puffed out. Released. "Okay. What's your name?"

"Tom."

"You okay with the world, Tom? You're not going to make a bad day worse, right?"

"Ma'am — you don't even need to get out the car. Just put it in gear, pull the parking brake and I'll — "

"Tom?"

"Yep?"

"You didn't say whether or not you're going to murder me in the parking lot."

"No, Ma'am." He frown-smiled. Removed his baseball cap and blinked hard enough to wrinkle his brow. Restored his cap. "I work at a garage. Help a lot of people."

"I didn't mean to — "

"Enjoy your day."

He turned and launched in the same motion then strode and entered his truck without a backward look.

Elvita opened her door. Her voice rose in her throat but she stopped. She'd fix the tire herself. Perhaps grime on her hands combined with coffee and grease on her skirt would show Salvatore and Estebanita Contreras that she was a regular person, not a business. That she was someone who would be wounded if he took his accounts elsewhere..

Elvita stood before her open trunk, not sure what she had expected.

A tire?

The trunk bottom was flat. She noticed a recessed handle

and pulled. The trunk floor lifted, revealing a recess on the left where a blue plastic tool sheath was tucked. She opened it: jack, jack handle, lug nut and wrench.

"Okay, where's the tire?"

She saw two more latches on the trunk floor and released them. A second false floor lifted revealing a spare tire in the center and the car's battery on the right. She removed the giant circular wingnut holding the tire in place.

"You want to let me grab that for you?"

She jumped.

"Tom."

He shrugged.

"I'm sorry. I didn't intend to be rude — but I was."

"No, you were right. Woman's got to think about things like that. So for the record, I'm not going to kill you in the parking lot. Let me grab that tire."

"I just realized I've never had a flat on this car before."

"I'll show you if you like. Or you can wait in the car. Up to you."

"Let me learn from you."

"Looks like you found everything."

Tom removed the tire, held it six inches from the pavement and let it drop. He caught it on the bounce.

"This tire is under inflated. It'll get you to the garage, and I can put more air in it for you."

Elvita nodded. "How long will that take?"

"Couple minutes. You in a hurry somewhere?"

"I'm already going to be late for an appointment." She shook her head. "You know what? If they don't understand a flat tire, they can take their business elsewhere."

Tom broke loose each lug nut.

"Miss, would you put the vehicle in park and yank that brake handle for me?"

Elvita did and then stood behind Tom as he placed the jack under the jack-point and lifted the vehicle until the tire cleared the ground by a hand-width.

Elvita drifted. Chico hadn't been to work in days. They'd agreed to separate while they figured things out, but he didn't say he'd stop coming to work. That was not what they had agreed upon.

Chico had a gift. He was smooth — looked you in the eye and said words you wanted to hear in a way you liked to hear them. He knew how to place a gentle hand on your arm and how to show concern when something mattered to you. He was attentive in bed. He made breakfast before she woke.

The bastard rubbed her feet.

He did everything, until he did nothing.

After the wedding and honeymoon, they worked day and night to build a bigger business. Elvita already owned a financial planning practice. She'd studied hard her first five years in the business, becoming a Certified Financial Planner, Chartered Life Underwriter, and Chartered Financial Consultant. She was efficient. She offered economics and investing seminars and grew her business because people were happy to see that not all financial services representatives were permanent bulls, always pumping the market. Elvita studied Austrian economics, read the works of pioneers like Ludwig Von Mises, Friedrich Hayek and Murray Rothbard. The financial collapse of 2008 caught many off guard but not economists who actually knew what money was and how it worked, including Elvita.

She called the top of the market.

Most of her clients came to her because she understood risk and spoke in terms they could understand. But when the top arrived and it was time to move to safety, most preferred the advice of the screamers and dreamers on CNBC. Most thought everything was different this time, that assets deserved permanently absurd valuations. Only a third of her clients took her advice and moved to guaranteed investments.

Most of the other two thirds rode the market roller-coaster all the way to the bottom and when the Fed finally started printing money, they panicked and demanded she sell.

Naturally, their money lost, they needed someone to blame. Either that or they fell victim to the next rep promising giant gains with no risk. Accounts vanished. Calls went unreturned. Revenue shrank month after month after month after month.

Chico, who had been masterful at charming people to the office for a free consultation, began to be unavailable for erratic reasons.

Flu. For a man who never got sick.

Engine trouble, on a new Grand Cherokee.

Forgot, didn't show.

Accounts disappeared.

"That about does it."

Elvita blinked several times. Her eyes had been on Tom's back the whole time he'd been fixing her tire, but she hadn't even realized when he'd removed the flat and swapped the spare.

"Oh, let me get my purse. What do I owe you?"

He shook his head. "Nope, not needed."

"Which garage do you work at?"

"Ferguson's, just down that left turn right there."

"You said I need to get my tire inflated?"

Tom pointed back the other direction, beyond where she turned right and split her sidewall. "That gas station is closer. They have free air. It's off the side to the left when you pull in."

"But you work at a tire place?"

He nodded. "Thing is, your other tires are worn and almost needing to be replaced. Smart thing would be to change them all at one time so you get even wear. And I noticed you haven't been having these rotated. That reduces your mileage."

"Does your place have any deals going on right now?"

"Yeah, we do, actually: Free oil change when purchasing four tires."

He watched her.

"I could give you my truck as a loner. Get you to your appointment."

Elvita blinked away wetness that filmed her eyes. "Thank you."

3

*S*hirley Lyle held a stack of hundreds in her hand.
Saving Ulyana was super important, but getting her
half million of stolen drug money back satisfied a different
want.

As a teen she entered the sex business due to economic
needs and her skills in the lusty arts. There was no family
money. No family wisdom. She fell out of the nest and didn't
flap her wings once before she hit rock bottom: pregnant,
waiting tables and hooking on the side.

She dropped the stack of ten grand into the black
duffel. The greasy money smelled good. Life giving. Promise
making.

Shirley ran her tongue over her teeth and smacked her lips.

Life was pretty splendid. She'd pulled herself from the
ground. Overcame the stink-think in her head. Identified the
kidnapping Memmelsdorfs and killed them.

*You showed Donal O'Loughlin exactly what calm-under-pres-
sure looks like!*

Ulyana stood at the sink with a glass of water at her lips. Pants grimy and hair tangled. She had dirt on her elbows and insect stings — spider bites? — on her arms. Yet she smiled while she drank water. Not a jittery or nervous smile.

Not a 'I'm happy I survived' smile.

She seemed at peace... and that was just wrong.

The Memmelsdorfs broke her mind.

Shirley would take her under wing and be extra protective. She'd pull Donal aside and ensure they were on the same page. Couldn't allow Ulyana to wander off after a butterfly or a sun beam.

Donal knelt beside Ruth Memmelsdorf's corpse. He placed his fingers to her neck then withdrew his hand. The back of her missing head didn't bring the conclusion home but a third of a second pressing her neck did.

Maybe he couldn't believe Shirley — a woman — killed her.

Also, no doubt, Donal questioned if the shooting was justified. He'd been on the other side of the door and hadn't seen the action. If the gun next to Ruth's hand wasn't enough evidence, Donal could believe what he wanted.

Was it okay that killing bad people made Shirley feel good?

Whatever. It does!

"Not to question your skills or anything," Donal said, "did you happen to put your gun back on safe?"

"I think so. I've been mindful of that." Shirley pulled her Ruger SR40c from her bra. "Yep. White on the side."

Donal nodded. "I'm proud of you. You didn't hesitate. Most people underestimate how hard it is to kill another human being. They think they can. They've seen hundreds of action movies. But in the moment they think twice — because it's so permanent I guess. Most of us — if we think about it at all — think being murdered would be horrible."

Why is he still talking?

"And so we hesitate before killing someone else. Whether it's justified or not. The horror of it makes most folks hesitate."

"Uh-huh."

"But you didn't."

Shirley opened her mouth but her voice froze. Donal was an old homicide cop. The way he phrased it, a statement hooked like a question, felt like he was inviting her to speak a mistake.

Give him something to satisfy his curiosity. Otherwise your boyfriend is going to be investigating you behind your back.

"You're not my boyfriend. I'm just saying. As to hesitation, I guess after Maddix attacked me the second time, I kind of lost my capacity."

Donal nodded. "Hell of a thing, the bad luck that follows you."

"What do you mean?"

"I've known you all of four days and for a woman who never saw a gun, you're sure comfortable using it."

"Told you I was trouble, Sugar."

She held his look and inside, for the first time in a long time, felt herself swelling. Her self, her identity. Donal was a man on the floor looking up, trying to understand and she didn't give a royal clown-poke whether he figured it out. She owned herself and her right to defend herself and respect herself and if that didn't fit his worldview, he could either change it or find a skinny nervous girl who chewed her nails.

His choice.

She held his quizzing stare and her brow gave away nothing.

Donal glanced away. Swatted a fly on Ruth's nose. Tipped her head sideways.

"Okay," Donal said. "Well that's that."

Shirley zipped her black duffel bag of drug money.

A gunshot rang from outside the house.

Donal flinched. His eyes bulged and he ducked. He crawled to the open door and peered outside. Another gunshot, this time the blast arriving with a concussion suggesting the barrel was pointed toward them.

"Get down. Pay attention to the windows."

Shirley remained standing. "That's just somebody hunting rabbits. The bad guys are dead."

"I'm an ex-cop. Those are pistols. Most folks don't hunt rabbits with a pistol."

"We should go talk to them and see what they are upset about," Ulyana said.

Money bag in hand, Shirley strode from the sofa at the corner of the living room into the kitchen between Ulyana and the gunfire. "Here, you silly retard. Stand behind me until we get this sorted out. No more thinking for you."

Shirley cast out her arm.

More gunfire from outside.

"You two! Come on! Get down!"

Donal crouched beside the door. "We have the advantage. They can't see inside the house and they have to cross open space to reach us. Shirley, I want you in the living room. From the two windows you control the back and right quadrants. I'll stay in the kitchen covering the other two. Ulyana - you go back downstairs and hide in a corner where you'll be least likely to be hit by ricochet."

"No." Shirley shook her head. "Let's say there's a couple bad guys out there. They're not shooting at us. There's no bullets coming in the house, and I'm sure a couple bad guys could hit a house if they wanted. So while they're out there hunting rabbits, we don't sit here and wait for them to attack us. I've done that and won't do it again. People who wait get their asses beat. Hell, no. We slip out to the back of the house and head for the woods. Anybody comes after us gets what these fools got." She nudged Ruth Memmelsdorf's brainless head with her toe. "Or worse."

"I'm not going back downstairs." Ulyana leaned close to the kitchen sink window, kept her gaze outside while refilling her glass. "They have really delicious water here."

Donal, on the floor, smiled hard. "Unbelievable. You're an unmissable target, just standing there."

"She isn't going back downstairs and I'm not waiting around for somebody to come up and shoot me. I appreciate that you cops are taught to save yourselves first, but we don't have time to wait around for the bad guys to leave. So climb up off your knees, Donal. At least get off the floor so we can get around you. There's blood everywhere. Make room."

He clenched his teeth and shrugged. "Okay. That's not an impossible idea. I can work with that. You two head out back and I'll wait here and deal with them when they come."

"Why would people fighting themselves out there be coming here? They're fighting each other. Obviously, if they were after each other and found each other and are fighting each other, they're not coming here. Now, since there's bullets flying, I'm leaving — soon as I kick Roddy Memmelsdorf in the face. Let's go, Ulyana."

"Hey, what's in that bag?" Donal said. "That's evidence."

"This duffel is private property."

"It was mine," Ulyana said. "The Memmelsdorfs took it out of my car."

Shirley shouldered the bag, touched the pistol under her shirt to verify it was there.

She stepped onto the porch and Ulyana followed.

4

---

*E*lvita peered through the double glass doors. Salvatore and Estebanita Contreras waited in the foyer. Elvita hesitated.

Tom from Ferguson's Tire had lent her his pickup truck and she was lucky not to have another blowout on the way to the office.

By now the dry Phoenix heat had surely baked in the coffee on her skirt, and even though she hadn't changed her tire, she'd managed to smudge grease on her blouse.

The one thing she never, ever did was make a client wait. Big client, little client, didn't matter. Her first job was to run her life in a manner that kept her reliable. If she couldn't master that, how could anyone trust her to prosper a multi-million dollar investment portfolio?

Her heart raced.

Chico was a jerk, leaving her to handle the small talk, schmoozing and hand holding. She had been all too glad to surrender the role. Doing so had allowed her to focus on portfolio management and carrying the conversation during the heavy-duty portion of their client meetings. With Chico gone, she'd found the communication of pleasantries and touchy feely relationship-stuff difficult to resume — as if it was a foreign language she took in high school and never internalized.

She filled her lungs, squared her shoulders and opened the glass double doors.

Her assistant, Mendi, bounced from around the reception desk, short-step hurried to her and examined her. "You have a smudge." She indicated her cheek.

Elvita wiped her cheek and saw makeup on her sleeve. She smiled. "Salvatore. Estebanita. I apologize. Please excuse me for another moment."

She turned around and hurried into the ladies room to fix the disaster that her face had become. At the mirror she said, "You've been through rough patches before. You'll get through this one."

The coffee stain was now cooked into her skirt. No use wetting it — and the smudge on her sleeve was there to stay as well. She pulled her hair into a ponytail and stared herself down in the mirror.

"You are not losing this account."

"We're transferring our accounts," Salvatore said. Elvita extended her arm toward the conference room and drifted that direction. Salvatore didn't move except to lift his open hands.

"We want to wait on the sidelines. It's nothing against you. We needed to come in person."

"We have options here, in your existing accounts," Elvita

said. "Even with the tiny yields, we can still find alpha in long bonds. With the printing press running, inflation — "

Salvatore shook his head.

"Why didn't you call?"

"I did. In fact, I told Chico."

"When?"

"Two weeks ago. I was surprised you didn't reach out, afterward. Let's not make this any more difficult. I wanted to tell you in person. When the insanity ends, we'll consider asking for your help again."

Estebanita squeezed Elvita's hand. She tilted her head. Frowned. *In another world...* she seemed to say.

Salvatore held the door for Estebanita. He turned. "Best of luck."

Elvita stood in the foyer, arms limp at her sides.

5

*S*hirley stretched her arm to Ulyana. "C'mere, Sunbeam."

She stepped onto the porch and Ulyana followed. They paused to look at Roddy Memmelsdorf, shot in the forehead. Shirley glanced at Ulyana and noticed a wet glaze to her eyes.

"Happy tears?"

Ulyana closed her eyes and her upper lip trembled. She opened her eyes and turned partly away, head angled to the trees.

The boards bowed. Shirley grabbed a dry rotted porch post and lurched to the dirt. Her foot bumped Roddy's heel and his wrist rolled as if thumbing for a lift.

"Thumb a ride to hell, you no good piece of—

She planted her left foot outside his knee and swung her other foot between his legs, grazing his groin.

—rotten ass man sewage mother fu—"

"That's called desecration," Ulyana said.

"Oh hell yeah. I can dig it."

Shirley nudged Roddy's feet farther apart. Advanced to his knee and launched a another kick.

"Uh," Ulyana said.

"He may not have taken you but he sure didn't save you. Other than sperm I'm not convinced there's a use for men at all. But if there is, a man keeping his psycho wife from kidnapping people has to be on the list."

"Roddy brought me food and water. He brought me the blankets."

"Yeah, and Quasimodo burned the tower. Either way the girl at the Pink Panther said Roddy was stalking you. That's the only way I knew to come here — that plus I knew Ruth from the self hate group."

"You got lucky. Ruth did it."

"Come kick him in the nuts real quick. You'll feel better. Then we can go."

Ulyana shrank from her. "Why would I want to do that?"

"He had a part in it." Shirley kicked Roddy one more time; it felt like bubble wrap popping. "New rules. You're either part of the solution or you're getting kicked in the gonads."

"I hope nobody ever decides to judge me."

"Sunbeam — these people were going to kill you. Besides, from time immortal people take revenge on dead bodies. And if *you* start kidnapping people with the intent to kill them, yes I'll judge you and kick you in the balls."

"Okay, you've kicked him. Plus he's dead. Isn't that punishment enough?"

"Don't think so. Lot of folks beat on me and I never got to kick 'em when they were down. Roddy's here. He'll do."

Shirley stood beside Roddy's shoulders, pulled her leg back far as possible, lifted her toe...

She paused, expecting Ulyana's gasp.

Nothing.

She turned.

"Hey, where you going?"

Shirley chased down Ulyana — grabbed her arm and spun her. What are you doing?"

"I want to talk to whoever was shooting, and see what he's angry about."

Shirley pulled Ulyana by the wrist toward the back of the house. "You can talk to them after you talk to a head doctor."

At the window she wondered if Donal, inside, would shoot her shadow because he was afraid of the noise. For an ex cop, he wussed out a lot.

She stopped at the corner and peered. Proceeded.

"If I let go are you going to be all right? Don't do anything stupid."

Shirley released Ulyana's wrist after they were halfway across the backyard. After a few paces she turned.

"You — "

Ulyana had returned to the corner of the house and peered at where a fly had alighted on the siding. Shirley stomped and the fly flew away.

"It's eyes were sparkly green," Ulyana said.

Shirley grabbed Ulyana's elbow and paused.

The day she bought her Durango she watched a man at Walmart grab his daughter's arm the same way, twisting her shoulder blade and hurting her.

Shirley released Ulyana. "C'mon! We got to go!"

She charged forward and at the perimeter stopped to wait on Ulyana. They entered the woods. A few feet in, Shirley stopped.

"I parked that-a-way. But we need to circle around Elmer Fudd out there, so we'll go this — "

"Elmer Fudd?"

"Yeah. Don't do that fake Russian stuff. I know you watched Elmer in Philly."

"Okay."

"So what was I saying?"

"Where we're going."

"Right. So the Durango's out this way."

Shirley looked back every few feet to see if Ulyana stopped to study a moth or a mushroom.

"Hey, keep up. I got a question. A minute ago you said you hope nobody judges you."

"Yes."

"Why?"

"It stinks."

Shirley studied Ulyana's face. Sunlight fell on her but she seemed to glow with her own light.

"Did they bleach your teeth or something?"

Ulyana tilted her head. Sage.

"Oh hey. Thanks for covering me back there with Donal." Shirley adjusted the duffel strap on her shoulder. "About the money."

"Sometimes a deception serves the greater truth."

Shirley shook her head. "So does kicking a corpse. Anyway, your money's in the Durango. I didn't want it stolen too. Was it Ruth or Roddy that took mine? Did they tell you?"

"Ruth."

"I don't get it. That woman was no sister to the Revolution."

Ulyana stopped walking.

Shirley stopped as well. She scanned the woods then faced Ulyana.

"I don't know if I am either," Ulyana said. "Not the way you're — the way *we* were doing it."

"What? Killing bad guys? Hey! You didn't know this 'cuz you was in a cellar but I shot Maddix Heregger too!"

"Oh."

"What? Are you freaking kidding me? He busted in — this time your place. He had a gun; I had no choice."

"That's never true."

"Well I took the choice I wanted. Anyway, when I found my money was gone I grabbed yours so nobody would come back and steal it. I left it in the Durango, so you'll have it in a minute."

"Okay."

"That's all? Okay? You are seriously warped. Hey, I was thinking about starting a business. You'll be in it too. We're gonna make bra holsters and number two pants — soon as I can figure out how. I'll buy a CEO or something. But anyway that'll be the brand name. Number Two Pants. Get it? With the zipper?"

Ulyana shook her head.

"What? You'd pick a different name?"

"Everything's different now. I need time away to consider everything. I want to go camping."

"Okay, stop playing with me. What did they do to your head?"

"They forced me to use it."

Shirley glanced to motion on her right: a squirrel.

"So let's hear it. What's different now, except you're alive thanks to me and got your money back thanks to me, and — "

"Thank you."

"Don't mention it. So what's different except the good stuff?"

"Don't you ever think about the important questions? Where's the meaning?"

"That's what you spent your free time thinking about?

There isn't any meaning. How could there be? It isn't just that stupid things happen and it's hard to find justice or goodness. That's all there is. Random stupid everywhere. Made up horse crap. We're probably in a dolphin's dream for all we know. I saw a documentary that said they're smarter than us."

"Well isn't that interesting. I've come to almost the same belief. With one difference."

"Look, this is all fantastic. I'm really happy for you. But in case the dolphin's dreaming a bad guy over there where the shooting was, why don't we get into this later?"

"You asked."

"And I should've known not to, the state you're in."

They resumed walking. Shirley paused with each step to ensure the ground underfoot held no surprises. She shuddered to think what tortures the Memmelsdorfs had inflicted on Ulyana, to break her mind like that. She wasn't smiling giddily through drool, but close. Metaphysical nonsense. The only people who ever spoke like that were the crazies or the posers. Ulyana wasn't high society, so that left being crazy.

Shirley stopped walking. Held up her hand in a signal she learned from Platoon. They used the same signal in Apocalypse Now, so it was right. Ulyana drifted along, head tilted to where sunlight broke through the leaves.

"Uh, stop. This hand signal means stop."

"I wasn't watching your hand."

Shirley growled.

They walked. Shirley stopped again — no hand signal. Ulyana bumped into her.

"Listen, you need to pay attention. This is a tactical situation and we ain't out of the woods yet."

Ulyana smiled.

"You like that? Just came to me. Anyway, pay attention."

Shirley searched. Where was the house? She'd cut a broad circle but with all the conversation must have went too wide. That's where metaphysical conversations took you. Off course — no matter where your course was.

She angled to her right. Eventually she'd find the road, even if she missed the house. That might actually be preferable.

"Okay," Shirley said. She stopped and turned. "What are you looking at?"

Ulyana stared with a gigantic smile. She pointed.

Shirley shifted. Changed her focus. A little green worm hung from a thread.

"Bird food. So listen, I can understand why you might be a little okay with Roddy. He didn't actually kidnap you and his woman was way more powerful than him. But I can't understand how you think what Ruth did is okay."

"I didn't say it was okay. I said I hope I'm not judged."

"But it was out of Ruth's hands? Because she was psychotic? Is that what you mean?"

"Evil people don't choose evil. Their problem is they don't grasp right and wrong the way everyone else does. Their minds aren't connected to the world the same way. Put yourself in their shoes. You do something you think is right, something you're drawn to but everyone else condemns you. And when you're dead, they kick you in the center of your most personal and private place — your sex. From that person's perspective, he isn't evil and the world isn't right and virtuous. He's right and the world is evil — because of what it does to him."

"Wait. Stop. You're turning things upside down."

"Am I?"

"A person has to stand up for something."

"Exactly."

"What?"

"When you stand up for something, if you're on the side of the majority, you're right. But if you stand up for something everyone else thinks is wacko, you're Ruth Memmelsdorf."

"She was going to kill you!"

"I'm not saying I agree with her. Only that I don't hate her and don't want to punish her, or get revenge on her corpse."

"You're a bigger person than I am. I say kick all these dead assholes. It's clear as day. Don't do evil stuff to people."

"No, listen. Let's say you had a God's-eye view of right and wrong, of good and evil. Supposing anyone was good at all, how would that person's motives be different from the evil person?"

"She'd do the right stuff. She'd do good stuff."

"No — not what she *does*. I'm asking, how would her *motives* be different?"

"She wants to do what's right. Like VIVA, Baby."

"Okay, so the good person wants what is right."

"Yes."

"What does the bad person want?"

"What's bad."

"Nope. And you know it."

Shirley stood looking at her.

"Remember, even the psycho serial killer thinks he's doing what is right for him to do. Another thing. We've all done stupid things. Think about the last stupid thing you did. Before you did it, what was your motive? To bring more regret in your life?"

Shirley shook her head. "You're saying there's no real right or wrong."

"No, I'm saying we don't have access to it through our own understanding."

"That's stupid." Shirley strode forward. Where the hell was the house?

Ulyana spoke from behind her. "Whether people do things you think are good or bad, their motivations are all the same. We can't do what doesn't make sense to us. Is good and evil just whether something is good for you, or evil for you?"

"Stop talking. Elmer Fudd's up here somewhere with a gun."

"So how can one person be called good when the same motives in another person are evil?"

"So when Ruth was going to kill you, that was okay? That was just her chasing down her vision of what was right and proper?"

Shirley stopped at a dry stream bed with a two-foot bank opposite. A small pool reflected gnarled tree roots. Stones with moss. "Beautiful."

Suddenly conscious of her pistol at her breast and the high probability of slipping and smashing her head on a rock, or her chest, or whatever, Shirley withdrew her Ruger. She removed the magazine, slid back the rack and ejected the cartridge from the chamber. "You want to pick that up for me, so a deer doesn't come along and blow off its foot or something?"

Ulyana stepped forward and stopped. "Seriously? They can explode like that?"

"No, they don't just blow up. Please hand me that bullet."

Ulyana gave it to her.

Shirley slipped the round into the magazine and inserted it back into the Ruger. Same as before except nothing in the chamber to accidentally cause damage to the mammage.

She crossed the dry stream bed and ascended the opposite bank on all fours.

Ulyana bounded across and popped over the bank. She took Shirley's hand and helped her to her feet. "Why do we always demand grace from other people? But we don't think anyone else ought to expect it from us?"

Shirley shook her head. Ahead it seemed like the tree canopy thinned out a bit.

"We're going this way. Stop talking before my head blows up."

Nearing the clearing Shirley discerned the hard edge of the house roof and after a few more feet, the front corner. She'd made a huge circle and now approached almost the same way as the first time, from the front. The Durango must be nearby. She turned left. Spotted it. Felt a ripple of relief.

"There's the house and the Durango's back — what the?"

Shirley stopped. Ulyana stood beside her.

A man strode past Roddy Memmelsdorf's corpse. Didn't slow as he crossed the porch and waltzed right into the house.

"How the shit?"

"That was Lester," Ulyana said.

"Dead Lester."

"Or not dead. He must have been doing the shooting."

Shirley glanced around and dropped her duffel bag of cash behind a boulder. She drew her Ruger SR40c and launched toward the house.

6

---

*H*e should have left the Prius another couple houses beyond where Shirley Lyle ripped across the lawn and swerved into the woods. If he had entered the woods on foot then he wouldn't have it lingering in the back of his mind he'd just screwed up royally.

Lester stood with his skin tingling. The dead man appeared Russian, if corpses bothered with nationalities. Lester brought his toe to the man's arm. Nudged. Glanced about the terrain and stopped on the red glow of a motorcycle taillight catching a stray bolt of forest sun.

If things played out his way he'd be back for the body and the bike.

Dammit — should have found someplace else for the Toyota. If the house had a phone and someone called the police, there'd be no getting around the fact it was Lester's car. He'd have to justify parking next to the trail — and explain the situation.

Could he skew the time frame? He was there yesterday and

left the Prius? The whole story would be a gap that needed filled with lies; not even a kernel of truth to hang them on.

"Why on earth did you leave a pristine blue Prius in the woods where the next day there'd be a shootout?"

"Well officer, that's where truth is stranger than fiction."

In business Lester linked his pride to his audacity in telling the truth — especially when doing so rankled folks who preferred white lies. But if in the moment a lie held a higher utility, he'd deploy it with absolute sincerity.

"You see officer, I read on a website that cars have feelings. You can see the Prius looks despondent, no doubt burdened by global warming. Step around front and see for yourself. I thought the fresh air would do it some good — "

He was an old man. All he really needed to do was scratch his head and say, "Catfish? Hell yeah."

Lester retrieved his cell phone from his pocket. No signal — but that didn't mean Shirley Lyle had no signal. She might have a different carrier or access to a land line in the house.

The safest bet would be to leave while he was nearly certain he could remove the Toyota from the trail before law enforcement had time to arrive — should anyone from the house give them a shout.

However, Lester rarely made a decision without pondering both sides.

So there was a shootout in the house: Shirley Lyle and her man versus whoever took Ulyana. Nothing on the surface indicated who was more likely to prevail over the other and there was no logic that guaranteed the shootout's victor would want to call the police.

If Shirley Lyle was victorious, she'd likely want to skeeter off and hide. What hooker wants police attention? Especially with her involvement in killing his son, El Jay...

On the other hand, say Shirley was dead and the person who took Ulyana — if this was even the right place — was the victor. He'd be wanting a bigger shovel, not a land line or cell phone with decent reception.

Lester closed his eyes and saw a jail cell with concrete blocks painted dirty foam green. Or did they just pour concrete now that prisons were owned by private companies? He saw himself in a dusty courtyard looking out on a sunset, surrounded by a chain link fence with razor wire on top and guarded by an Uzi-bearing guard on foot patrol — with his German shepherd.

Lester opened his eyes and the image remained like a double exposure over the forest.

He exhaled hard through his nose, wiggling his hairs, then squeezed his nose between thumb and pointer and flung the snot off his fingers.

Another complication: either Shirley or Ulyana had the thumb drive. That wasn't just a rock she'd picked up in front of the burning trailer. If either gal gave the memory stick to the police, it was hello slammer.

But even if neither girl had the drive, they'd seen its contents. And who knew what information they'd extracted from El Jay? Any way he unwound it, Shirley Lyle needed to die. Same with Ulyana.

Otherwise he'd be looking at razor wire from the prison yard.

Lester gazed skyward.

You with me? 'cause the longer You let me do what I do, the more I think it's what You want.

No answer. Lester huffed.

Ain't even there.

Lester strode toward the house and almost rolled his ankle.

The sun was climbing and it was that or the killing had made him hot. He unfastened two shirt buttons and flapped in some air with his hand.

A dozen feet of blackberry briars grew at the perimeter of an overgrown lawn. Lester kicked out his right leg, turned the foot sideways and rolled it over the stalk of a bramble. The plant bent at the base and pushed the next, domino style. Lester stomped a path and stood at the edge of the ragged lawn.

The house was a square two-story with a basement. A stiff wind could knock the paint off.

Lester tingled. The exchange of bullets inside had only been a few minutes ago but the house was still.

Lester squeezed the grip of his .357 and loped across the lawn.

7

*C*laude McFadden allowed his rear end to slide over the edge of the seat of his 1992 Land Rover until his dangling feet met the sideboards. From there he jumped down.

He'd spotted an elderly woman across the parking lot — a client of one of his colleagues. She stood beside her Mercedes, peering back and forth and taking halting steps. She pulled the door handle and released it. Cupped her hands at her eyes and leaned on the driver side glass, then stuck her arm in the gap between window and frame. She only inserted to mid forearm.

Claude grabbed his briefcase, adjusted his necktie and angled to the Mercedes.

"Locked out?"

Arm in the window, she spun. Her face was old. Her plain-spoken clothes said money.

"I might be able to help."

"I'm just going to call Triple A."

"No need! I bet I can reach the lock."

Claude stood beside the woman, his head at the level of her elbow.

"My arm is a little too thick to get inside." She pulled it out.

Claude stood his briefcase on the cement. He removed his suit jacket, folded it once and draped it over his briefcase. After removing his right Napoleon Bonaparte cufflink and dropping it in his breast pocket, Claude folded his shirt sleeve up to his arm pit.

He offered his hand to the woman. "I'm Claude."

She squeezed his digits between pointer and thumb. "Pleased."

He bowed his head. Smiled and offered a single quick nod coupled with a triple eye blink. Ought to knock her socks off.

He lifted his arm allowing her to verify its slenderness, then held it next to hers for easier comparison. She nodded.

Claude stood perpendicular to the Mercedes and slipped his hand into the window gap. At the elbow he folded his arm... but his shoulder was lower than the glass and resting on it like a fulcrum, his elbow jammed against the roof. He smiled with cheer, withdrew his arm and removed his jacket from where he had laid it on his briefcase.

"Mind if I place this on the hood of your car?"

"Go ahead."

Claude deposited his jacket, placed his briefcase on its side below the driver door and with great caution stepped on opposite corners. With his shoulder aligned with the gap in the window, he dropped his arm to the lock and released it.

The woman entered her car while Claude threw on his jacket and lifted his case.

"Thank you," the woman said.

Claude smiled. "My absolute pleasure."

8

From twenty feet away Lester observed the man's blasted-out cranium. He'd fallen backward but with his head turned to the side. A circular divot — such as a rotating foot would make — marred the ground about eighteen inches from the man's right shoulder.

Lester recognized the evidence of someone kicking in the man's brain from himself having, on occasion, loosed a vengeful boot. Unfortunately, the swirl indicated a foot rotating on its ball but gave no clue the size of the shoe.

Lester crossed the porch and entered the house through the open door.

A dead woman partly blocked his path, skinny and slightly knocked up. A large amount of blood pooled around her head. He listened and glanced about the house examining details and imagining the events that had created them.

Bloody footprints began at the body and led outside. Two different sizes indicated at least two people were inside the house after she bled out. One footprint was tiny. The other, not so much.

Shirley Lyle had been with her clean-cut partner. No way Shirley had the smaller footprint of the two. Could the man have a footprint that size?

"Where are you?" Lester said to the cupboards. "I heard the shooting. Came up to see if everyone was all right."

He stepped past the body and turned to the unlit living room and wondered at the shaded windows. He cocked his head, blurred his gaze and concentrated his other senses. His feet, for the tickle of a floorboard. His chest, for some supernatural constriction.

He tasted blood in the air.

"Anybody here?"

No time to enjoy the subterfuge. Wasn't worth it. Trust didn't matter. Time was short and he needed to put this whole chapter behind him.

Except for some reason you never finish the job on Shirley.

With his .357 pointed roughly at the entrance to the living room, Lester considered the footprints again. Shirley had arrived with a man and two sets of bloody tracks left the house. One of the prints was small: Ulyana. The other set could belong to either Shirley or her man. The other person remained.

The house had an upstairs and a basement, but hiding there wouldn't make sense. Whoever stayed chose to do so rather than escape with the other two.

That could only mean attack.

Shirley Lyle?

Not likely. She hadn't killed him when she had the chance after he burned her trailer. Just returned his gun.

So it was likely the man.

The least risky attacks used overwhelming force, surprise or both. Shirley's man didn't have overwhelming force and there was just one of him. But he could fire at any moment — a genuine advantage.

Standing in blood, Lester faced the living room. He tightened his vision. His neck hair bristled and his pulse bounded.

Motion? Sound? Something twitched his attention left, into the kitchen — the closet door.

Lester eased his .357 upward.

Within the door aperture a shadow, silver.

"Don't move. You're under arrest."

Lester could spin and fire in less than a second, but the man with the gun could squeeze his trigger faster.

Lester could dive forward, rotate to land on his back with pistol arm poised, but he was eighty-three. Which bones would break?

He'd had his advantage and squandered it. Time to throw down some old man bluster.

"Like I said, partner. I heard the gunplay. You do these people this way? That you?"

The closet door creaked. Lester beheld a pistol barrel, the circle at the end housing a large dot.

"That a fifty caliber?"

"Be very careful. No sudden movements. Do exactly as I say."

"You police? Or pretending? If you're police put that damn thing down. I'm one of the good guys."

"Moving only your gun hand, pitch that revolver to the sofa in front of you."

"Why exactly would I do that when you haven't answered my question and I don't know who you are?"

"Donal O'Loughlin. Phoenix Homicide. Retired."

"So I pitch my gun over there and you do me like you did the girl and her man outside?"

"I am ordering you — "

"You order shit. Show me a badge — who the hell you think you're talking to?"

Lester gritted his teeth and kept his eyes narrow while calculating his next step.

Go ahead, one hand to the pocket. That's all I need.

The man's eyes remained intent on Lester. At the same time his right arm came forward, elbow pushing the door, hand holding a silver badge.

"The ID says retired but you don't get to see that until the gun's down."

The man lifted his right elbow sideways and pushed the door, giving him space to move. While Lester stood in blood that would make him slip if he farted. Piss poor situation over all.

Behind the gun stood the man who had been assisting Shirley Lyle. His face was narrow, with skin like soggy leather after it dried. His eyes seemed rattled.

"So why's a retired cop carry a badge?"

"Like I said, I'm a retired cop. If you're one of the good guys, we get this sorted out in two minutes. But not until you pitch that gun to the other room. Three seconds. One. Two — "

"You got no authority unless you're willing to shoot a man in cold blood. I'm not raising on you. I came to a scene where there was gunplay, trying to lend a hand. Imagine how that'll play, you shooting me, when I had nothing to do with nothing."

"What makes you believe anyone would ever think that?"

Lester held the man's stare and understood him. Cops, courts...

"Easy," Lester said. "This is just so we can have a conversation without getting excited."

He allowed his .357 to slip in his hand until he held it by three fingers. Leaning to ease the toss, he pitched his gun to the sofa cushion.

"Turn to me. Keep your hands in the air. You know the drill."

Lester raised his hands.

The man emerged from the closet keeping the pistol directed center mass on Lester.

"What's your name? What are you doing out here with a gun — and what was the shooting a minute ago from over there?"

"I happened by and heard the noise. Thought I'd better come up and see who needed a hand. That's the problem nowadays. Nobody helps nobody."

"Good Samaritan. Sure. What's your name?"

"Lester."

"Interesting. Well, Lester, until I get a better handle on this scene, I'm taking you into custody."

"Retired cop's custody? You said Phoenix PD. You got no more authority than that gun in your hand. Far as I know, you're in it with the fat girl who stole my money. So put your gun down and call the real police if that's what you have in mind. Otherwise I'm going to pick up my piece, go home and give woe to any man who tries to stop me."

"What do you mean, stole money?"

"Look. I'm not armed. You can see it. Move your gun from off me, or I'll understand you to mean harm."

Holding Lester's glare, the man lowered his pistol hand. "I'm going to pat you down."

"The hell you are. Call the real police. That's the only move I give you."

Donal again lifted his firearm and pointed it at Lester. "Don't move." With his free hand, Donal extracted a phone from his pocket and pressed a button. Shook his head. Stepped a few feet, glanced down and stepped over the dead girl. Positioned between Lester and the front door, he removed an old land line receiver from the wall and placed the receiver to his ear.

He nodded — must have a dial tone.

His body was partly turned with his gun hand on his opposite side.

Adrenaline shot through Lester. He slid his right foot in the blood until the slipperiness gave way and his toe found purchase. He shifted his weight to that side. He saw his next moves unfold in his mind and executed them in the same moment. His weight on his solid foot, Lester lunged. He heard his feet on the floor and a scuffle behind him. He grabbed his .357 with his left hand and rolled to his right, entering the living room diagonally and carrying him out of the other man's firing lane.

His knees lifted him like they were young. Lester swung his gun arm level and pointed at the aperture around which stood the other man. He glanced about the living room. No exit.

"You make me," Lester said, "I'm coming out shooting."

"Those aren't the words of an innocent man."

"When I come out, you'll be dead if you're standing there."

9

The stock market was closed. Elvita rolled her leather high-back chair to an antique cabinet. Kicked off her shoes and pulled Chico's celebration bottle from the bottom shelf. She grabbed two glasses.

"Mendi."

Her assistant stood at her door with mail in her hand.

"You're done for the day." Elvita held an empty glass aloft. "Want to drink two-hundred dollar scotch?"

Mendi lowered her head and curled her shoulders. She brought her gaze to Elvita's. "I'm sorry, I don't drink."

"Four years, and I didn't know that."

She minced inside Elvita's office and placed two envelopes on the corner of her desk.

"Who are they from?"

"A life insurance company and the other is from the Lymphoma Society charity golf event."

Elvita pitched the second. "Chico golfed, not me."

Mendi half-smiled. "Is everything going to be okay?"

"I don't — why?"

"Your rule about unopened mail. You never throw it away."

Elvita shook her head. She bent to the trash bin and retrieved the envelope. Slipped a nail and ripped it. "An invitation." She pitched it again.

"You started to say you don't know if we'll be all right."

Elvita loosed a long breath. "I don't know. We could have handled all the clients shifting to the money markets and not generating fees. We could have kept enough in bonds to pay the bills. But we lost so many accounts — before the five million today — I don't know how things are going to turn out."

"I noticed something about the accounts that transferred out."

Elvita tilted her head. She poured Johnny Walker Blue and stopped at two fingers. "What did you notice?"

"They all clear through Pershing."

"Pershing is huge."

"But all of them?"

"Hm. All?"

"Uh-huh. Do you know, uhm."

"What?"

"It isn't my place. But... do you know where Chico has been, lately?"

"No, not exactly. Not at all. But I don't see how he could be behind it. It takes weeks to change your broker-dealer registration, and even with all his personal trading, our clients never saw him as the brains. I doubt very many would think he has the skills to manage their money."

Mendi raised her brows. "But he does. And he has a silver tongue."

Elvita flashed to a conversation she'd had with Chico when he was trying to get her to see the big picture. He dreamed of

running a hedge fund and turning the financial planning practice — her practice — into a tributary, dumping cash flow into
the fund. He'd be a separate enterprise. Most clients, when not
in a panic, were open to new ideas. *Modern Portfolio Theory was
dead*, he said, along with a lot of the financial commentariat. *You
can't diversify away risk when all asset classes can freeze and drop
like a rock at any moment. You need new tools. Old tools. All tools.
You need freedom from the constraints of the 1940 Securities Act. In a
hedge fund, you can buy on margin, use derivatives, commodities,
futures, whatever. You need the juice. You can't limit yourself to
stocks and bonds. That's where retail money goes. Think of this*, he
said. *Next time the Dow crashes seven hundred points in fifteen
minutes, how many of our clients — and other people's clients —
will be screaming for an investment that goes up when the market
goes down? All we do is peel them away into the hedge fund. Except
now, instead of earning one percent on the account, we earn two, plus
ten percent of the profit. All we have to do is talk the money loose.*

Elvita looked at Mendi. "I'm sorry, I was thinking."

"So... What's been going on with you two?"

Elvita spun her chair. Outside, far off, a cloud. Sometimes
you go all day and don't see a cloud. She sipped Johnny Walker.
"You knew we were separated. We still are."

Elvita put her feet on the windowsill and rested her head
against the leather seat back. She closed her eyes and rested her
drink hand on her lap.

"You're sending me home early?"

"Yes." Elvita lowered her legs and turned. "I don't know if I
can keep your hours the same. I'm going to have to look at the
math this weekend. I didn't want it to come to this."

Mendi leaned against the door frame.

"I have absorbed as much as I can. I can't keep the business
going if I can't pay my bills."

"I understand." Mendi left.

Elvita finished her Johnny Walker and put away the bottle. Middle afternoon, with a buzz to make it all bearable, she locked up and realized, standing in the parking lot, that she had to drive Tom's truck back to Ferguson's Tire.

She arrived at Ferguson's and found her Mercedes parked in front of the service garage. What a terrific day to buy four tires. She put the truck in park and turned off the engine, opened the door and slid out. Her heel caught a drain grill and snapped.

Elvita slammed the door. She kicked the heel free then drove her other foot at an angle to the pavement. The blacktop was hot enough to cook meat; no way was she walking in her nylons.

Inside she sat and watched the clock mounted high on the wall above the window into the garage.

The door to the work bays opened and Tom entered the lobby, along with a blast from a pneumatic device a mechanic was using on a tire. The door swung closed. Tom looked around the room and seeing Elvita, waved her to the counter. She approached with his keys dangling from her hand.

"You busted both heels."

"I did."

"When we're done I'll have one of the guys bring your car to the door."

"That's fine. I kind of like walking like this."

"I should do business with you. You don't lie very well."

"You don't know what business I'm in."

She waited while he looked at the computer screen.

Brought a pair of narrow glasses from his shirt pocket and held them up by scrunching his nose.

"So, four new tires and a free oil change."

Tom typed information from the form completed by the service man into the machine.

"Apply for credit and you get ten percent off."

"I saw the sign. Okay. I'm in."

A mechanic approached Tom and asked a question about a gizmo thingamabob — the new kind. The old had burrs on the edges. Tom stopped pressing keys and pointed to the back section of the garage.

"Do you manage this place?"

"I own it. Me and the bank."

"Might be time to refinance soon."

"Is that the business you're in?"

"No. I'm an investment manager, but I keep my eyes on rates and liquidity."

"Everyone I talk to says there's no money to be had. Nobody wants to lend, even a refi."

"That's starting to loosen."

Tom entered more information into the machine and tapped the final keystroke with an exaggerated motion.

"Your total, before taking off ten percent for the credit application, is eleven hundred ninety-three and twenty-four cents."

Elvita held her face steady. If someday soon she had to sell the Mercedes, it was money lost.

Tom passed her a clipboard with a one-page form. "Name, address, phone. Your social and income. Takes thirty seconds."

Elvita completed the form. She never used credit but had plenty of it. If she took a client to lunch, she paid with a card but made a payment to cover the expense as soon as she returned to the office.

She passed the clipboard to Tom and sat in a chair in front of the window. The place was surprisingly clean but the coffee smelled stale. The Johnny Walker Blue Label wasn't sitting well. Her head felt crowded, like before a migraine.

She pulled her cell phone out of her purse and checked her emails.

"Uh, Miss Elvita?"

She read his face. "What's wrong?"

She returned to the register. "We got a decline. Could be anything. In fact, a lot of times it's the company — you know. Since the crisis. Like I was saying, nobody wants to lend."

"That doesn't make sense. I have a dozen cards with high limits and zero balances."

He lifted his shoulders. "I don't know. You'll get a letter in the mail in a few days, and you can request more information."

"I will definitely be pursuing that."

"Okay. Um. So the balance is — "

"Here." She passed him a Visa.

He swiped.

She studied the ceiling. Tried to tap her toe, but couldn't with the heel broken.

"Uh — "

"You're kidding."

"Declined."

She pulled another card.

He swiped. She waited. Declined.

Declined.

Declined.

Declined.

10

———

*S*hirley recognized Lester Toungate's voice.

"When I come out, you'll be dead if you're standing there."

She stood on the porch step under the shadow, looking inside. To her right, fifteen feet, Ulyana. Ahead, Donal's back, and beyond, the room where Lester made demands. Beside Donal's foot, the telephone receiver and a couple feet of tangled cord rested in blood.

It's going to be a mess to get that clean. Especially after the blood dries.

Something about the whole setup bothered Shirley.

Why would Lester come barreling in? Did he have a sidekick somewhere? Didn't he have another son? Or a lieutenant? All drug lords have lieutenants. Capo-regimes and consiglieri. Hitmen — wisefellas. Were they out in the woods, sneaking up on her just as she crept up on Donal and Lester?

If it wasn't a setup, why was Lester so cocky?

Ulyana's been acting strange too...

Shirley leveled her arm and pointed her Ruger SR40c at the living room entrance.

It was bright outside. She blinked and discovered she was aiming at Donal's back and seeing the entrance beyond.

You need to be more mindful. Maybe you should tell Donal to step aside.

"Shut up."

Donal flinched. "Shirley?"

"Hello, Shirley," Lester called from the darkness. "Heard you coming."

"Well that's a pissy way to start a conversation. Donal, you want to move a little to your left, so I can get a clear shot? I'm about to make it three on the day."

His shoulders taut and his two-handed stance pointed at the living room, Donal tilted his head. "You're not supposed to be here. Why'd you come back?"

"I saw Lester sneak across the lawn with his gun out. Figured me and him needed to have words."

"Sure," Lester called. "Here's some words. How much of my money's left?"

Donal partly lowered his gun, shifted to his right and glanced back toward Shirley.

"Donal, you want to move to your left? I'll have a clean path to shoot him."

"Where are you pointing the gun now?"

"That's why you need to move."

From the room beyond Donal: "I got some more words for you, Shirley. You got my thumb drive? Isn't that where all this started?"

"Look, I ain't seen that thing since you burned my place. I

don't even want it anymore. You and me wouldn't be talking if you didn't keep trying to kill me."

"True, I came to you. But it started when you accepted that thumb drive from Clyde Munsinger. How much of this do you want your partner to hear?"

Shirley faked a smile — though Donal had his back to her and Lester remained hidden in the other room. "He already knows everything."

"So you told him about El -"

"Camino! No, I got the Durango instead... You know? Like I said I might... We should talk again real soon. After we sort this whole thing out..."

"Wait a minute," Donal said. "Yesterday you thought Lester was either dead or trying to kill you."

"Well Donal, live in the past and you're always a day behind. Or more. Lester, how about you and me save this conversation for later? After you go to jail or something."

"No," Donal said. "Lester said you took his money. He said it twice. Was that his money in the bag you carried out of here?"

Shirley squirmed inside. "Like saying something twice makes it true? You heard Ulyana. It was hers. Ruth Memmelsdorf stole it from her car."

Ulyana crossed in front of Shirley's Ruger and entered the kitchen. Shirley's mouth fell. Another step and she'd be in Lester's sights.

Shirley swiped for her but missed.

"It doesn't make sense to keep doing this," Ulyana said, standing on the other side of Ruth Memmelsdorf with only the kitchen table between her and Lester, still in the living room. "Everyone, listen to me. The light is here for all of us. Shirley, a minute ago you said you don't want the thumb drive. Did you mean that?"

"Uh — yeah? I don't know. Why?"

Ulyana's hand moved toward her pocket.

"I picked it up after your place burned. At first it was just to make sure Lester didn't get it and then I forgot to tell you."

Lester said, "You got my thumb drive, little girl?"

Ulyana sank her knuckles into her pocket. "I don't think it was damaged."

"Bring it here."

Shirley watched in horror.

"Lester, I don't want you to be angry with us anymore. Promise?"

"Sure, of course I promise. Pitch it to me."

"Okay," Ulyana said. She pulled her hand free of her pocket. "NO!"

Shirley lunged. Her toe snagged the door sill and she lurched, swung hard with her right leg as Ulyana underhand-pitched the silver thumb drive across the kitchen table.

Shirley reached —

One more bound —

Her pinky tipped the thumb drive. She followed with her stare. Her right knee landed on Ruth Memmelsdorf's stomach, burping a two-inch blood fountain from her mouth. The thumb drive spun into the living room. Donal grabbed Shirley's arm.

Ruth Memmelsdorf said, "ssssssss."

The kitchen table barked and slid.

Lester swiped the drive from the air with his left hand as Shirley lifted her Ruger level with Lester's hips.

He shifted his .357 to Shirley.

"Just stop it!" Ulyana said. "You people need to get away for a couple days and chill! Yeah?"

Lester smiled. "You can leave, Ulyana." He kept his pistol on Shirley. "Now if I can get my money back, I'll be on my way."

Still around the corner from Lester, Donal said, "Tell me about the money, Lester."

"You need to stop running your mouth," Shirley said. "You're leaving me no choice."

A bird shadow crossed the curtained window behind Lester.

Shirley held her gun steady and thought hard. If things continued on their present path, Donal would arrest Lester for showing up with a gun. Didn't make sense but that seemed to be the lay of the land: two boys having a bigger wiener contest. Lester wasn't responsible for the bodies here, but that didn't seem to matter to Donal.

That'll teach you not to belittle a man with a gun.

Regardless, if the police took Lester into custody, who knew what kind of stories the old man would tell to secure his release? Even if they took the thumb drive and used the evidence it contained to put away the undead drug lord forever, Lester hinted he knew what she did to El Jay. He'd use that information to sweeten his deal. Get a room with a window or extra time in the prison flower garden. Happened twice a day on television. He could even lie and say he witnessed her killing El Jay.

End result: Shirley Lyle mopping floors singing Old Man River. It would be difficult to steer a social justice uprising from prison.

Frigging birds must be having a party outside. Another shadow crossed the window — this one bigger.

Regarding Lester, there were only two ways things could unfold.

She could shoot Lester — say he flinched or something. Donal couldn't see and Sunbeam wouldn't be considered a trustworthy witness after spending a week in a root cellar screaming at spiders.

But Lester never raised a hand toward Shirley. When he told her to make coffee while El Jay tossed her place, he was cordial.

He tried to burn you alive in your trailer.

No he didn't. He just held a gun on me.

With you trapped inside!

Later, while her trailer burned he tried to roll her to get his gun, but he didn't take advantage of her. And though he was with El Jay when they tossed her trailer, she hadn't killed El Jay because he dumped her stuff on the floor and broke some glasses. He died because things got out of hand.

While Lester probably gave the order to toss her place, he'd been so polite... Killing him seemed wrong.

Killing people who attacked her — glory hallelujah, that was righteous. But in cold blood? Shirley didn't start Viva the Revolution so she be a spree killer.

Looking across the barrel Shirley realized that the indicator that showed if a bullet was in the chamber was not up. Trying to be more safe, she'd removed the cartridge earlier before crossing the dry stream bed. In order to shoot now, she'd have to rack the pistol and aim before Lester could squeeze the trigger.

Shirley held his steady glare and caught motion out of the side of her eye — something black in the trees beyond the yard.

"You have a choice," Lester said. "Put a bullet in your man here, take Ulyana, and walk away. El Jay, the money, all bygones. A misunderstanding culminating in some regrets and bad manners. We both move on. That's the safe move. Otherwise I'm going to make sure we're all on the same page about what brought us together today."

Panic time! We're going to jail forever! Think of something!

Shirley gulped.

She swung her gun arm toward Donal and aimed two inches right of his left ear. His jaw fell but his gun was still pointing toward the living room.

Shirley glanced out the front door and back to Donal. "Sorry, Sugar cube."

11

---

*E*lvita Blinked until the wetness left her eyes. "I don't know what to say. I have money, I have credit. I have a couple hundred thousand dollars of credit."

Tom raised his brows. She saw wrinkles by his mouth and at the corners of his eyes. He was a businessman; every day people tried to take advantage of him, and he studied her with the same suspicion as any other person trying to chisel him.

"It could be anything going on," he said. "Sounds like identity theft. You'll be able to sort it out."

"I can pay."

"That would be good."

"I have money at home my husband didn't know about. I mean, not that he has anything to do with anything."

"We're almost ready to close for the day and I live out past you a ways. I'll go with you."

Elvita hesitated. Why on earth would he need to go home with me?

Because he just put eleven hundred dollars worth of merchandise

*on your car, the economy is in the crapper and he's probably as close
to losing his business as you are to losing yours.*

"I'll just follow in my truck and sit in the driveway. Save you
the drive back this way — and that way I don't have to wait for
you to drive back."

She winced.

"I got a sick dog," he said. "I usually have him in here but he
had a surgery and has one of those things on his neck."

"A cone?"

"Yeah. I need to get home. He's doped up on pain killers. But
we still got this bill to figure out. If you don't pay it, we have to
add late fees and I don't want to do it, but collections — "

"No, that's fine. I want this resolved as much as you do. I'm
just kind of having a rotten day."

"Okay. No problem. How are you going to pay? Do I need to
bring enough change to break a hundred?"

"I have hundred dollar bills."

"Okay."

Tom left her in the lobby and entered the garage. A man
worked under a vehicle on a lift. Tom put his hand on the man's
shoulder, spoke and pointed outside. He slow-motion punched
the man's shoulder and returned to Elvita.

"Let's roll."

"I'm really sorry for this," Elvita said. "This just isn't how I
run my life. Today is a disaster every single way."

Tom said nothing.

She glanced. Still he said nothing. His head was bouncing
slowly as if in agreement, while thinking.

"Are you going to say anything about how much of a
disaster I am?"

"You're not a disaster. I was thinking about what you were
saying. I ought to be apologizing to you. I guess it's just this

economy that makes us pay attention to every nickel and dime."

"Eleven hundred dollars is more than fifteen cents. And when some woman comes in and you don't even know her, and every card is declined, you have to look after yourself. I get it."

"Yeah that's what I mean, but I just want to make sure you're okay too."

"I've been through some rough times. I'll figure out what's going on here."

*E*lvita lowered her windows as soon she turned the key, even as the engine started. They'd parked the car facing west and although it was only April, the afternoon sun streaming directly into the car made it an oven. She blasted the A/C and directed the vents toward the steering wheel.

Elvita lived a mile from Ferguson's Tire. She made a couple turns and was home. She left the garage door closed and parked in her driveway: Tom pulled in behind her.

Now he knows where you live.

"He already had my address."

But now he's here.

What was the protocol? Should she allow him to enter? Did he kind of have a right, since she owed him significant money? Plus he helped her on the roadside by changing her tire.

Elvita exited her Mercedes-Benz and Tom was already standing beside his door, looking across the roof to a saguaro.

He said he was going to sit in the truck.

"Would you like some lemonade while you wait? I'll only be a few minutes."

"Okay."

He wandered off the driveway to the gravel beside and stood

looking up at the many arms of a cactus. "Yeah, see. I love these saguaro. This one's got to be a hundred twenty years old. Did you build the house? Was this already here?"

"I bought it in the last recession. I think the development built right around the existing terrain. The back yard's full of boulders and barrel cactus."

He nodded. "Lotta folks like the grass and sprinkler setup, but I prefer the natural look. I guess 'cause it doesn't seem so artificial, right? I mean, we're in a desert."

She stepped on the patio and unlocked the front door.

This is a local businessman with a reputation to uphold. I don't have to worry.

Tom followed her into the kitchen. She removed a glass from the cupboard and a pitcher from the refrigerator.

"You have a nice home."

She passed him the glass. "Thank you. Okay, I'll just run upstairs."

"Sure."

The shortest route to the steps was to walk past him, but instead, she circled into the living room and around. She should have just leveled with him at the store and said she'd bring the money back. She could have walked home — but she was in a hurry. ALWAYS in a hurry. Rattled. Her life was caving in.

Elvita entered her bedroom and opened the closet door. She owned the house — and had a safe built into the bedroom closet wall — before marrying Chico. She'd never told him about the safe. All it held was a few thousand dollars. She always figured it would be easy to explain as a memory lapse.

She was a rotten wife sometimes. Not the person she presented herself to be... But if anything ever happened that left her destitute, she'd at least have a few dollars to grab a bus.

At the back of the closet Elvita shifted aside her long dresses and knelt before the safe. She twisted the dial left, right, and left, hesitated, and with her eyes closed, pulled open the door.

Had Chico found the safe too? Who was she kidding? He had to be behind her credit cards all being declined.

She opened her eyes.

Everything was there... plus something extra for her peace of mind. She pulled out her father's snub .38 revolver, an instrument she'd always been slightly fearful of, and possibly disdainful of, and opened the cylinder to check the load.

Maybe keeping it in a safe that takes thirty seconds to open isn't the best idea.

She tucked the pistol in her purse.

The next shelf in the safe held thirty one hundred dollar bills she'd earmarked for buying gold she never got around to buying. Deep down she always thought the banking system would be fine. Not because people of virtue sat on top — she believed the exact opposite. All financial markets were inherently corrupt... but the people who had the money would ensure the system never broke. Some companies were too big to fail. Likewise, some people were too rich to be poor. Their wealth would compel them to do whatever was necessary to keep the system afloat. Otherwise they'd be like everyone else.

She grabbed a stack of one hundreds and counted twelve.

She closed the safe and spun the dial. Stuffed the .38 deeper into her purse and snapped the flaps closed. It'd be nice if there was a way to carry the pistol, but short of a leather holster on her hip, what could she do? Strap it to her thigh?

Elvita walked down the stairs with her shoulders back and her lungs full of air. Purse on her shoulder and cash in hand.

She would be fine. No matter what, she would be fine. She'd

been poor before. She'd been a scrapper before. She'd started from the bottom and climbed. She would do it again, if she had to.

Alone, if she had to.

Tom stood at the window facing the rocky backyard she'd told him about. Hands locked at his back, he seemed deep in thought.

"I have the money," she said.

He turned, his face softer than she had seen it before.

"I had a revelation," he said.

"Oh?"

"I'd rather leave the money and take an IOU."

"That doesn't make sense."

"You had what, six cards declined? Seven?"

"Yeah, but — "

"Right. Somebody's messing with you. For all you know, those dollars in your hand might be all you have until you sort things out."

She nodded with a tight smile.

"I'll put a bill in the mail and make sure you get a few weeks to pay it. No late fee."

"I don't know what to say. What happened?"

"Guess I was standing here thinking about my sick dog, thinking I ought to be more like him."

12

"Put your gun down," Shirley said to Donal. "Lester has to walk past and no one wants any trouble."

Donal searched her face. She held her expression taut. "Come on. Put the gun down. You've no call to arrest Lester, anyhow. What did he do other than come see what the commotion was about? Constitution says he can hunt rabbits out there like anybody else."

Donal studied Shirley.

She drew her eyeballs together and pointed them both at the top of the barrel. Did he see: No red indicator... the tube was empty... Because it would suck an egg to have him whip up his gun and kill her.

Donal shook his head. "I never surrender my weapon. But if this is what you want, and you're willing to point a gun at me to get it, then Lester can pass."

"Your word?"

He clamped his mouth.

"Give me your word."

"I did when I said it the first time."

"Don't be so hard to get along with. This is a tense situation. Lester needs to hear your word."

Lester emerged from the living room with his left hand jostling his pocket and his right holding his pistol toward the ground.

Donal lowered his gun.

"Your name Donal?"

A nod.

"Good man. Another time and day, maybe — ? Nah. Shirley, you put one in my back, I guess I'll finally know something."

"I don't do people like that. Get out of here."

Shirley flicked her Ruger toward the front door and left the barrel pointed that way.

Lester glanced toward Ulyana, hesitated a moment to find his footing around Ruth Memmelsdorf and her blood. He took a long step and exited the kitchen.

With Lester past, Shirley mouthed SORRY to Donal and put her finger to her lips. He stared.

You pointed a gun at him.

With Lester out the door she mouthed WAIT.

Wrinkled brows.

They all three turned: Ulyana looking out the window, Shirley and Donal watching Lester out the front door. He stepped to the corpse of Roddy and shook his head...

He knows.

Lester raised his hands allowing his .357 to dangle from a finger in the trigger guard.

"Freeze!"

Men in black uniforms rushed from the sides of the house. Must have been the bird shadows she saw behind the curtains.

A man whose beefy body seemed to burst from his tactical

outfit yanked Lester's gun from his hand and after handing it to another man wrenched Lester's arms behind his back and placed him in hand cuffs. Lester bowed his head.

"Put that down," Donal said. He nodded at her gun. He stooped to place his on the floor.

Footsteps on the porch. Another man in black flashed past the kitchen side window.

Donal stood with his hands in the air.

A man in black jumped into the kitchen wielding a machine gun. Black leather pouches and black devices covered his black vest and black uniform: a one-man war machine. He landed on black jackboots as if his goal was the basement. He pointed his machine gun at Shirley and she allowed her pistol to slip in her hand, hoping he would notice before he murdered her out of sheer mendacious authority.

He peered through goggles with bloodshot eyes.

"We're the ones who called in, earlier," Donal said. "I'm Don — "

"SHUT UP! – YOU! – DROP YOUR WEAPON!"

Shirley's mouth fell.

"DROP YOUR WEAPON NOW!"

Shirley farted a little.

"NOW!"

"Drop the gun, Shirley, do as he says."

"YOU!" He pointed his rifle at Donal. "SHUT UP." He pointed back at Shirley. "I'M NOT TELLING YOU AGAIN!"

Shirley dropped her Ruger SR40c to Ruth Memmelsdorf's breast.

"PLACE YOUR HANDS IN THE AIR!"

Shirley and Ulyana complied. Donal shook his hands like a flapper.

"YOU!" He pointed his weapon at Shirley. "BACK AWAY FROM THE BODY."

"Uh, there's this table here — "

"I SAID BACK AWAY — "

Shirley pushed the table.

"No need to be wound so tight, officer. We called you."

Another deputy — this one in a brown uniform, not black — stood on the porch.

"Frank, I got it from here. Come on out. I need you for another detail."

The assault officer stepped backward, never removing his aim from Shirley.

"I want you to make a circuit of the location. Fifty yards out, just make sure what we're dealing with here. Got it? Go get em."

The assault officer said "HOOAH!" and Shirley imagined a drooling-mad dog under the goggles.

The officer in charge entered the kitchen. "Anyone else inside?"

Donal cleared his throat. "That guy — "

"Just answer my questions, please."

"I'm retired Phoenix PD. ID in my pocket. The basement's clear. That's where Ulyana was — her. The blond. I believe this level is clear but I haven't checked it. Things have been moving fast. I haven't been upstairs."

"LOU!" The officer swiveled his head like a man in a spit-hurling contest. "LOU! Get in here."

Of the two men holding Lester's elbows one double timed to the house.

"Boss?"

"Clear the house. This floor, then upstairs. Give the base-ment a look, last."

The brown-uniformed deputy studied Ruth Memmelsdorf.

He lifted his gaze to Shirley, then drifted to Donal and bounced hard over to Ulyana, where he lingered.

Asshole. I got tits.

"Clear a path for Lou, here, would ya?"

Shirley pushed the kitchen table until it came against the cabinets under the sink.

Lou double timed past.

"Real bunch of warriors you got here," Shirley said.

Deputy said to Donal, "Retired homicide, right?"

"PPD."

"Wait a minute," Shirley said. "No cop lingo. What's that mean?"

"Phoenix Police Department," Donal said.

"Let's see the ID. Got any more weapons on you?"

Donal nodded while he probed his pocket.

"Put 'em on the table for now. Until I know what I'm dealing with. How about these two?"

"No. The bodies belong to the kidnappers. We found Ulyana in the basement. She's unarmed. Shirley only has the one weapon that I know about. You got another gun, Shirley?"

"I wish."

Donal shook his head. "Give the situation a little more gravity."

"That's what we need — more tension. They came in here like Black Hawk Down. What's up with that?"

The brown uniformed deputy remained flat mouthed. "You'll have an opportunity to make a statement in a minute. For now, play nice until we get the situation in hand."

A raised voice from outside. "We got another body."

Shirley looked beyond the deputy. Lester seemed to shrink.

The man beside Lester turned to the officer in charge, inside the kitchen. "Frank found another body."

"I heard."

"Who would that be?" Shirley said.

Ulyana shrugged.

Donal kept his mouth tight.

"I wonder if Ruth had another woman in the cellar, before Ulyana."

"Miss? Shush. You — I'm still waiting on those guns."

Donal removed a pistol from his lower back and another from above his shoe.

"Holy cow, Donal. That's what I'm talking about."

"All this violence," Ulyana said.

A light beam entered through the window and lit airborne dust.

"You," the officer in charge said to Shirley. "Any more firearms?"

"Just that one."

"You sure about that?"

"If I'm lying I'll definitely tell you the truth."

"So this is what happened," Donal said.

The officer held up his hand. "No statements. No more talking. Let's all step outside."

"But my gun — " Shirley said.

"Let's step outside," the man said.

Donal nodded.

"What's going on?" Shirley said.

"They want to question us separately, to make sure our stories are in sync."

The officer in charge glanced at Donal.

From upstairs came the shout, "Clear!" Boots in the stairwell.

The brown uniformed deputy backed out of the kitchen and stood on the porch with his hands on his hips and his belly proud. Ulyana shifted around Shirley and exited next. Her eyes seemed watery. She crossed the porch with her fingers splayed and her shoulders taut. Shirley followed, touched bellies with the cop and followed Ulyana into the overgrown grass. She glanced back. Donal stood at the entrance.

"Keep an eye on these two, would you? Keep them apart."

The attack officer with Lester nodded. He waved Ulyana and Shirley to him. Shirley crossed the lawn and kept an eye on Donal and the other cop.

I don't trust him.

"I don't either," Shirley said.

The attack officer corralled them beside Lester, standing with his hands cuffed behind his back. Shirley noticed Lester staring at Ulyana with his lips narrow and his brows high.

He wants something.

Ulyana met his stare and her face softened. The attack officer watched the deputy talking to Donal. Ulyana glided a few inches toward Lester.

Shirley overheard snippets of Donal's explanation about how she figured out who kidnapped Ulyana. At one point he nodded at Roddy Memmelsdorf's corpse. He stepped away from the door and mimed having Roddy's arm across his throat and gun at his head. He seemed to be telling it straight.

Ulyana stretched her toe to a tuft of grass. Nudged it. Lowered her foot and shifted closer to Lester.

Hmmm.

Shirley swiveled her head and took in the rest of the scene. She hadn't noticed, but another war-clad policeman stood at the corner of the house, outside the kitchen. He seemed to expect an attack from the woods.

The man tasked with clearing the house emerged from the kitchen and approached the man at the corner. They slapped hands — high five, but chest-level, like a quickly aborted game of patty cake.

Hooah! You got here late but you played with your toys and yelled at a fat girl, so that's a win.

Shirley watched the woods but couldn't see the man who'd reported finding another body.

Would they find a boneyard of all the strippers Ruth Memmelsdorf murdered? Or did they secretly keep pigs somewhere? So many questions.

The big one: would he also find her bag of money?

Shirley swallowed. Breathed in long and slow, allowing the air to expand her chest and fill it before releasing.

From the corner of her eye she saw Ulyana ease her hand toward Lester's hip.

Ulyana had backed her play for the money with Donal... and Ulyana was a founding member of VIVA The REVOLUTION.

You have to back her up.

Shirley stepped forward and cleared her throat. "So you reckon you got the situation in hand? What's going on? Why doesn't anybody want to know my version? I got a version."

The man spat on the ground but failed to clip the spittle. It stretched. He wiped his mouth with his black sleeve. Shirley noticed his lip puffed out and black tobacco tucked in his teeth.

"That's gross."

He smiled. Ran his gaze down and up her body. Smiled again.

"Did you just? You did. Unreal."

Ulyana was slightly behind Lester, her right side hidden from the cop's line of sight. Ulyana reached behind Lester and her hand slipped around his hip, and down. Lester rotated slightly and a moment later Ulyana withdrew her hand in a ball.

Shirley shook her head. Ulyana shoved the thumb drive back into her pocket.

Lester sighed and his cold eyes seemed stuck between appreciation and calculation.

"Some people," Shirley said. She connected eyes with Lester while the cop stood watching his boss and Donal. "Some folks need to understand we're not the enemy. All we want is to get along. Let bygones — "

"What are you talking about?" the copper said.

"Just that we're all in this thing together. You know. Human beings. Right, Sunbeam? Ulyana — tell him. Say something about the sunshine. We need to get along. That's all, officer-sir. M'Lord."

His upper lip twitched but Shirley didn't know if it was because he preferred strife or had tobacco up there too.

"That's right," Ulyana said. She connected stares with Lester a long moment, then faced the cop. "Sometimes things get out of hand and when we cool off and have a chance to think, we see the error of our ways. And all we want is peace, you know, to give it a chance."

The officer smiled his contempt.

The other — the one in charge, shook Donal's hand. Donal returned inside the house. The officer in charge noticed them and his face instantly contorted. "What did I say? Keep them apart."

"No one's talking."

Head shake. Clamped teeth. He waved Shirley to him.

Boy these guys think they just get to tell everybody what to do.

She arrived as Donal emerged from the house with his hands behind his back.

"Do I get my gun back too?"

"We'll see. So. We got a body here — "

"That's Roddy Memmelsdorf. He beat his wife and killed her cat."

"And inside we have another body."

"That's Ruth. She was actually the Lex Luther of the whole affair."

"Miss, Shirley is it? Miss Shirley, I'm kind of setting the context here, so I can ask my questions."

"Oh. Okay. Because I don't know the context."

Deep sigh. Swallow. Tongue over the teeth. "Fine, Miss Shirley. How'd this all go down?"

"Super cool," Shirley explained. "Like this."

13

The officer in charge questioned Shirley for fifteen minutes and had her walk through the events culminating in two dead bodies. He asked about the man found in the woods. "Don't know nuthin' 'bout that," Shirley said.

"Thank you. I'll need you to go stand over there in the grass."

"Wait a minute. Why did you people show up? Those two clowns who came to the Memmelsdorf's house before — the ones who said Ulyana was at the strip club — they shut the whole thing down. Told me to leave. Then all of a sudden you guys show up here. What changed?"

He observed her like a man unaccustomed to answering questions. "Nothing changed."

"All you guys just decided to go for a walk in the woods."

"The two officers radioed their suspicions that the kidnapping victim was indeed being held by the, uh, these people. We assembled and came as quickly as feasible. That's all I'm going to tell you." He waved Ulyana to him. "You — stripper — what's her name? Ursula. Come here."

"Listen, my feet are a little tired. A lot tired. I got bad knees, too. I'm going to sit on the porch or something."

"Go stand over there, like I said."

"No."

"Excuse me?"

"I want a chair and they're in the kitchen. I have a health condition. I'll get it myself." Shirley took a step towards the kitchen.

The man blocked her. "This is a potential crime scene."

"No duh. I made it."

"You were aware at the time that your actions were criminal?"

"You're putting words in my mouth. All I said was I did it. I shot them. I didn't say it was a crime; you said it was. But you didn't even say that. You said it was a *potential crime scene*, and I said no duh, I made it. That's what I agreed to. It's *potentially* a pink elephant. I don't care what you call it — I just want a chair."

"You can sit on the ground. Over there."

"No."

"Frank, c'mere. Escort Miss Shirley."

"It's Mizz Lyle."

He pointed. "I want her right there. For her safety."

The attack officer with bloodshot eyes stomped from the corner where he was talking with his buddy. He pitched a cigarette ahead of him and crushed it in stride.

He must practice that. I need something cool like that: a signature.

Arriving next to Shirley, Frank reached for her arm. She

batted his hand. He lunged, grabbed her wrist and wrenched her forearm behind her back. He stank of cigarettes.

"Waaa!"

"Frank. Easy."

Frank steered her with pain. Shirley lurched but apparently not where Frank wanted. He twisted her arm and she changed direction.

Agony in her shoulder and elbow; knees, suddenly, not so much. Nose twisted up inside from the two day old tobacco stink coming from his hair and clothes.

Anger in her heart, for the thugs in black who thought courtesy was for sissies and forced everything. It's easier to use a muscle than a brain.

"Your name is Frank," Shirley said.

"What of it?" He pushed her away. They stood in grass that was overgrown last year and just coming back to life for this one.

"Your name is Frank," Shirley said. She held his eyes. Rolled back her shoulders, stood full height — two inches taller than him. She inflated her lungs and squared her stance.

He raised his lip.

"So what? Are you going to hit me? Or can I sit down?"

He opened his mouth and tongued out a wad of black tobacco. Disgusting. Copenhagen or Skoal. Her stomach rolled. The black clump fell from his mouth with a string of black goop like the old gut-cleanse advertisements where the gobsmacked guy holding a python of ooze says *this came out of my colon!*

The man coughed. Contorted his mouth. Spat. His eyes teared up. He grinned, showing stained teeth, gleeful in his vulgarity. He pulled a white deck of Marlboros — the lights — and lit one.

What is it with these people and tobacco?

"I hope you get mouth cancer."

Shirley started to lower herself to the ground and stopped. "Just great, ants! You people really are special. You don't need to be power-trip jack hats, you just are."

She placed her hands on her knees and bowed out her lower back to ease the stress. She placed one foot before the next, shifted forward. Her shoulder hurt. Lawsuit? Only if they found her duffel of cash. Ah! This patch appears ant-free. She lowered herself.

"Hey — stop. You don't get to sit today. You have to stay standing on your feet. For your safety."

"Lift me."

Across the yard, Lester gave her a narrow look that seemed approving.

She made a dumb face: What are you going to do with people like this?

He shrugged: Shoot them?

She nodded.

Over at the house, Ulyana spoke in a voice so low Shirley couldn't hear her. Donal now stood at the corner of the house with the other police officer who so far had done nothing but walk around the back of the house.

Stomping brush sounds came from the woods — off to the left, where so far she had not ventured. Must be where they found the body.

Shirley felt something.

She squirmed. Jumped. Bounced from the ground and hit it again. Slapped her calf.

"I'm sitting in ants!" She smacked her calf. Her arm. "I truly hope you get mouth cancer."

Shirley twisted partly to her side, lumbered to her feet.

What would happen if you punched him? What could he do, really?

Shirley shook off the thought. He'd kill her. Instantly.

"Miss Shirley?"

"Mizz." She turned. It was the officer in charge. Donal and Ulyana stood beside him. He marched toward Shirley, speaking on the way. "We're going to take you to the station for a formal statement. Frank, escort Miss Lyle."

"Hold on." Shirley rotated her cocky-big-girl stance toward the brown uniformed deputy. "What is this? I already told you what happened."

"I want to hear it again. All this is standard procedure."

"Do I need a lawyer?"

"You have the right to an attorney."

"Are you arresting me or something? They had guns. They were going to kill us."

"You can have an attorney present if you like. That's your right."

"Donal? Are you getting an attorney?"

Negative head shake.

"I don't know. I don't like this. You people came in like stormtroopers."

"Just keeping everyone safe."

"Yeah, like Wyatt Earp. I'm your dingleberry."

Ulyana stepped from under the shadow of the porch with her head tilted upward.

The sky was blue. Empty. Bright.

Ulyana smiled.

Shirley closed her eyes.

$\mathcal{E}$lvita logged onto her computer in her home office — a space designed to be a first floor bedroom. It was large and close to the kitchen and bathroom. She'd always loved the idea of having a den. When she bought the house it made perfect sense to locate her office-away-from-the-office close to the only other places she spent conscious time.

She never minded the window's blinds being up at night because she had a block wall around the perimeter of her yard. But tonight the black window seemed to hide a thousand probing eyes. She drew the blinds and thought of the .38 in her purse, which she'd left on the kitchen island. After grabbing it she placed the pistol beside her keyboard.

Elvita brought up a web browser. She clicked on the folder titled Finance, then selected the first credit card company website. She had six to choose from — each having declined her tire transaction this afternoon.

Each card had at least twenty-five thousand dollar lines available. She kept the cards open without balances because canceling them would reduce her credit score, and in her early years, the credit helped her smooth out her erratic sales income. Since the Great Recession began, she secretly feared she would need them again.

She entered her password and clicked enter.

Password not recognized.

Off to the side:

"Are you a customer? We do not recognize your username/password combination. To open an account click here. To reset your password click here."

Leaving that browser window open, Elvita created a new tab and opened the second credit card company website. Her username and password pre-populated. She clicked enter.

Password not recognized.

Elvita opened four more tabs, opened one of her credit card companies in each. Hit *enter,* and discovered she was unable to log into all six of her cards.

She returned to the kitchen and grabbed her purse. Withdrew her pocketbook and sat back at the computer. She extracted the first credit card and on her cell phone, dialed the number on back. She entered her sixteen digits at the prompt. Her date of birth.

"Yes. Yes. No." She pressed 1. "No. No. Representative. Representative."

0-0-0-0-0-0-0-0-0-0-0-0-0-0-0-0-0-0-0-0-0...

"The number you entered is not recognized, please — "

0-0-0-0-0-0-0-0-0-0-0-0-0-0-0-0-0-0-0-0-0...

"Date of birth, please."

Oh thank God I can understand you.

"Yes, this is Elvita Marín. I can't get into my account. I tried to buy tires and — "

"What's your date of birth?"

"I already entered that. What's the point of entering it if you're just going to ask again?"

"Ma'am, what is your date of birth?"

"March 28, 1970."

"What's the last four of your Social Security number?"

"Six two nine one."

"Your mother's maiden name?"

"Garcia."

What was the name of your high school?"

"Barry Goldwater."

"In 1994, you took out financing on a new vehicle..."

"What the hell is going on here? Why can't I get into my account? Why are you people blocking me?"

"Ma'am? To be able to help you I need to verify your identity."

Elvita spoke through her teeth. "What was the question again?"

"In 1994, you took out financing on a new vehicle. Was it a Ford Tempo, a Volkswagen Beetle, or a Honda Civic?"

"I've never had any of those vehicles. What is going on?"

"Your card was reported stolen."

"It's not stolen. I have it right here."

"We received a phone call three days ago, right after the transfer. The caller identified herself as you and said she left the card at a gas pump by accident, and when she returned could not find it. Are you saying that was not you that made the call?"

"Of course I'm saying that's not me. I didn't lose my card, I have it right here."

"I would be happy to issue a new card."

"Wait a minute. What did you say about a transfer?

"A wire."

"A wire. That doesn't make any sense. What kind of wire?"

"A money wire. Your cash advance."

"What cash advance? I haven't advanced any cash! What's going on?"

"Ma'am, I'm going to have to ask you not to shout at me."

Elvita's mouth fell open. Her heart skipped a beat. She lifted her gaze from the computer to the wall above and stared at the blankness.

Is it Chico? Did he take all of my money? Did he make a ton of debt? Is he stealing my clients? I'm going to kill him! It couldn't be Chico... How could he give me a flat tire? Who is doing this to me?

Elvita stiffened in her chair and brought her eyes back to the screen.

"I'm sorry, I didn't mean to get excited. I did not take a cash advance out on this card. I don't use credit."

"So you are denying that you are the person who took out the twenty five thousand dollar cash adva — "

"TWENTY FIVE THOUSAND DOLLARS!!!"

"Ma'am please don't shout."

"Who took out twenty five grand? You have to have a record or something, right? How does this happen?"

Elvita concentrated on breathing: inhale deep, chest out, relax the shoulders. Try not to scream or drive your head through the monitor.

"Ma'am, our records show that four days ago, you faxed instructions to wire money to an account in Grand Cayman."

"I've never been to Grand Cayman. I don't even have a passport."

"Yes ma'am, I understand. So are you denying that you sent wire instructions four days ago?"

"Yes."

"Okay ma'am, I will have to refer this to our fraud department. They will be reaching out to you."

"Wait! Turn around the wire!"

"That's not possible, ma'am. Even in cases of fraud it is not possible. The money is sent."

Elvita knew she was right.

"Wait. Can you turn off the card or something so no one else can do this to me?"

"Ma'am, with your cash advance and over limit fees, there is no additional credit."

Elvita ground her teeth.

"Still, what I asked you was whether you can turn off the card."

"Yes ma'am."

"Well? Will you do it?"

"If you would like me to."

"I can't believe this. Do you people record these phone calls? How is it possible for you to not understand that I want you to turn off this card so no one else rips me off?"

"I turned off your card ma'am."

"Who is going to call me? And when?"

"I can't say for sure, but someone from fraud will call you."

"What's your name?"

"My name is Susan, ma'am."

"Susan what?"

"Just Susan."

Elvita ended the call.

15

Shirley and Ulyana stood on the cement outside the Flagstaff police department. Grinning, Shirley elbowed Ulyana. "So I said, 'For the record, this is total garbage. I told you what happened.'"

Ulyana shifted away. "I'm not feeling as boisterous as you I guess. I want to go home and get a shower."

"Yeah. You must feel nasty. But you're out of the cellar — no more spiders! If I was you I'd be having nightmares."

"Thanks."

"Oh, cool. Sure."

The sun had set and with the arrival of darkness, Shirley's slumbering appetite roused. But more than food she craved her money. She worried about her oily freedom dollars, alone in a black duffel under a plant she hoped was poison sumac. Or oak or ivy. If the police found it, surely someone by the coffee and donuts would have said something. Assuming the cop who found it was clean, and didn't just throw the cash in his trunk.

Some people think it's okay to steal money just because it's dirty...

Ulyana faced the door behind them. Shirley studied it too. Farther up the building proud spotlights showcased the police department name. Ulyana glanced at the hedges and leaned closer to Shirley. She fumbled her hands together. "You said you have my money?"

"Oh sure, it's in the Durango, I checked. You want to get out of here?"

Ulyana nodded but didn't move. "What about yours?"

"Do you want to get away from the building? Just in case it comes out in a couple years that you can't trust your government not to spy on you, you know?"

They stepped away from the building.

"You want a burger or something?"

"I want kale juice."

"Oh — bile. Now I need a soda."

They walked and stopped. Shirley reached but stopped short of touching Ulyana's shoulder. "So what's the deal? I know you just went through some serious crap. I mean, they were going to kill you. Cram a dildo in your ear and stir. What a mind-fu — "

"We need to change our arrangements," Ulyana said. "Did you get your money back? It was all there? Or mostly?"

"Well, uh — yeah. Near as I can tell."

"I need some space to evaluate things. To breathe a little and find a sense of peace about what happened. I have so many questions."

"Oh, Honey. Sure! Of course. We need to get a hotel anyway. Maddix is still at your trailer and — honest — killing someone on carpet is so much different. You'd think the carpet would soak up the blood and keep things tidy — and it does, but you know, it's kind of sick. It smells worse in a confined space. If I was you I'd move. Let Clyde Munsinger's relatives worry about it. Or we could get Lester to burn your place too. Did you say you had insurance on it?"

"I know. About getting a hotel: I know I need to. But I want space. So different hotels. And I need a few days to clear my head, you know. Before we talk again."

Shirley's jaw gapped. Her brain sputtered.

"Don't take this wrong. I'm very grateful to you."

"Sure. Of course. You need some..." Her first chin puckered and dimpled. A tight frown pressed old happy tears from her eyes.

"Ohhh. I'm sorry. Don't cry. This isn't about you."

"Bullshit. Everything's about me."

Shirley wiped her eyes. Smiled as much as she could fake, then suddenly felt better. "Wow. That works. You know Oprah had on this head shrink who said you can make yourself feel better if you smile. I just did it. Why don't you? Then we'll get a hotel. We can get rooms side by side or something."

Ulyana smiled — but tight, with narrow eyes. "Yeah. Um. I don't need to convince myself I'm happy. I need to understand."

"Try some alcohol?"

Footsteps. Shirley turned. Donal quick-stepped the cement stairs as the glass front door closed on its automatic hinge behind him.

Shirley lifted her arms, wrists side by side. "Look! No arrest! Woo-hoo!"

"So far," Donal said. He slowed as he approached, giving off a sense of not belonging. Hands jammed in pockets; tight about the face as if anger simmered.

"What do you mean, so far? They had their chance. If they come at me again its double jeopardy and I don't play that game, Alex Trebek."

"Double jeopardy only means they can't try you for the

same crime twice. They can consider you for it as long as they want, if the crime is murder."

"Murder? How can you murder an evil person? That's a serious question."

"They'll give what they have to the D.A. He'll make the call."

"Does he have my number?"

"He'll make the decision about potential arrests."

"Arrest me for ridding the world of creeps? Great. How will he let me know if he doesn't have my number? Don't answer. They'll come crashing through my door with their black shirts tight on their biceps and prodding me with a machine gun. In Ronald Reagan's America." She shook her head. "I don't know. I just don't know."

"What don't you know?"

"How'd this come to pass?"

"Are you done? What do you want?"

"An *atta girl*. The world has three less creeps because of me. Say, when do I get my Ruger back?"

He shook his head. "No way to say."

"They can't just steal it."

"Yeah, Shirley. They can. I notice that words don't mean the same thing to you as they do to everybody else. I don't have time to explain it."

"So what's the deal with Lester?"

Ulyana peered at Donal's face.

"Loose lips at the coffee machine. I wandered around after giving my statement. This is a solid police department. I talked to some of the guys."

"Coffee and donuts," Shirley said.

"I was in earshot of the kitchenette. If they haven't arrested Lester yet, they will. They were holding him on suspicion, based on the gunshots we heard before he arrived and the body found in the vicinity of the gunshots. One of the officers I talked to said Lester hadn't said a word other than 'lawyer' since they found the body this afternoon."

"That's too bad," Shirley said.

"What? This is the guy you said was trying to kill you."

"We kind of had a moment."

"Empathy," Ulyana said.

"Yeah. Telempathy," Shirley said. "Like we were in each other's heads, because the police are such asshats. No due respect, of course. Or unintended disrespect."

"If you were a peace officer facing today's society, you wouldn't think the same way. You'd be defending yourself just like they are."

"So much violence," Ulyana said.

"I'm mad at you," Shirley said. "You were just standing there while that thug tried to break my arm off."

"A police officer has to control the scene or else it's dangerous for everybody."

"There wasn't a scene. It was just us and a couple of dead people."

"I give up. But there's one thing I need to know. When you put your gun on me, you knew the police were out there?"

"Oh yeah, of course. I saw motion behind the curtains and outside I saw a couple of them getting in position. I wanted to get Lester outside without another shootout. It was so tight in there. I'm super-glad you trusted me."

He stared at her too long. Finally released a long breath. "Trust? You don't ever, ever want to do that again. I don't trust people. I'll take you out."

Donal walked to a patrol car that pulled up.

Shirley shook her head. "I really don't get it. I guess I should've not gave a damn and drank myself to death. Then I'd be dead and you'd be dead and the people who have the power to help people wouldn't look like useless cowards."

Donal looked back at her while he stood with his hand on the cruiser's door handle.

Get in the car already.

Shirley stepped toward him. Thrust out her chin.

Donal entered the police car and kept his face pointed forward as it drove away.

"Were you dating him or something?" Ulyana said.

"No. I was using him to help me find you. Let's go. I'll give you your money and take you to a hotel."

I'll celebrate the fact that you're alive without you, Sunbeam.

Shirley drove Ulyana to the Motel 6 on East Butler Avenue next to Interstate 40.

Ulyana pouted. She pressed the door closed and failing to make it latch, turned and rammed it with her butt. She stood in front of the double glass doors with her backpack of cash.

What ever.

Shirley stomped the gas and the Durango lunged. She braked to avoid a car with a U-Haul trailer hidden behind it.

You are not going to cry.

She'd have to drive all the way around the building to get out of the parking lot.

Why do they do that? Oh look! Subway.

The clock on her dashboard read 10:45. Her stomach gnawed. She dry swallowed. Reverse, forward, reverse, growl over to the empty Subway parking area.

Make you a deal. You can get a sub but you have to park in the corner and walk all the way to the door.

"But my feet hurt."

No pain, no footlong double meat add the bacon and run it through the garden.

"I'll walk for bacon."

Shirley tooled by the entrance. No one was inside except a young girl who never ate. The back of the lot was barely lit. Shirley patted her chest. No Ruger. And Donal — the way he was acting, he might not even sell her another. Fine. She'd drive to Phoenix and get one on the street from some gangbanger who removed the serial number with acid. Buy the gun, then kill him with it. She may not know what he did to deserve it, but he would.

Shirley scanned around the Durango. Hunkered and twisted to get a long look out the rear side window.

All clear. Safe.

She opened the door and gazed at the front of the Motel 6 where Ulyana, still standing, turned with her head bowed and went inside.

You should feel like crap. Ingrate.

A Nissan Altima swerved from Butler Avenue with squealing tires. The tail lights flashed and the car lurched to a stop, scraping its nose on the concrete sidewalk.

"Hey. No!"

They were right beside the entrance.

Shirley slammed the Durango door. Pushed off, heart a patter.

No. No. No.

Six boys and girls splashed out of the vehicle and raced inside the restaurant. Little playful footsteps.

"You..... You....." Shirley faced the building a long moment trying to fathom random acts of subjective evil. Her lungs as empty as her stomach, she entered and stood in line behind the caffeinated teens.

Their noise became background: Everybody flirting, rolling eyes, hands in pockets, nervous feet, vanity, sham anger, nudges and laughs. Oh! The humanity.

Just go out in the woods and screw yourselves blind already.

Shirley patted her pockets.

The sandwich artist opened the bread cabinet and pulled out a left over six inch Italian.

The little princess in leotards decided on Black Forest ham. The bunny beside her giggled and with exaggerated gravity chose meatballs.

A boy, bless his heart, said he was a breast man and chose chicken.

You are not going to cry!

Shirley left.

16

FBI Special Agent Joe Smith left the ambush when it became obvious that Lester Toungate had taken the bait and would solve his Shirley Lyle problem. He'd been following as Lester tailed her and when Lester pulled to the side of the road Joe had to make a choice: He could swerve behind him, abandoning all pretense, or turn his head and maintain the sham that he was someone else that just happened to be driving a black government issue sedan and choosing the same exact turns.

Joe kept driving and instead of turning around and trying to figure out a place to park and watch Lester, so he could charge into the breech and commit two murders if Lester failed, Joe instead drove a mile, pulled into an empty driveway and summoned a map on his phone to guide him back to his hotel without returning past Lester.

He'd been summoned back to Phoenix and while on one hand his boss demanded his quick return, on the other Joe knew if he abandoned his task without being certain Shirley and Ulyana were eliminated, he would leave a string that would unravel his role in soliciting a prostitute and being an accessory to her torturing and murdering a man.

Joe was government, sure, but not high up enough to do those things with impunity.

Special Agent Joe Smith returned to the hotel where he'd already checked out that morning. He sat in the lot thinking with the radio tuned to an AM news station and his unfocused eyes resting on a Burger King across the street.

He would get a hamburger; those were good. And he would wait for word that two women had been found murdered.

He eased through the Burger King drive through and with burger in hand, parked in the back of the lot while the announcer talked politics and economics.

Should he return to the scene? See what became of Lester?

Or drive to Lester's house? All it would take was a quick nod, no words, just a solemn gaze from Lester, and Joe would understand the threat of being implicated in murder was ended.

He chewed. They forgot the cheese, how? You put the burger on the bun and the next step no matter who you are or where you learned hamburgers —

Joe swallowed.

The burger wasn't bad without cheese. Gave the tomato room to sing.

Hadn't he paid extra for the cheese? He shook his head and dug his receipt from the paper bag. Shirley Lyle. Everything in life was worse because of her, as if she draped a black film over his entire world. Joe read his receipt and wondered why he dug it out.

He waited for hours. Eventually he closed his eyes.

. . .

*T*he radio:

In breaking news: a Flagstaff couple shot dead under questionable circumstances, with another shooting victim found in the woods nearby. Details, top of the hour.

They cut to a commercial. It wasn't news so much as intermittent hooks followed by ten minutes of ads. Joe rolled his Burger King bag with the crumpled napkins inside. He opened and closed his mouth. He'd been sleeping and his tongue tasted funky, like after breathing though his mouth and snoring. He had to pee. His back was tight. The car was snug. He could walk to the trash but that risked not hearing the news. He pitched the garbage to the passenger footwell and opened his window. Fast food smelled appetizing until it was inside your gut and your body realized the trick.

"Annnnnd top of the hour news, Phil Morgan here. Let's go immediately to Jessica Pink who is on site at the shooting that took place today in Flagstaff. Jessica, what do we know?"

"Thank you Phil, this is Jessica Pink on the scene. It was a bright morning like any other until shots rang out... in Flagstaff."

"So, uh, Jessica, can you tell us what actually happened?"

"Thank you Phil. Yes. It was a tranquil scene. A house in the woods like an old hunting camp until late this morning, when chaos broke out... This haunting landscape could be a war zone."

"But Jessica? What happened?"

"There are two bodies, one inside the house and one outside — and police say there's still another shooting victim in the woods nearby."

"Any word on the victims' identities?"

"Police say two of the victims are the property owners. The other has not yet been identified. Each brutally shot at close range for maximal blood curdling damage — "

"Thank you Jessica. Any word on who the police believe was responsible?"

"Yes, I learned moments ago the shooter was a single woman who is being detained for questioning as a person of interest. At this time no motive has been established."

"Alleged shooter."

"Yes, alleged shooter."

Joe leaned his head to the steering wheel and stared at the tachometer. His mind swam. Thoughts crashed like waves. Some got in his lungs. He felt himself going down.

Joe sat bolt erect and felt his pockets. He opened the car door and jumped out. Patted his jacket breast pocket. His pants pocket. Dove back into the car and found his phone in the center console, plugged into the charger.

He yanked it free and swiped open his photo gallery.

The first time he visited Shirley Lyle, prostitute, he'd sat in his car several trailers down, hood pointed to the gravel road and angled so his line of sight through the passenger window aligned with her trailer door.

In that exact moment, he'd been unsure he'd go through with it. He had a powerful, powerful need and didn't feel like satisfying it the way he usually did. Dead-ended in the FBI, stationed to Flagstaff to hunt a redneck murderer. No social life and no friends he could go drinking with and find someone to screw. No outlet — and he, a man in his rutting prime.

Up to the moment he knocked on Shirley Lyle's door he told himself he was surveilling her as practice for the day the FBI gave him a role in the field — not computers and video tech. He wasn't there because he wanted laid, he told himself. It was practice. Home study. Above and beyond work ethic.

When a man exited the trailer, Special Agent Joe Smith took photos.

It became his thing. He'd arrive, take pictures and eventually ease into a zero morality zone, a blackout that allowed him to slip inside and... slip inside.

Surrounding his bad deeds with the appearance of good created dissonance between his abiding depravity and goodness. Every time he arrived at Shirley Lyle's place, he tuned himself taking photos.

The first man he'd captured in pixels seemed familiar but it wasn't until hearing that Shirley survived that something in his brain clicked.

He knew where he'd seen the man before — or rather — who he'd seen the man with.

Joe rolled through his cell phone's image gallery. Too many pictures of the snowy mountain peaks and white-barked trees with bright yellow leaves. A mama elk nursing a calf. Fawn? Little elk.

Ah! Here!

The man was balding. His face had lodged in Joe's mind, seemingly familiar but impossible to place. Joe had snapped three quick images as the man hurried from Shirley's door to his Dodge Magnum. When he backed out Joe snapped a shot of his license plate.

Joe expanded the clearest image and smiled.

He didn't know the man.

He knew his wife.

17

*E*lvita stared at an Excel spreadsheet she'd created to keep a record of each conversation with her credit card companies.

Six cards, each with an outgoing wire. The total: $153,492.88. Every single penny of her credit limit, and because charges came in after the wires went out but before the cards were reported lost, the total debt was $169,181.15.

Her heart felt like a fist.

You're going to lose the company. There's no way to make payments on a hundred and seventy grand on credit cards. That's thirty thousand of interest a year. You're bankrupt. Right now, you are bankrupt.

She stood up from her chair. Wine? She needed to steady things out. Think. Let her heart stop pounding and her nerves stop twitching every time the house creaked.

As she drifted toward the kitchen, she hesitated.

"No alcohol. Right now you need to think."

Elvita returned to her chair and read the Excel spreadsheet:

card name, the total balance, payment due, the amount of the money wire, location, date and time, and the first name of the person giving her the information.

She placed her head in her hands and closed her eyes.

*S*he met Chico at a dance club. She'd just bought her house and he'd just lost everything. They celebrated. Hooked up. Dated. Married.

Sometimes when they sat around being romantic, lazing side by side on the couch, he mused about starting a hedge fund. He talked about how exciting it was to trade. How much better the income potential was, since he'd be able to charge whopping fees plus a percentage of the gain. Retail investing was for suckers... Both the clients and the advisors choosing to play in a city with oppressive rules when the wild, wild west was the next town out.

Before they met, Chico traded stocks for a living. In the late 90's the Nasdaq went up every day. Press a button, make money. Chico managed to lose some. A lot, paying his dues, you know. He returned to stocking racks at Home Depot.

When Chico's father died he inherited some cash and opened an E*TRADE brokerage account. Told his boss to shove it and went back to what he loved.

Chico could talk a wicked game about Fibonacci Fans, Stochastics and Moving Average Convergence Divergence, or MACD, but he never profited enough to improve his stake. He was always one bad trade away from the night shift.

The S&P 500 bottomed in September 2002. When an early February rally fizzled in March, Chico went all-in against the market, expecting another twenty-percent decline. He bought far out-of-the-money puts, which would grow exponentially as the market fell — but would lose value in a flash if the S&P 500 increased.

The market rallied. Chico talked himself through the trade, why the market had to fall and any other outcome was impossible. Each ten thousand that disappeared from his trading account only furthered his commitment to the position. Selling would lock in the loss.

"At that point it was only on paper."

To Elvita's mind, the situation was profoundly different. Chico logged gains when the ticker hit a high mark and ignored everything after. She logged gains after making the sale and deducting the cost of the trade and taxes.

He said, "Everyone in sales has heard of the guy hunting diamonds in Africa. He searched all over for diamonds but they were all in his back yard."

"The analogy doesn't work. You're thinking of the gold miner who quit digging, when the seam was another foot down."

"Yeah, you know what I mean. That's why I stuck with it."

He was reflective, somber. He admitted his failure — yet his determination remained undiminished.

She was more intelligent than he was — but everybody's brains worked differently. His obstinacy made him more masculine and in the beginning she loved him more for it. She wanted to protect him.

In the beginning.

Though broke, he knew too much about the industry to give it up. So instead of trading his own money — he had none — he would earn his fortune trading other people's money.

Ever since he first learned about hedge funds, he wanted to own one. The idea of being the genius sitting atop the market, watching graphs on the screen and knowing the future... The image was intoxicating and within reach. From his past failures he'd created new trading strategies that would eliminate the risk and all but guarantee high returns. All he needed was a few clients and the operating cash to get started: $150,000.

*E*ach wire went to Grand Cayman. None of the credit card companies were willing to share the routing information, even though they had verified her identity.

Elvita understood each company would assume the charge was legitimate while its fraud department investigated. She'd had her credit card number stolen before. Charges for E-Harmony showed up on her statement. She contested the purchase and the item was removed. But she feared twenty five thousand dollars might cross a threshold where the truth would most likely be found aligned with the company's most profitable outcome.

Bottom line: she would have to prove it wasn't her.

She would have to be proactive.

She grabbed a sticky pad and a pen.

1) call police

2) call Experian, Transunion, Equifax. Add 90 day fraud alert.

3) call company compliance — morning!

She searched the internet for the Glendale police. Pressed the numbers on her cell phone and put the call on speaker.

"Ma'am, that's a civil problem. The appropriate course is for you to report it to your credit card. They'll wipe out the debt. No worries."

"Officer, the total is one hundred and sixty nine thousand dollars. If someone stole that out of a bank, would you be interested?"

"That's a completely different situation. That's real money."

"Actually it's all debt but you don't know what money is. Are you honestly telling me that creating debt in someone else's name is not a crime because it isn't real money?"

"Ma'am that's not what I meant and not what I said. The credit cards will write off those charges. Crime without a vic — well, crime without any people who actually lose money."

"I need to speak to your superior."

The receiver muffled like it was being pressed against cloth. The police officer's voice came through in grumbles, talking to someone else.

"You can come to the station and report it."

"What is your name, officer?"

"Hank. That's Officer Hank."

"I'll be there in fifteen minutes."

"You'll have to come in tomorrow. There's no one on duty for that type of complaint."

"There's no one on duty. You're a volunteer?"

"Ma'am, I have work to do. I'm hanging up now. Come by tomorrow if you want."

"When I come, what will happen? I file a report and then what?"

"You should bring any paperwork you have that supports your claims. An officer will be assigned and will review what you brought."

"And then what, an investigation?"

"The detective will make a decision."

"Thanks for being on my side, Officer Hank."

18

Money made the world go 'round. Earlier when Ulyana's fate was uncertain and Shirley drove with Ulyana's bag of cash in the back of the Durango, a tiny voice in the back of her mind said, *if she's dead, you get the money.*

It wasn't Old Shirley or Viva Shirley.

Evil Shirley whispered and the syllables caressed her into feeling solvent with only the cash they'd taken from El Jay and her $13,000 life's savings.

Ulyana's situation had been dire — she was most likely dead and the objective truth, regardless of how Shirley felt, was that she would inherit the pink backpack and its stacks of hundred dollar bills.

Down a friend. Up a half million.

No comment.

However...

Now that Ulyana's cash resided with Ulyana, and the

ungrateful little butterfly had holed up in a Motel 6 to meditate her way to enlightenment, Shirley's cash situation felt dire.

She missed the sense of freedom the smelly street dollars had given her. She'd finally hoped for a normal self-respecting life. No more hooking. Freed of workday chains, she'd have time to better herself. Not meditating — she wasn't a new age weirdo or anything — but maybe she'd watch more Oprah. Do some stretches and start taking shark cartilage for her knees. Figure out which vegetables were edible.

It was hard to think while her dollars were stashed in the woods available for anyone who walked by to notice — and steal. She had no home, no refrigerator, no job. Her tiny nest egg would never last.

Shirley's life economics felt like cement blocks on her shoulders.

If the absolute worst happened and someone stole her stolen money, what recourse would she have? What livelihood? The question almost sank VIVA The REVOLUTION from the beginning.

If she didn't hook she'd have to find an entire new set of skills to bring in the dollars. Thinking about it didn't feel like a weight on her shoulders so much as cement blocks chained to her ankles, thrown overboard, pulling her under.

She'd been a producer her whole life. She left home at eighteen and moved to Cumming, Georgia and started at a restaurant waiting tables. She knew the menu. Loved chatting. Acquired flirting skills — even started her pretentious word folder when a dear old lady called her a *coquette* for stroking her husband's shoulder while describing the seared sausage sammich. She got away with more than the skinny girls. Most wives didn't mind her sweet hearting and sugaring their men.

She was safe.

She was a big girl.

It worked because in those days men tipped what they wanted and average middle aged housewives didn't know how much fun an unreserved thick girl could have. Shirley enjoyed getting poked as much as the boys doing the poking, and kinda sorta earned a reputation for easy availability.

One rare day she wasn't in the mood. That morning the scales read 275 for the first time — and that after two days of only eating toast and water — a diet she'd heard about from another waitress who said it was Rocky Balboa's diet. Desperate to slim down, she bought two loaves of Wonder Bread and set about eating them. After drinking a gallon of water, against all odds, she gained weight.

She realized fate had condemned her. Nothing worked. Fatter and fatter. She remembered being skinny when she was what? Five? Halcyon days for her waistline — followed by years of storm. Raining fat. Waves of fat. Until the skinny girl drowned and Shirley navigated the stages of grief: denial, anger, bargaining, depression and acceptance. Maybe the toast experiment was her last attempt at bargaining to bring back the skinny prepubescent her.

"What's wrong Shirley? You're in a mood this morning. Hey, can I get another piece of toast to mop up these eggs? They're runnier than usual."

"Toast. Ugh." She refilled Walter's coffee.

"You don't like toast?"

"Its all I've had for three days."

"Why?"

"Diet."

"Reminds me of a joke."

"I don't want to hear it."

Walter smiled — a charmer. She'd banged him twice in the

last three weeks, both times in the back of his brand new 1978 Ford F-150 crew cab. Made her feel both rich and crazy, with Ted Nugent on the 8 track.

Both of their last tosses started with Walter telling her an embarrassingly weak joke.

"Walter," she leaned, "it ain't happening."

He raised his brows. Hesitated. Smiled. Pressed on. "So this woman gives birth. Doc says the boy's healthy. She opens her arms and takes him. Later she sees something wrong."

Walter grinned. Waited.

"Okay Walter. What was wrong with the baby?"

"The baby had a tiny — " he glanced around. Lowered his voice. "Dick."

"A dick joke? A *baby* dick joke?"

"Shhh! So the doctor says, just feed him some toast. That's all it takes. 'Bread toast?' she says. 'Yep.' So she takes the baby home. Sits him in the — whaddaya call those chairs for babies, with the tray? Anyway she brings a plate with two dozen pieces of toast."

"Sounds like a sick mother. 'Sides. Wouldn't it grow? Their hands and feet grow."

"You're spoiling the joke."

Shirley glanced across the tables. A man held a coffee cup in the air. "I'll be back."

She filled the coffee. Took a couple orders. Rang out a customer. Took a pee break. Returned to Walter.

"Okay. Finish your story."

He shook his head. "It won't even be funny now."

"Wasn't yesterday, either. It's a baby's dick."

"So the new mother brings thirty pieces of toast on a plate. The baby reaches his hand and she smacks it. 'That's for your father!'"

Walter snorted three times and stopped.

Shirley fake smiled.

Walter reached. Touched her wrist with one finger. Slid it an inch.

She pulled away. "I gotta ring this couple out."

Shirley kept herself busy at other tables and didn't return to Walter. She'd only been away from home a couple months but she'd already learned how wildly men could distort reality when seeking signals allowing them to continue their pursuit. If she so much as glanced at him it betrayed her deepest desire to make him lord of her life, so she could serve his every physical desire and then do his dishes and laundry.

At last she took her fifteen minute break. Before returning she looked out from the kitchen.

He was gone.

Walter returned early afternoon when he knew her shift ended.

"What are you here for?"

"Wang dang."

"Well go home."

Shirley left him at the counter. Another waitress asked to seat him and he waved her off. Shirley went to the kitchen, punched her time card and slid it in the metal slot.

Walter was still there with his hands in his pockets. Basset hound eyes under rock n roll hair. He grinned. "Was it the toast joke? I thought it was too edgy."

She shook her head as she walked past and out the door. He leaped behind her. She turned left on the sidewalk and he followed. She lived two blocks away — the best thing about the restaurant job.

"I gotta have some of your love," he said.

"I have to clean a stuck drain."

"I could do that… For a fee."

Shirley slowed. Step. Step. Stop. Turn. "Did you just offer to fix my drain in exchange for me sleeping with you?"

"Well."

Shirley walked. Walter followed. She stopped. He stopped. "Is that what you think I am?"

"Well — "

Shirley walked. Walter followed. She stopped. He stopped. "I'll fix my drain myself. And if you want me from here on out it's fifty bucks."

"Fifty bucks? No matter what? What if I only want — "

"Every time."

She watched his mouth part and eyebrows drop a little on the sides, then scrunch up in the middle. Meanwhile his jaw shifted left, right, left.

Shirley had no idea what sex cost. She'd thrown out fifty dollars because it sounded like a high number but Walter seemed to be considering it.

She walked faster, hoping to reach her apartment building before Walter could find his cash. He made decent money in the union, middle-aged, unmarried. Not exactly a wild man in bed, but he could focus and make it last as long as he wanted, which was a hell of a lot better than her last twentysomething from the bar on the corner. Sometimes he'd whisper dirty things in her ear that helped her embrace the fact that regardless of how high her intellect usually floated above the biological necessities of earthly life in human form, she was in fact an animal behaving in the most utterly animalistic fashion, which made getting laid one hundred percent better.

Thinking about it changed her mind. She was randy as she reached her building.

Hand on the rail, Shirley placed one leg on the step and stretched it so he could take in the curve of her calf.

"What's it going to be, Walter?"

"Fifty dollars? My house payment's only two fifty."

The fantasy moment snapped.

She'd offered herself for money. Straight up brazen sex for cash. She was a whore.

Shirley rushed up the steps, unlocked the apartment building entrance and ducked inside. She slammed the door and when she entered her apartment slammed that door too. She slid the dead bolt and leaned against the door.

All her life she'd giggled with the other girls, pointed at and ridiculed the sluts. And here she just dangled her sex out there for money. There was the side she was on, the line and the people on the other side. Always. As a girl, the sluts were on the other side of the line.

Then she became a slut and felt the same.

The next line demarked the whores...

Walter never came back to the restaurant. She saw him in town a couple times. He turned away both times like she was a different girl than the one he penetrated for fun, offered to penetrate for an exchange of services and refused to penetrate for cash.

Shirley rarely thought about Walter in the thirty-two years she spent prostituting herself. But when she did, it was with a sense of puzzled gratitude. He brought her to the line and dared her to put her foot across.

When she did she felt no different.

If she had to pay the bills, she had to pay the bills.

Thirty two years but she finally got it.

There never was a line.

19

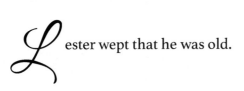ester wept that he was old.

20

---

*S*hirley slowed the Durango at the final right turn expecting a sea of revolving red and blues. There were three dead bodies back there — the Memmelsdorfs' and the stiff they were pinning on Lester.

So far, no field of bones or other proof the missing strippers existed outside of her fancy. Well, if Stephen Hawking could say black holes existed because they made sense, Shirley could believe in missing strippers.

The street was empty. Out of the half dozen houses on this stretch only one had a front porch light on.

Shirley crept around the corner but didn't accelerate.

Where are the police?

She picked up speed. Another hundred yards and she'd have to decide. She couldn't park on the road and walk all the way back to the house where they kept Ulyana in the cellar. Not with springtime bugs coming alive and a mountain lion being spotted in Tucson. Four hours away, sure, but those critters roam. Probably grizzly bears out there too, at least at night.

Actually, you can walk that far. You did it the other night around the trailer court.

"Well, yeah. I did."

The Memmelsdorfs' place was to her left. Shirley kept the wheel straight. A quarter mile farther she pulled into a random driveway, backed out and returned to the Memmelsdorfs'.

"What will I say if they catch me?"

Gathering evidence for your lawsuit?

"They'll love that."

She stopped in the driveway, engine running. Weird looking at the house now that the people who were supposed to be inside it were on slabs. Kind of peaceful, except for everything being black, and the legion of undead strippers buried in the woods.

The police have to be back there working the evidence.

They probably had a tent set up and generators running spotlights like a scene from an alien movie. They'd have a guard on the road to keep out that pesky button nosed reporter who let her stories deliver her punches. And the grad student guy who was always sniffing after her, he'd be along for the ride — because he studied aliens at Northern Arizona U, and the writers knew Shirley was dying for them to make a real, lasting connection instead of a quick hook up.

She blinked away the vision. Just a dark road with houses keeping their eyes low, not looking for problems.

Shirley turned the wheel and coaxed the Durango onto the lawn. Leaned forward in her seat. Hunkered.

Crept around the house.

Uhhhh — headlights?

"I won't see nothing without them."

But you don't have your Ruger.

"There's nobody but police up there."

Shirley steered around the tiny cabin built for the wood burning stove. No smoke. The Durango seemed to pause before rolling over the final tufts of grass and entering the woods.

The trees were closer together than in the daylight and she wondered if she remembered the path around the fallen tree well enough to navigate it without scratching her paint. If she could make it that far before someone stopped her.

Turn off your headlights. You're never going to get your money if they see you first.

Shirley took her foot off the gas and peered at the blackness under the trees. The Durango drifted and stopped.

"This isn't going to work."

The dashboard lights created a glare. Shirley rolled down her window then partly stuck her head out. She pulled forward and then backed into the space she had just observed. The Durango was off the trail but with its nose forward so a quick right turn and a heavy foot on the gas would spin her to the exit.

She left the vehicle unlocked in case a grizzly bear chased her back. She patted her breast. Nope. Handgun hadn't returned.

"I should pick up a rock or something."

Nah. Stealth mode. Quick and dirty.

Shirley reached out with her arms and squinted in case she walked into tree branches.

As long as you remain on the path there won't be any branches.

"Good, my arms are tired already."

Which reminded her that her feet hurt. And she hadn't eaten since that morning. She probably lost fifty pounds already.

"This is crazy. They'll hear me and start shooting."

So shut up.

Shirley squinted. Focused. The darkness in the woods seemed total. A couple of insects buzzed. Something skittered across leaves: probably a squirrel.... or a serial killer. She looked left and right hoping to resolve the direction of the path.

You need that money. Don't stop now. Your eyes will adjust. This is like going to the refrigerator at two a.m. You can see fine then because your eyes adjusted to the dark while you were sleeping. You'll be blind for five minutes, then you'll be able to see.

"So I should wait five minutes."

There's no time. Keep going.

Shirley crept forward and put her arms up again. Turned to reorient herself based on the Durango — and couldn't see it.

"I'm getting out my cell phone."

Hush. No! Wait a minute.

"You said — "

Shush!

Shirley waited.

Listened.

She lifted to the balls of her feet and rotated. The Durango engine ticked. Now that she knew where to look, its blackness seemed a deeper shade than the night around it. She distinguished the gray of the sky and stars filling the gaps in the early spring tree canopy. When she returned her gaze to the terrain before her, different shades of dark resolved and a ghostly lighter-black seemed to stretch before her. The ground was a void. She could walk off a cliff and not know — but at least the contrast gave her a path.

"Oh! Coming back — how will I find the Durango?"

You'll see it, by then.

In the distance, slightly to her left, she detected a brightening in the forest. Distant lights. Cops at a crime scene. Shirley released her breath. Stepped forward. Reached ahead; stepped and reached, stepped and reached. Almost hard to keep her balance without something solid to stare at.

Another step — a small rock underfoot pressed her arch. An insect buzzed her head.

Slow going. Sweat wetted her brow. She shivered and advanced toward the brightening. The leaves on the path reflected light differently: they were less black.

She detected the tree that had fallen across the path while still a dozen feet away. With increased care she circled the obstacle and resumed the trail. At the fork she crossed the stream, unable to find the rocks she'd stepped across in the daylight. After a moment cold water soaked her feet.

Well... that feels absolutely wonderful.

She stepped backward and stood in the water. The coldness eased some of the pain in her feet.

You're like an Army Ranger.

"They stand — "

Shhh.

"They stand around in water?"

Radio silence!

The faint glow ahead eventually became a dome of light, bordered by trees on the sides and the relative blackness of the sky and woods all around. Two policemen — no longer wearing their martial law uniforms with tools and gadgets and body armor — sat on the porch smoking cigarettes. Had to be only a few feet from where Roddy's corpse had been.

So they removed the bodies. What are they still doing here?

She saw motion inside the house.

"Processing the crime scene."

Four vehicles were parked next to the house, not counting the four wheelers used by the Memmelsdorfs. Two cops outside and one or two Dexters inside gathering blood samples, searching the dust on the table for cocaine residue and sniffing the walls for a funny smell behind recently patched plaster. That sort of thing.

Stop!

Shirley halted. Listened.

Just checking. In case there's more on patrol or something.

While stopped, Shirley imagined the house as she'd seen it earlier that afternoon — the angles of her perspective from the woods right before she hid the money. She hadn't been all the way out around the front, where the forest trail entered the clearing and yard. She'd been off to the side, like three o'clock. Not six o'clock, like now. She had to walk three more hours to the right!

Through the woods with no driveway.

With the cops up there on the porch, listening.

Would you rather be destitute? A prostitute? Or rich?

"Oh, wow. I think it's been a week since I've gotten — "

Shush.

Shirley angled right and resumed waving her arms before her. While walking off the established trail, even with her improved vision, there would be no warning before a twig stuck in her eye.

At which point it will no longer be fun and games...

Shirley slid her right foot along the ground, tapping her toe like a blind person's cane. The going was slow. Somehow it was easier when she was on the trail...

The cops stood up on the porch. The red glow of a cigarette cherry arced to the lawn.

That grass is dry, dumbass.

"Crap! They're coming this way!"

Shush.

The two cops paused and faced each other. The one

speaking waved his arms around, more story-time than angry-time.

Shirley closed her eyes and pictured the house as it was when she saw Lester lope across the lawn. She had the angle right, but the house was smaller in her memory... doesn't memory make everything small?

No.

"I need to move farther away."

She'd dropped the bag in the tiny space between a four foot boulder and an evergreen growing beside it, thinking the combination would be easy to spot and the evergreen branches would hide the black bag.

Shirley faced away from the house and discovered the woods appeared a shade of black darker than before. She barely made out the contours of tree trunks and the aprons of the evergreens.

In the distance glowed an oblong form. Arms pumping, she hurried toward the boulder. Arriving and about to rejoice, her last step landed on a stick. As it bowed under her weight she shifted, reached to the rock, tried to stop the step before her foot crashed through.

CRACK!

Shirley dropped to her knees, squeezed her eyes shut and fell forward with her arms unable to break her fall. Because of the leaves she fell unhurt except for her abused knees. She opened her eyes. A flashlight beam sliced the woods. She felt along the contours of the earth and discovered she'd fallen into a tiny depression. Unless a beam fell directly upon her she was safe for the moment.

She wriggled, reached and found a rock embedded in the ground. Clasping it she rolled and spun herself forty-five degrees and pushed up like a seal. Flashlights scanned back and forth but didn't appear to come closer. One of the beams fell to the ground and illuminated the officers in a reflected glow. Each had his sidearm drawn. She heard their voices but not their words.

You should snort like a bear.

"Oh, glad you could make it, Stupid Shirley."

Shush! Both of you!

The second flashlight beam fell to the ground as the men spoke.

Shirley rocked to all fours. Casting out her arm she discovered a small tree. She clasped it and lifted herself. In a single lunging motion she bounded forward, elbows pumping and feet rushing as on wings of air. The leaves were damp and soundless. Again the flashlights sliced the woods, nearer and nearer. Her target boulder shimmered gray in the distance. She lunged behind a smaller boulder that appeared suddenly at her right.

Her face landed in evergreen branches and on a nylon bag.

The money!

She'd been aiming for the wrong boulder.

Shirley pulled the bag close and heaved into a crouching stance with her eyeline barely above the rock surface. The two police officers stood at the edge of the lawn where briars formed a barrier. One said something to the other and they both turned to the right. The gap that Shirley had taken into the lawn area was before them. They stopped. More voices.

They got confused changing directions.

Shirley's arms glowed pale in the reflected light from the house. Her skin would shine like a lightbulb under a flashlight beam. Shirley grabbed the bottom of her shirt and rolled it over her clasped hands and forearms. She shifted to her right, placing more of the boulder between her and the white-purple glare that cut back and forth at ground level across the woods. She squinted to reduce the size of her eye whites.

The two police entered the woods and consulted. They pointed their beams exactly toward Shirley. The flashlights seemed to bob in place.

They're coming!

Shirley pressed lower. Her knees throbbed. Twigs crunched. Any more weight on her folded knees and they would pull apart. She rocked forward, swung up her arms for balance forgetting they were rolled in her shirt.

Her belly flopped to the dank leaves and humus. An insect tickled. Her palm had come loose from her shirt and landed on a slug-like form that popped grease underhand. She smelled it. Gross. The flashlights homed in on her position casting an eclipsing glare around the boulder. She hunkered. Wondered if her shoe was in the beam on the other side. The flashlights wiggled.

Oh crap they're really coming!

She snatched out with her right hand and felt along the ground for a rock she could hurl or a branch she could wield.

Leaves.

They'll kill you for this money!

Shirley inhaled deep and held the lungful of air a couple extra heartbeats and released slowly, expelling the terror that seized her.

"Where you been Old Shirley? Get Viva's ass up here. Now."

Shirley huffed twice.

You got more brains in your ass than these two guys put together.

Shirley calmed.

If they get close, stand up. Don't let them see you on the ground with the bag. You have to lure them away — wing on the ground like a wounded mama duck.

Shirley nodded. That made sense. The money wasn't going to protect itself.

"I am Mama duck."

She felt stronger.

Their voices became clear.

"I know it was around here somewhere."

"You don't even know what was in it."

"What could it be but a go-bag?"

"I don't know. The vics didn't look like they had enough money for a go bag. Probably had some old underwear and a couple cans of soup."

"Great. When we find it I'll take your half."

"I'm not saying all that."

"I know she was around here somewhere. We approached on the right of the driveway, after the gunfire on the left. Lester and all. And that was over there. Fat girl was coming this way with the blonde, chattering like idiots. I could've shook my crank and they wouldn't have known."

"Uh — "

"Yeah, funny. Piss off. I need to go back to where I was standing when I saw her drop the bag. She hid it by a boulder."

"Like that one?"

Shit!

"Yeah, look at that. You go left. I'll go right."

Shirley closed her eyes. This was the moment: Life or death.

Time is a wire. You're the cheese.

The flashlight glow disappeared.

Shirley blinked. She twisted her neck and took in as much forest as possible. It was all black again.

She lifted and turned. The light beams split and each man approached a different side of the same boulder Shirley targeted before accidentally falling behind the right one.

Now's your chance!

Shirley rocked to her knees and lurched aboard her feet. She steadied herself. Coiled up like a spring and popped forward while their backs were to her and the sounds of their tromping feet might mask hers.

Twenty feet. Heart about to shatter... Lungs like buckets of fire... Eyeballs bloated and burning...

Like an action movie.

I could eat a garbage bag of popcorn right now.

Her last footstep cracked a twig. She slowed for the next ten feet and halted. The cops had arrived at the boulder and their flashlights dissected it. She'd acquired enough distance there was no way the lights could reveal her.

Shirley tossed the duffel strap over her shoulder and walked with her shoulders back and her chest out. She could see better and in no time she'd find the safety of the Durango.

But wait. If they were there when you went back to the house because of Lester, when did they arrive? And why didn't they do anything?

21

C laude McFadden sat at his desk working on his laptop. His cubicle was located at the end of a row of six. The barrier from one to the next was eyeball-high for a person of normal sitting height but Claude had to stand to see above it.

The door to the copy room snicked.

Head pointed left toward the row of cubes, he leaned back in his seat and pushed out a little. No one watched him — no one was even there at work. If he asked, they'd all say they started at six a.m. and already had five coffee-prospecting-sessions at Panera, but in truth they were all in bed. Some together.

Claude's colleagues didn't begin their workdays as early as he and most didn't toil as hard... probably because most didn't visualize themselves in the top one percent of their industry. So said the motivational tapes Claude listened to on the morning's drive to the office. Many of the cube occupants were new recruits, some fresh out of college. They came and went, recruited and failed, over and over.

Looking at the empty cubes was almost fun because to his right, tantalizingly located at the back of his left-turned head, was the copy room. Inside the copy room, the only other person now present in the office made copies.

Bubbles.

When he met her he thought it was a nickname. A couple guys minted the tag at a frat party and she thought it referred to her personality, so she embraced it. Turned out her parents did a lot of drugs and put the nomenclature on her birth certificate.

Bubbles made copies.

The copy room door was usually closed because, on occasion, producers brought their clients beyond the conference room by the main entrance to their personal offices. No one wanted to see the bowels of an office, so Elvita — Claude's somewhat sexy boss — was always railing about keeping the door closed and the cubicles policed of over-the-top personal items. No Sports Illustrated swimsuit pinups. No Obama bobble heads. No smokeless tobacco use in the office — and certainly no plastic Coke bottles repurposed as Copenhagen spit bottles sitting out — even though the spit was visually indistinguishable from the product, and Claude always got away with it.

Still looking the other way and imagining her form, Claude rotated his head and beheld Bubbles. He placed his hand at his groin for a quick wake-up jostle.

She wore a skirt that stuck to her skin so perfectly he made out dimples. The red cloth ended before her thighs, which were tan, and toned, as perfect as a ham and swiss sandwich.

Given the rectangular shape of the copy room, and the machine manufacturer's required distance from the wall (to prevent overheating), Elvita had situated the copier sideways...

providing observers a profile view of whoever operated the copy machine.

Claude twisted the cap of his Coke bottle and released a string of Copenhagen goop. Slid his tongue across the top of the bottle — cleaning it — and twisted on the cap.

Bubbles placed her hand on her head and scratched.

Claude smiled.

Bubbles lifted the lid.

Claude said, "Close."

Bubbles stepped back, bent forward, butt pooched out, boobs hanging and opened the paper drawer.

"How?" she said. "I just filled this last night. People."

She grabbed a ream and unwrapped it. Assumed her prior posture and slid the paper into the drawer.

In a moment her copy job completed. Bubbles rapped a stack of papers on edge to get them square and vacated the room.

Claude opened his desk drawer, grabbed a three inch stack of copy paper and placed it on a shelf in the copy room.

He returned to his desk and from his computer bag withdrew a folder.

22

---

*E*lvita arrived at work early.

    She officed in a seven-story building; brick on the back and black glass facing the highway. Her suite looked out from the third floor to the parking lot.

    Take the elevator, turn right. At the end of the hallway, go through the double glass doors.

    The floor had four corner offices; her suite, two. She'd decided on the eastern corner before signing the lease. When Chico joined, he asked for the adjacent corner which she'd been holding open as an incentive to all her reps. After a year of nonstop work and explosive growth, she told him to move into the office.

    Elvita reached with her key but found the door already unlocked. She entered.

    Chico?

    She cocked her ear. The copy machine was running. Without conscious thought voicing the angst simmering below, she unsnapped her purse and placed her hand on the grip of her .38.

She hadn't slept well. She'd gotten out of bed late and spent an extra ten minutes at Starbucks. She bought an iced coffee, got back in line and bought another for the rest of the drive in to the office. Her brain was thick like before a headache, but jazzed with caffeine.

The copy machine stopped. She heard the plastic crinkle of the top being opened for a document to be placed on the glass.

She glided over the carpet and stopped at the corner. Without thinking, she drew the pistol from her purse and held her arm back at her side, hidden. She peered around the corner.

Her assistant Mendi's office light was on.

Elvita had spent most of the prior night imaging Chico instigating every scene in her crashing life. At 1 a.m. she'd scrunched her pillow into the headboard and sat up, turned on her lamp and deliberated over Chico with as much indifference as she would give a math equation.

Was he about to seek a divorce so he could make his fling with Bubbles legit?

Was he saddling Elvita with debt to crush her, while setting himself up to steal every client? What role did he play with her credit cards being declined and the cash advance money wires? She'd given him the computer logon information when they created their company emergency plan — a process made mandatory by her compliance department.

Though sharing her password wasn't.

But from that mistake, he could easily have gotten into her password folder on her office computer and from that, accessed her credit card websites. From there, it would have been a matter of filling out a request and Bubbles faking her voice on a phone call. He knew the answer to every identity verification question they'd ask — and from the home computer, could have watched incoming emails to delete any with reference to the accounts.

Chico could also be involved in the rash of clients leaving — albeit she couldn't see how he would gain from it. He was already receiving income from all of their shared accounts and they didn't separate their finances, so he was in a sense making the same money she was.

Elvita crept to the edge of the copy room. She swung around the corner.

Claude McFadden.

She jumped and removed her hand from the pistol grip. "Oh! I thought you were Mendi. You're in early this morning."

"I'm always here this early."

"I never see you."

"I'm short."

"What are you working on? Good case?"

"Just filling out some forms for a new account. You know."

Claude never smiled. He was a little Josef Stalin-looking hemorrhoid that Chico had argued they should hire. She had the veto, but she'd given in, thinking if Chico took an interest in developing him, Claude had a shot despite looking like a used car salesman. He kept his hair straight back, wore olive suits year round and kept his beady eyes stuck on hers long after she cringed and looked away.

Regardless, he was harmless. "What's the size of the account?"

"It's a 527. Hardly worth the paperwork. I — "

"You mean a 529?"

He smacked his forehead. Turned and pressed a button on

the copy machine. "I was reading an article about campaign finance a minute ago."

Elvita left him there. Claude boasted average abilities but thought himself capable of all things at all times to all people. He had a hand in a hundred activities and performed none of them particularly well. Sometimes the best thing was to allow reality to set the boundaries.

On the way to her office Elvita swung into Mendi's, since the light was on.

Empty.

Back to the copy room.

"Claude, is Mendi here?"

"No. She must have left her light on overnight."

Elvita held his stare. "Let me see the document you just took off the machine."

"This?" He grabbed the stack from the output. "Here you go."

She glanced at the first few pages — the right forms for a 529 plan. She passed them back. "Thank you. Next time you see lights on that don't need to be, please turn them off."

She left him there, swiped the light switch inside Mendi's office and a moment later turned on her own.

Of her list of action items from the night before, the most pressing were to call her compliance department and go to the police to file a statement.

She sat at her desk and picked up the telephone. Pressed the numbers from memory.

"Lou, Elvita."

"Elvita, this is early for you in Phoenix. What is it, five thirty there?

"Seven thirty. Hey, I'm calling because of a financial problem."

"Oh?"

"I tried to get tires yesterday with a credit card and it was declined even though it had a twenty five thousand dollar credit limit. So I called the credit card company and they said the card was reported stolen right after someone did a twenty five thousand dollar cash advance, and had it wired to the Cayman Islands."

"Let me guess. You didn't wire the money."

"No."

"Oh damn."

"That's not all. I have five other cards. Same thing on each one. Plus there was some spending before the wires, so with all the charges it's close to a hundred and seventy thousand."

"Did you put a stop on the cards?"

"Yes."

"Did you call the police?"

"Yes. But I still have to go there to file a report."

"Did you notify the FTC?"

"The Federal Trade Commission?"

"Yep. They will be interested."

"Does anything go on my U4 because of this?"

"All depends on how it comes out. With a number like that, I imagine the credit card companies are going to give the circumstances a good look before writing the debt off. If they don't find fraud, it'll be yours to repay."

"That's what I was afraid of. We've lost so many accounts, I was starting to wonder whether we'd survive at all. And now this..."

Elvita clamped the phone to her ear with her shoulder and started cleaning her desk. Strands of stray hair. Sticky notes with long expired messages. Pennies. She hated them. All in the trash.

"Elvita, it's hard times everywhere. But what you do is important and people need it. Take it day by day and you'll get there."

"That's what I keep telling myself."

"Keep us posted on what's going on with the credit card companies' fraud investigations."

She ended the call. Mendi was at her door. She pointed toward the corner of Elvita's desk. "Did you throw that away again?"

"What?"

"The letter from the insurance company."

"No. Where is it? I left it on my desk." She tilted the can. Empty. "Strange." She shrugged. With so much going on, she didn't know if she was coming or going. "So Claude's here early and now you. What's going on?"

"You sent me home early yesterday and I still had work to do."

"Oh."

Now that the envelope from the insurance company had disappeared, Elvita was curious what it contained.

When she and Chico married, they each took out a two million dollar term life policy with the other as beneficiary. The idea resulted from a long term business planning meeting. Chico was a sales rep in her organization with no special title. Although she sometimes dreamed about holding his hand while walking a sandy beach when they were eighty, she never named him a partner in her business.

He said he was fine without a title. Success didn't need another name.

Still, he was her de-facto partner. If something happened to either of them, the business would suffer until that person's duties could be absorbed by others or a new associate found.

The life policies would function as key-person insurance, except owned by husband and wife.

Their first little argument arrived when they completed the life insurance applications.

It wasn't an argument, so much as Elvita not relinquishing a point.

She paid closer attention to details and managed the household finances. She would be the one to call the company, fill out forms, pay the bills... Why wouldn't it make sense to have her be the owner of each policy? She owned the company that employed both of them. She carried the heavier burden and the deeper responsibility. She earned most of their income. Why should she abnegate ownership because of some sexist tradition?

As the financial crisis exploded into 2009 and they lost half their assets under management, she suggested to Chico, and he agreed, that she should cancel the life insurance policies. They could always get new ones. They would have to not die until their business straightened out — easy enough. Elvita completed the forms to stop the automatic bank draft more than two months ago. Being term life with no cash value to cannibalize through automatic premium loans, the policies should have lapsed by now.

The only reason she could think of for the insurance company to send a letter would be a last ditch appeal to pay a premium and keep the policies in force. She had no justification to think it was anything else, but with her new ever-present feeling that a shadow might reach out from any direction and punch her in the teeth, she needed to know what was in the missing envelope.

Elvita moved her mouse and opened a new browser

window. She typed in the address for South Dakota Mutual Life. Found the 800 number and called.

"Hello this is Elvita Marín. Your company sent me mail. I'm a former policyholder — I removed two policies from bank draft. I lost the envelope before seeing what was inside. Do you have a copy online?"

"May I have one of the policy numbers? Or your Social Security number?"

"Just a second." She opened a file on her computer and then a spreadsheet. "Yes I have the policy number. It's OA-739473-2HH. Did you get all that?"

"Yes, I'm bringing up your information. It appears — hold on let me check one thing — okay — your policy never lapsed."

"I don't understand, I stopped paying over two months ago. The grace period should've only been thirty days."

"So let me see here... You turned off the bank draft immediately after the policies drafted for February, on the fifteenth. The premium that was paid on the thirteenth covered until 13 March. That's when your thirty day grace period started. The premiums were caught up on the twelfth."

"Who paid the premium?"

"Um, just a minute. What did you say your name was? Elvita?"

"Elvita Marín. I'm the policy owner."

"Well that's just it ma'am, the owner was also changed. Unfortunately I can't say anything else."

"Why does this not surprise me? I am in the middle of having my identity stolen, so I'm not shocked. Without telling me anything you are not allowed to, regarding my other policy that was taken off bank draft..."

"Let me look, just a moment. Okay. You're talking about the policy on Chico? It lapsed. And you remain the owner."

Elvita followed an urge. "With the policy being recently lapsed, how difficult is it to reinstate?"

"We automatically reinstate policies when premium is received within the first week of lapse. No forms, no problems."

"Can we set up a bank draft over the phone?"

23

_S_hirley opened her eyes.

"I need a gun."

Condensation filmed her Durango windows. She'd left a gap at the top for air. Her cheek tingled under her eye; she scratched and withdrew a bloodied finger and the tiny mangled remains of a mosquito. She checked the sun visor mirror and blinked until she could focus. Little bastard got her right below her eye.

She rubbed her sockets with her fists and wriggled in her seat. Her lower back throbbed and her right hip ached where it pressed against the seatbelt clasp all night. Her neck felt like someone had removed a vertebrae the way a waiter jerks the cloth from a set table.

She'd left the keys in the ignition in case she needed to make a speedy getaway. Arriving late last night exhausted from the forest death march back to the Durango, she patrolled the entire Walmart lot and circled the building. Two RVs parked at the front left corner where they could cut the wheel and exit

with minimal fuss. Opposite them, on the far right wall toward
the back corner of the building, a man sat leaning against the
cement blocks. On her approach he was mostly hidden by a
garbage dumpster. Clearing it she saw him better. He was a
corpse — until he rolled his head and stared into the headlights
a moment before closing his eyes.

He wasn't going anywhere. He was waiting by the dumpster.
Shirley parked way out front but with the man in her line of
sight — just in case. She locked her doors, put down her visor,
cracked the window for air and went to sleep.

I don't want to be awake yet.

Shirley started the engine and powered down the windows.
The man was still there.

Maybe he's dead.

Fresh air roused her. The interior smelled like she'd been
farting all night. She lifted her arm and sniffed.

Oh Lord.

With her head turned she saw the black duffel bag on the
passenger seat and her heart pattered. She was safe. She'd
made it out of the woods with her eyeballs intact and no broken
bones. Not even a twisted ankle. She was like a Green Beret. By
the time the two chain-smoking cops investigated the wrong
boulder and found the correct one, she was a hundred yards
away and separated by a forever of blackness. At that distance
the insects and a subtle breeze absorbed the sound of her feet
and the heaving of her lungs. It would have taken a shout to get
their attention. She found her way back to the long driveway
and by the time she returned to the Durango, the moon had
risen and she saw a glint of chrome a dozen feet before she
arrived.

Now the cash was on her seat and the window was down.
Any hoodlum with skinny arms could run up, unlock the

door and grab the duffel. She powered up the passenger window.

"I need a gun."

She cranked the engine and turned on the heater and defrost. Rubbed her arms and stretched forward in the seat to relieve her back. A far-traveled scent of breakfast burritos wafted in to the Durango. McDonald's beckoned — all those boxes mounted on the roof weren't air conditioners; they were fans, ejecting the sweet torment of smells into the lower atmosphere, luring travelers from the highway.

Her stomach clamored.

Shirley reached across to the glove box and withdrew the money bag she and Ulyana had taken from El Jay. She dumped the bills into the black duffel, zipped the duffel and dropped it into the foot well. Reclining her seat, she shoved her hand in her front pants pocket and withdrew a twenty and three singles.

"Twenty-three dollars of ninety-nine cent burritos."

Shirley blinked and rubbed her eyes again. Drew in a deep breath.

Nothing quite so disorienting as waking up inside a vehicle instead of a bed. But by the time she'd extracted herself from the woods, she just wanted to sit and think.

It was time for a break from things. A real break — maybe from VIVA the REVOLUTION.

She'd done things...

If there was a God, Shirley knew she'd be able to assert the justification of taking the lives. It was them or her. But she wouldn't be able to explain the glee she felt each time she witnessed evil fade from a pair of eyes.

"Burritos!"

Shirley put the Durango in gear, checked left and right and cut diagonally across the parking lot.

Order four coffees so they don't think all those burritos are for you.

At the McDonald's drive-through window she said, "One big ass coffee and ten of those burritos you got... What? You're mumbling... Of course I want hot sauce. Twenty."

Take a break from Flagstaff. Get away from the pile of bodies. Go someplace where they wouldn't ever search — if they somehow connected her to El Jay's death. The others killings were pure self-defense.

Aggravated self defense.

But El Jay...

Had she released him, he would have come back for her. She had to kill him and God knew it as well as she did. But a prosecutor looking for a scalp could argue she never had to lure him in. Never had to alternate a blow job with thirty electric stim pads to extract information from him.

A clever lawyer could make her look bad.

Shirley paid the teenager and received the paper cup of coffee and bag of burritos. Drove back to Walmart and ate.

After four burritos she leaned her head out the window and dry heaved. Drank coffee but couldn't expel the rolling feeling in her stomach.

It's all those stupid vegetables you've been eating.

"Not now, Old Shirley." She spotted the man on the side wall. What was he doing, waiting to die? He hadn't moved for hours. How could a man sit on blacktop and not get a numb butt?

Maybe he likes his butt numb.

"Men are very funny about their butts. Well if he does, it stands to reason he'd like some breakfast burritos."

Shirley engaged the gears and drove. The dumpster prevented her from getting close enough to hand him the bag.

She steered close and shifted to park. Powered down the window and leaned.

"Want breakfast?"

Skin and bones. Gray hair. Weak eyes.

A nerve tingled in her brain.

Sometimes when you see people like that it's supposed to be Jesus.

"Dammit."

She opened the door. Got out with the paper bag and her coffee. Drank another long pull of coffee as she walked.

"Hey stranger. You want some breakfast? I bought a bag of burritos and don't really have the appetite I thought."

He regarded her.

"I'd sit down there with you. No lie. But last time I sat against a wall it took a half hour of gymnastics to get back on my feet."

He mustered a frail smile.

She stepped closer, leaned down, offered the bag. He clasped the rolled paper on top and placed the bag next to his leg with his hand over the bottom, as if enjoying the warmth.

"You ain't hungry?"

No voice. She read his lips. "Thank you." His eyes said he was already someplace else.

"When you get back you can have a bite. Okay? Well, I have to go. Big day. I'm getting a shower today. Bye."

She climbed in the Durango and waved. He remained in the same position as before.

Well that was horrible.

"What do you say to a homeless person? Here's food."

I know. But that was horrible. Not you. That. All of it. This whole human thing.

"Yeah. Sometimes. But I have things to do. And now he has breakfast."

Shirley exited the parking lot, turning right.

You could have helped him more than that. I mean, are you a hero or what? Are you Shirley F'N Lyle or Shirley Don't-Bother-Me Lyle?

"I got things to do."

That man might have been Jesus.

"Oh, dammit!"

Shirley signaled. Changed lanes. Looked to make sure she hadn't hit anyone. At the next traffic light she swung right at a gas station. Gauge said she was close to empty. She filled the tank. Fished cash out of her duffel, went inside and paid cash. Donated to the kid with cancer. Turned left, left, and left, back into the Walmart lot. Drove back to the side and angled next to the dumpster.

The man chewed. His eyes twinkled at little, like she'd caught him.

Shirley studied his face. Skin worn like sandpaper with the sand knocked off. A yellow hue about him. Whiskers that seemed short for a man with no mirror or blade. He wore a denim jacket with no liner and pants sliced at the left knee. His top shirt buttons were undone and she saw a port taped to his sternum. Tennis shoes with black toes sticking out. Not a healthy color for a white man.

That thing in his chest is for chemo or something.

Shirley got out of the Durango.

"What's your situation? Wanna talk a minute?"

He chewed. Raised his eyebrows... words were coming... Soon...

He swallowed. Rested his arms back at his side.

"You eat all six?"

Head shake. "No. Only the one I'm afraid."

Ohhh. He's educated.

"Where you from?"

"Phoenix." He swallowed several times. "I wanted to see the canyon. I went there in sixty nine with my girlfriend. My wife. We took a VW bus. I wanted to commemorate the trip forty years later, and remember her."

"I never been there. Where's your van?"

"In a ditch a hundred miles away, from the feeling in my feet."

"When did you get here?"

Shrug. "Three days?"

Like Jesus!

"So what's the plan? You gonna get the van fixed or something?"

"No plan."

"What?"

"Doctor said I'd be dead last week. Angry cancer."

"Oh. That sucks."

"I'm not convinced."

"That it sucks? Really?"

"Perhaps I'll be convinced after I die."

"Shouldn't you be in a hospital?"

"That isn't where people live."

"But Walmart is?"

He smiled. "The canyon. If I could get there. That was my goal."

"If I take you to the Grand Canyon, will you die happy?"

"And wake happy on the other side."

Shirley checked her wrist. No watch. She never wore one. "I never been there. You tell me how to do it?"

"What?"

"I'll take you to the canyon. I need a little getaway myself. But you have to navigate. I never been there. And I have an errand first. Ten minutes. C'mere." She leaned and offered her hand.

He studied her, eyes not quite believing.

"I can't stay bent over like this but three more seconds."

He took her hand. She pulled. He stood, braced against the wall and then placed his back against it.

"You can't hardly stand."

"Thank you for the burrito. I think."

Shirley looked at the bag on the ground. It contained food. Wasn't right to leave it. "You think you'll have another?"

"I am certain I will not."

Shirley stooped, swiped the bag and chucked it into the dumpster. She weaned the man from the wall. Placed her arm about his shoulder and braced him to her. She walked him to the Durango's passenger door.

"Whew! You stink too!"

"Yes."

"Tell you what. After my errand, we're going to get a motel room and grab a shower. Then we're going to the Grand Canyon. Think you can last four hours?"

"If not, just dump me over the edge."

"Say, we ain't been introduced. I'm Shirley Lyle."

She reached. He clasped her hand.

"Jesús Garcia."

---

24

*V*anko Demyan waited but Burian Tkach never returned to the office. The sense of doom dawned on him sooner than with Mikhaltso Babyak, whom Lester Toungate somehow turned the tables on only a couple days before.

Burian was supposed to be the best and Vanko had given clear, daylight-hit instructions. All in, all at once. Make a big flash and a bigger bang, then disappear while people stared at the noise and blood.

That never happened. Eventually the news carried a story of a triple homicide and Vanko's pulse quickened. He didn't get excited about bodies any more, but killing meant business risk and until the operation was complete, he would remain alert.

The news offered scant details.

Vanko telephoned a cop that sometimes caught hours as a bouncer at the Pink Panther.

The man didn't answer.

Vanko thought about Shirley Lyle, Ulyana and Lester Toungate. Baffling that they could find enough common purpose to join forces. The woman — Shirley — was a chameleon. She strutted in like a sex queen and demanded her place in his rotation and when he called her bluff she attacked again, winning his tentative trust and curious appreciation. When he tried to remember his mother's face without aid of her photo, he saw Shirley. Though he consciously rejected the association he felt it working subconsciously against him nonetheless.

Regardless of his muddled feelings about Shirley, objectively, he couldn't conceive her playing the tool in one of Lester's Toungate's strategies. Since Vanko broke his truce with Lester by working to unseat him with his sons Paul and El Jay, he'd expected Lester's counterstrike. He never would have foreseen Lester weaving Shirley Lyle into the plot.

If she worked with Toungate, it wasn't as his implement. More likely his master. She was the strangest wild card he'd ever seen.

Ulyana distracted Vanko as well — with other musings.

It wasn't her mere body. As a boy he lusted after beautiful women and his desire gave them power. Not so when he saw them naked every day, then sneaking out to cars for an extra dollar. No relationship was above economics. Owning a club, he no longer elevated women above being the biological bait and switch traps they were: beauty and passion until they had a roof and a refrigerator.

But Ulyana's quick mind set her apart. She was assertive enough to be playful when others trembled. He'd used her to investigate Toungate under cover and had been taken by her loyalty... She wanted advancement. She wanted a place beyond what she could secure with her body. She wanted to trade on her wit and loyalty.

Vanko had permitted himself to imagine...

In tired moments when he closed the day with a couple shots of vodka he sometimes fancied himself more intimate than merely taking possession of Ulyana's body. He imagined speaking with her about her upbringing in Russia, employing the cat and mouse conversations that would provide insight into her soul.

Exactly what his father warned against.

The whole thing was a mess — and ample proof of why his father always advised: no one gets in. Never imagine you are not alone.

Vanko's phone rang. He lifted it.

"Yeah.... Yeah I called. Listen, there was a shooting. Three dead. Who were they?"

Two of the dead were owners of the property. The third had not been identified — no matching prints.

So long, Burian Tkach.

Lester killed Mykhaltso and Shirley Lyle somehow dispensed with Burian. There had to be something about the woman he didn't know. A missing piece that explained her... because everything else said her success was impossible.

The cop still on the line, Vanko said, "There is a woman, Shirley Lyle. I want to know everything about her associations. Where she came from. Parents. Spouses. Children. Where she went to school. I want to know everything."

25

————————

Shirley drove to Silver Miner's Bank. She placed a few hundred dollar bills in her pocket, carried the duffel bag inside and exited with a key.

Her freedom money was secure.

Driving to the motel she passed a Goodwill and bounced over the curb and sidewalk into the parking lot. She felt flush and Goodwill sold clothes so cheap it didn't make sense to wash the set she wore. She lucked into a few items that fit and bought Jesús a change of clothes too. Nine bucks.

Next she drove to a motel that accommodated rentals by the hour. The attendant looked out the window at Jesús. "Go easy on him. One of you girls left me a corpse last week and I'm still dealing with the attention. I'm serious. Go easy."

Shirley helped Jesús Garcia inside. The burrito seemed to have revived him. He showered first, changed into his new duds before exiting the steamy bathroom, then showed them off — to Shirley's applause — in front of the mirror and sink.

"Hey, Babe. I'm not changing in the bathroom. I need space

to move around. So if you got to look away, that's fine. Or not. I don't care."

Shirley showered and exited the bathroom dripping, scrubbing with a towel.

Jesús watched Fox News.

Shirley turned her backside to him. Toweled up and down, brought it up front to get the undersides of her mams. Through the mirror she caught Jesús with his eyes rotated in his skull and his mouth ajar.

"It's okay, Sugar. Look all you want. I hope you dig what you see."

Still facing the television with his eyes twisted, he smiled.

"It ain't good for your eyeballs to do that. Don't you get black spots?" She faced him, held the towel in her left hand and allowed the rest to cascade down her flesh to the floor.

Jesús swiveled on the wood chair. Ran fingers through wet hair. "My goodness."

"You look spiffy. Going out on a date?"

He flat-smiled.

"Oh! Your wife. I'm sorry."

He shrugged. "You might know this already but the female form is an inspired work of art. Inspired in the old sense. A divine truth *breathed into* something."

"You saying God's a chick?"

"I wouldn't mind. That would actually be a pleasant thought."

"Had your fill? I'm going to get dressed now."

He sighed. "If you must. Meeting you has been a most unexpected delight."

"Me, too."

Shirley donned her new threads and dumped her old in the trash. "You ready?"

He braced himself and stood.

"We'll get more food soon," Shirley said.

"It's not that. I think my brain is noticing a shortage of blood."

"Look at me blushing."

"I'd like to."

"Oh, my. We better go."

Shirley placed the motel room key on the credenza beside the thirteen inch television. With Jesús on her arm she led to the Durango and installed him in the passenger seat. Made sure his legs were inside and closed the door.

The sky was blue; the sun bold. A few miles away Ulyana, the Sunbeam, did what she did. Whatever. Time to move on. Donal the grudge-holding sissy could go back to his gun store and flirt with the ATF girls. Whatever.

Shirley had Jesús.

She sat in the Durango and slammed the door. Turned on the AC. "You like hip hop?"

"Decidedly not."

"Yeah, I decided I didn't either."

"Rock and roll?"

Shirley found a station and drove north on highway 180. Eight miles out of town, Humphrey's Peak broke through the trees on the right.

She passed a police car exiting the Snow Bowl ski resort entrance.

She made eye contact with Jesús.

"Jesús, I want you to know — "

"It's Hay-soose."

"Hay soose. Just doesn't sound right. Not like Jesus. You anti-Jesus or something?"

He chuckled. Coughed. "I am a dying man. I am pro-Jesus."

"Oh, no." Shirley adjusted the rearview mirror. Glanced out the side. "That cop's on me."

"May I suggest you pull over?"

"I wasn't speeding much."

Shirley put on her turn signal and slowed. The berm was narrow but extended by ten feet of litter-strewn grass to the right. Then a ditch and a wire fence preventing her from busting loose across the plain.

She slowed. Cut the wheel and waited for the sound of shattering glass. None.

"Just my lucky day."

"It is, actually."

"Why, 'cause I got pulled over with Jesus?"

"Just do as he says and you have nothing to fear."

Jesús smiled.

She watched through the side mirror. The police car parked on the road with lights flashing. The officer exited the vehicle.

"Don't you love how these guys block the lane? Look how I got over, being polite... What the — ? He's got his gun out. What the hell, Jesus?"

"It's Hay-soose. You might place your hands on the steering wheel, so he can see you are not a threat to him."

She powered down the window and placed her hands on the wheel. "What else?"

"Be polite. Do what he says. Remember, it's better to get even with a lawsuit than a punch to the face."

Jesús placed his hands on the dashboard.

"STEP OUT OF THE VEHICLE!"

Shirley found the cop in the side view mirror. "He's aiming his gun at me!"

"You better step out of the vehicle. It's comply or die with some of these guys. Stay calm. And it's better to say nothing at all than tell a lie. Literally — saying *nothing at all* is better than telling a lie. Keep your hands in front and move slowly. You'll be fine."

"STEP OUT OF THE VEHICLE! BOTH OF YOU! HANDS IN THE AIR!"

"Can't I tell him to put his gun down?"

"You must get out of the car. Do it now."

"I'M COMING OUT!"

Shirley cracked open the door. Shoved her hands through the window. "SEE! DON'T KILL ME!"

She pushed the door open. Heard Jesús open his door. She swung her left leg out. "I need my hands to get out!"

"KEEP YOUR HANDS WHERE I CAN SEE THEM!"

"I NEED THEM. I'M FAT!"

"KEEP YOUR HANDS WHERE I CAN SEE THEM!"

Shirley bucked. Squirmed. Grabbed the door sill and cavorted until her right leg joined her left, out the door. She rested.

"STEP OUT OF THE VEHICLE NOW!"

Shirley ground her teeth. Heard Jesús say again, low, "Comply or die."

She pushed the door all the way open and lurched to her feet, awkward with the irregular process and stance. Her pants jammed in her butt crack. She reached back — froze.

"OH DAMN! I'M SORRY! I GOT A WEDGIE! DON'T SHOOT ME."

The officer pointed his weapon at Jesús. "YOU! COME TO THE OTHER SIDE OF THE VEHICLE. HANDS IN THE AIR!"

Jesús complied. He stood next to Shirley.

The officer approached with his gun aimed at Shirley's chest. As he neared she squirmed inside. She was glad for the wedgie. Her sphincter puckered and it took her mind slightly off the high probability a bullet would soon explode her heart. Her eyes grew wet. Her chin trembled. "Why are you doing this?"

"Shhh. It's okay," Jesús said.

"TURN AROUND. PLACE YOUR HANDS ON THE VEHICLE."

She heard his feet on the gravel and a siren from a distant car. Backup.

Shirley turned. Jesús turned. Each placed hands on the Durango. The officer stood ten feet away with his gun on them. The siren neared. Lights flashed in the distance and in a moment the car arrived and two more police exited with guns drawn. They converged. One holstered his weapon while the other two kept their beads on. She wanted to get a better look but feared death more.

The officer groped her from behind. Shoved his hand in her crack, far in the back and patted up around between her legs, up to the front. He worked her waist, her sides, under her chest.

The familiarity brought a lopsided smile to her face. She tried to wrap her mind around being both fearful of death and ready to giggle.

"Keep your hands on the vehicle."

This cop's manner was brusque. Efficient. The one who pulled her over seemed hysterical, like a froufrou dog scaring off Freddy Kruger. But this one was all business. She twisted for a half-look.

"DON'T MOVE!" said Froufrou.

She saw regardless. The one who searched her shifted left while squatting and patted Jesús. In a moment he stood.

"Miss Lyle, I'm placing you under arrest for murder."

"WHAT?"

"Don't say anything," Jesús said. "Do not utter another

word."

"You have the right to remain silent. Anything you say can and will be used against you in a court of law."

The man grabbed her left hand, snapped on a handcuff and pulled. He grabbed her other arm.

"You have the right to talk to a lawyer and have him present with you while you are being questioned. If you cannot — "

"Hey! You're gonna break my arm. My hands don't reach."

" — afford to hire a lawyer, one will be appointed to represent you before any questioning if you wish. You can decide at any time to exercise these rights and not answer any questions or make any statements. Do you understand each of these rights I have explained to you?"

"I understand you're hurting me."

"Do you understand these rights?"

"Stop breaking my arm!"

"Officer, please," Jesús said. "She is not resisting you."

The police officer grabbed Shirley's left wrist with both hands. Another cop came from the side and grabbed her right arm. They pushed.

"AHHHH!" she cried.

"DO NOT RESIST ARREST!" the second officer said.

Shirley closed her eyes. Her heart heaved. She was being attacked and had to defend herself — but the instinct to protect herself would get her killed. She had to override her fear, her fight or flight response and allow the LAW to abuse her, contort her, wreck her joints, humiliate her, force her obedience to their sneering faces — because they had the right to kill her on the spot and no judge would ever find them guilty. Ever.

"Gentlemen, may I remind you she is one of the people you are sworn to protect and serve?"

Her shoulders sockets stretched. Her wrists bounced. Pain

stabbed her elbows and shoulders. Metal pulled her right arm to her left and when the squeezing shoving hands released, metal bound her wrists together.

Shirley placed her forehead to the Durango glass. She blinked. Clamped her jaw and blinked more, pressing away the water.

They would not see her weep.

She opened her eyes and stared into her pupils reflected on the glass; stared all the way into the black to the hole where some invisible strand of her mind connected to the Ultimate, the Big One, the heaven-is-another-dimension-of-here.

Shirley calmed.

The deputies jerked her away by her wrists. Pain zapped through her shoulders. She gulped down a curse and reminded herself she lived in a good world struggling with evil, not the other way around.

As two deputies shoved her toward the arresting officer's black and white, the third questioned Jesús.

"What is your name?"

"Jesús Garcia."

"What are you doing here?

"What are you doing here?

"I said, what are you doing here?

"Release him," the arresting office called. He strode in front of Shirley, opened the rear door and shoved her inside. She landed with her face on the seat. The car surged while she struggled to sit upright. Left swerve, reverse cut right, forward hard left with tires spraying gravel.

Shirley sat at an angle with her wrists pinched behind her. Jesús still had his hands on the Durango hood.

"There's gas money hidden in the glove box, Hay soose," she whispered. "I hope you get there."

26

*E*lvita's clock read 11:30. She had intended to go directly to the police after speaking to her compliance department, but after calling about the life insurance, she telephoned each credit reporting agency to put a freeze on her report. Then she realized she had no evidence, so she called all six credit card companies again. How could she report the crime to the police if she couldn't even print out the damage? It took a fight but each company allowed her to reset her user name and password for online access.

Armed with ink on paper showing one hundred and sixty eight thousand dollars of credit card fraud, Elvita drove to the Glendale Police Department. A sign on the two-foot brick wall around the parking lot read: Foothills Public Safety Facility. She drove into the parking lot and tried to register the size of a building that seemed deceptively small from the road but much larger as she neared.

How on earth did Chico believe he could get away with everything? Did he think she wouldn't realize it was him?

She stopped in her tracks.

She was a financial planner — how could she not have realized?

Debt in the name of one spouse disappears when that spouse dies. The lender has no recourse to the other spouse.

With the temperature outside already in the high nineties, her back tingled like she pressed it against ice.

The pieces fell together.

Chico planned to take as much debt in her name as possible, kill her, collect two million and disappear with Bubbles. He'd have the hundred and fifty thousand he'd need to start and operate his hedge fund. He'd have two million in seed money and access to all Elvita's remaining clients.

"Morning ma'am. Are you okay?"

She spun. A police officer walked behind her. "No. This is a rotten moment, to tell the truth."

He stood beside her with good-natured rigidity.

"I called about reporting of financial crime. The person I spoke with didn't think it was worthy of your trouble."

"Did you get the officer's name?"

"Officer Hank. He wouldn't give me any other information."

The police officer smiled. "I apologize for Officer Hank. He's new — that's why he's on the phones at night. Come inside with me and we'll get you taken care of."

27

The deputies took Shirley to a large complex of attached buildings housing the sheriff's office and the Coconino County Detention Center. After delivering her to booking, they patted her down and removed her safe deposit box key.

"You were driving without a license?"

It was in my purse in the Durango...

Shirley said nothing.

They took her to another room with a table and chair. The arresting officer sat and told Shirley to sit as well. Still handcuffed and unable to move without sending volts of pain through her shoulders, Shirley attempted to see behind and lower herself. She missed the chair, collapsed to her side, mostly on her elbow and bounced her head on the linoleum. The officer said, "What is your name?"

Shirley said nothing.

"What is your date of birth?"

Shirley said nothing.

"Suit yourself."

He completed his form and stood. "Get up."

Shirley attempted to comply and gave up. Her brain throbbed when she moved. She expected a boot to the face.

She wanted to blurt, "Why are you so mean?"

She heard a combination of Viva Shirley and Jesús Garcia: *These people are your enemy. Give them nothing. Do all you can do to comply but give them nothing to use against you, because they will.*

Shirley said nothing.

The arresting officer left her on the floor. After a few minutes he returned with four others who wrestled her to a sitting posture. They attempted to weave their arms between her hyper-extended elbows and her torso. She screamed. They persevered. She cried. The arresting officer came around front and removed a spray canister from a black leather pouch on his belt. He stooped eye level and pointed the nozzle at Shirley.

"WE ARE GOING TO REMOVE YOUR HANDCUFFS. DO NOT RESIST ARREST."

Shirley said nothing through her tears.

More pain in her shoulders, elbows and wrists as the police pushed her hands together. The handcuffs fell away.

"GET UP."

Her arms were useless. She couldn't feel her hands or fold her elbow the right direction. Her shoulders didn't feel like they were in the right place. She placed her hands on the linoleum and pressed but the elbows buckled. She shrank from the leering deputy. Tears rolled down her face.

He swung the pepper spray and depressed the nozzle.

Shirley winced.

The aerosol burst into her face and eyes. She gagged and wheezed. Sparks flew in her mind. *Keep your mouth shut. This is*

*because you told the other one you hope he gets cancer. These frat
boys will kill you.*

Mucus dripped from her nose to her lips and she coughed a
burst of phlegm to the antagonizing officer's leg.

"GET ON YOUR FEET!"

With her arms free, the four took positions at her shoulders and upper arms. They lifted and more pain shot through
her. She worked her legs underneath and pushed. Snot
continued to expel from her nose and hung from her face like
drool.

Upright, they shoved her into the wall and re-applied her
handcuffs. Shirley ground her teeth and expected death at any
moment.

*You have to fight as soon as you get a chance or these people will
kill you. They aren't good people. They enjoy force! They live for this
stuff and look for opportunities to push people around. And they've
been trained to think everyone is a bad guy. These people are broken.
You have to get away!*

"Carl, has she been fingerprinted? 'cause we're just going to
have to do this again."

"Then we do it again."

Steered by the elbow, she walked to another room. There
they pressed her against the wall and removed her handcuffs. A
female officer who refused to meet her tearful stare rolled each
finger in ink and transferred her print to paper.

"You can clean the ink off with these." She indicated a
container of towelettes.

Shirley attempted to move her arm but could do no more
than swing it. The elbow wouldn't fold on command.

The woman huffed. Without meeting her gaze, the woman
grabbed an alcohol pad and mauled Shirley's finger pads. She
softened after a moment and became more gentle. Finally, she

grabbed Kleenex from a box and wiped the tears and sinus goop from Shirley's face and neck.

The deputies handcuffed her again and steered her by the elbow to a room where a different police officer asked her sixteen different ways why she murdered Roderick and Ruth Memmelsdorf.

Roddy? Ruth? I though this was about Maddix...

Shirley said nothing.

They left her in the room for what felt like six hours. At least she was sitting. Should she ask for a doctor because of her arms? Why bother? They knew what they were doing. They wanted her to suffer. It was a tool in their toolbox. They wanted to break her. She would allow herself to say nothing.

The new deputy returned. She noticed now that he wore plain clothes, regular pants and a button down shirt. Brown leather shoes with polish. He smiled. Said they got off on the wrong foot. Would she like a cigarette? A donut? A can of Coke?

Shirley said nothing.

Hours passed and they led her to a cell and finally removed her handcuffs.

Shirley lay on a bed almost too small to fit her and stared at the ceiling while ice cold tears dripped and then stopped.

*I*n the morning a deputy led her to a room with tables and chairs. The walls were cement blocks without windows. The fact that they had color at all seemed a despised concession.

"Sit."

The deputy left. Shirley sat facing the door. It opened and feet squeaked on perfectly clean linoleum. A man with a briefcase entered: He was too young to be good at anything. He wore a crinkled suit and hair gelled to look fresh out of bed. The man walked like a spring tossed him forward and his feet struggled to keep up. He threw his leg over the back of the opposite seat and dropped onto it. Rested his case on the floor.

"Mitchell Lucas." He held out his hand.

Shirley said nothing.

"I'm your court appointed attorney — but it isn't official." He smiled and his teeth gleamed. He gave her two thumbs up. "So here's the deal. It's — " he referred to his watch " — eight. You're going to be in court in a half hour. This is your initial appearance. You'll be informed of the charges against you: Murder one, two counts. You'll be advised of your right to have me represent you, or someone else if you want to pay. The judge will talk about bail. You won't get it — the judge is Howard Hang 'em Bly. Last, he will set another date for your preliminary hearing. That's like a little trial to find out if the evidence is strong enough to justify a full trial. Our goal is to get the judge to dismiss at this point, for insufficient evidence. Got all that?"

Shirley said nothing.

Shirley swallowed hard. Her mouth was dry. She wore the same clothes that she put on yesterday at the motel with Jesús. They cuffed her hands in front and moving her from the jail to the Coconino County Superior Court. She felt like a handcuffed president: suddenly people were courteous and deferential. Stony faced instead of jeering.

Solemn... As if viewing a venerated ritual. An execution.

When her feet refused to carry her forward at the entrance, her phalanx of beefy deputies ushered her into the courtroom. She came at rest on the left side behind a table. A man in uniform with a walkie-talkie pinned to his shoulder stood at her side and two more lingered behind her.

She beheld the burgundy leather chair behind an elevated cubicle made of the same tan wood panels as the walls. Behind the chair, the flag of the United States of America and another representing Arizona. Between the flags, mounted high on the wall, was a two-foot medallion. She read the encircling words: GREAT SEAL OF THE STATE OF ARIZONA.

They sure want this place to look official.

To the left of the seal was a clock. They were getting an early start at 8:30 a.m. She watched the second-hand click moment by moment, each second dear to her.

Feet shuffled. A deputy bumped her. She turned. He shifted behind a divider and Mitchell Lucas stood beside her. He stared past Shirley. "Who are you?"

"Jesús Garcia."

Shirley whirled. Jesús was with her! He wore a suit that probably came from Goodwill. Old shoes that still had a shine between the scratches.

"Hay soose! Why aren't you at the canyon?"

"We only have a second," Mitchell said. "Who are you? Why are you here?"

Jesús looked as if walking into the courtroom had used his last reserves. He steadied himself with his hand on the table. He held Shirley's gaze. "I am a retired attorney from the American Civil Liberties Union. I'm here to offer pro bono representation. So long as I'm alive."

"What's that mean?"

"Free."

"But I'm not in the union."

"No — not that kind of union. The ACLU exists to protect the constitutional rights of all Americans."

"I'll take it."

Mitchell cleared his throat. "Miss Lyle — "

"Mizz."

To the left of the judge's throne, a woman in a blue blouse sat at a normal height desk. She stood.

"All rise." The few people in the court stood. "The Honorable T. Howard Bly presiding. Please be seated and come to order."

The Honorable T. Howard Bly walked into the courtroom with his head angled down and his black robe flowing. He sat at his desk and opened a folder. He looked like grandpa climbed off a fishing boat and ducked into a robe. Black-framed glasses. Bumps on his withered face. Gray hair, thin on top. Likely had a six-shooter on his hip under the gown.

As Shirley studied his face her jaw fell.

She blinked.

Bly's gaze drifted from the paper in his hands to Shirley. He held her look and started speaking droll and boring while Shirley smiled huge.

I got you!

"Good morning folks. The matter before us is the people of Arizona versus Shirley Lyle. Counsel?"

A woman with athletic calves and an outfit designed to show them off stood behind the table to Shirley's right. "Kristin Mize-Jones for the people of Arizona."

"Mitchell Lucas, your honor. Good morning. Public defender representing Shirley Lyle... Uh, who is in custody and present in the court."

"I'm Jesús Garcia, your honor. Formerly of the ACLU in Phoenix. Also representing Mizz Lyle. Pro bono."

Bly lifted his nose. "Interesting. ACLU. And Kristin Mize-Jones... who is with you?"

"Mike Ortlund, your honor. District attorney investigator."

"Ms Mize-Jones, are you ready to proceed in the initial appearance proceedings?"

"We are, Your Honor."

"Then do."

"Your Honor. The people file with this court a two-count complaint against Shirley Lyle, date of birth, March 28, 1959. More counts may follow. Both counts are murder, first degree. The people will demonstrate the defendant verbally assaulted Ruth Memmelsdorf at a battered women's group. Shortly thereafter she applied for a firearm. After her application was approved she acquired the handgun and went immediately — literally Your Honor, within hours — to the Memmelsdorfs' and accosted the deceased, Roderick. Mr. Memmelsdorf called the police and made a report, therein stating the defendant behaved in a threatening and abusive manner. Two days later, the defendant filed a false missing persons report, which when investigated proved to be of no substance. The supposed missing person was a stripper and she was found safely at work when the police investigated. This person is currently being considered for accessory charges. A half hour later, the Memmelsdorfs were both dead by the defendant's hand."

Judge Bly shook his head. He looked at Shirley. "Miss Lyle, I'm going to take a few minutes to inform you of your rights and make you aware of a few items. First, you need make no comments. Anything you say can be used against you. You have the right to a trial by jury. That jury would be comprised of twelve jurors and all twelve would have to return a guilty verdict for you to be found guilty. In this sort of case, there is no absolute right to bail. We will discuss that this morning. You have four pleas that you may enter. Guilty. No contest. Not guilty and not guilty by reason of insanity. If you plead guilty, that means totally guilty, and the court could proceed to sentencing. No contest means you agree with the charges but not the guilt. So the next step would be sentencing. If you enter a plea of not guilty, the prosecution will have to prove beyond a reasonable doubt that you are guilty, and you will be presumed to be innocent until they do so. You will have the right to confront your accusers and cross examine their witnesses, along with the right to present your own witnesses — and to subpoena those witnesses to compel them to testify on your behalf. You also have the right to not be compelled to testify against yourself. Last, if you plead not guilty by reason of insanity, you must do so in writing. Do you understand your rights, as I have related them?"

Shirley said nothing.

Jesús leaned to her. Whispered to her. She whispered back.

"Your honor, Mizz Lyle understands her rights as you relate them."

"Is there some reason Mizz Lyle doesn't want to say that for herself?"

Jesús whispered. Shirley whispered.

"Mizz Lyle is exercising her constitutional right to not speak, Your Honor."

"How do you plead, Shirley Lyle?"

"Your Honor," Jesús said, "Shirley Lyle enters the plea not guilty."

*S*hirley tried to pay attention but the proceedings didn't sound like any episode of Law and Order she'd ever seen. Every person there seemed to have a pretentious words folder a hundred times thicker than hers, and apparently had sworn an oath to only utter words contained therein.

She perked up when she heard the word bail — though her money was in a safe deposit box and the arresting thugs had taken her key. She'd resolved to not play their game. If they were going to steal her life from her, they would do so without her participation. She didn't want any part of it.

If she spoke, and they found her guilty, it somehow seemed she'd have been a willing part of it.

The concept of making bail enticed, but the horror of having to give it up if they railroaded her to prison — no way. Don't bother. She'd rather climb to the top bunk and dive on her head.

Judge Bly said, "Miss Lyle, in the state of Arizona, you do not have an absolute right to bail. But the state does believe that to deprive you of your liberty, it must be with due process — meaning, with your rights being argued in a court. In short, you cannot be deprived of bail unless certain conditions are met. If the death penalty could be imposed, you are not entitled to bail. If the charged offenses were committed while you were already on bail for something else, you cannot have bail again. And last, if the prosecution can show you pose a danger to society, and that no conditions of release could assure public safety, then bail may be denied. Do you understand?"

Shirley said nothing.

Jesús again leaned and whispered. She whispered back.

"Your honor, Mizz Lyle understands."

"So be it. Miss Mize-Jones, does the State of Arizona have a recommendation for bail?"

"We do, Your Honor. The defendant was arrested while presumably attempting to flee Arizona. She was — "

"Wait a minute. How do you know that? Where was she going? She had her bags packed?"

"Uh. No, Your Honor. She was driving north on — "

"She was driving north?"

"Uhm. Yes, Your Honor."

"That's all? She didn't have luggage? Did you find a passport? And wouldn't someone running from murder charges in Arizona be more likely to flee south? Wouldn't you think?"

"I don't pretend to — "

"Well that's the issue at hand. You said she's a flight risk, so you do pretend, as you put it, to know. Aside from the flight risk, what else have you got?"

"Yes, Your Honor. Thank you. Uhm. There is one thing. You see, her fingerprints were on both the weapon — we allege — she used to murder Ruth Memmelsdorf, but also on the one we believe she planted next to Ms Memmelsdorf."

"She couldn't have picked it up afterward?"

"Uh."

"I hope you have more than that."

"Well, in addition to the two murders Shirley Lyle is charged with, there is also an investigation pending into another homicide."

"Is it fair to assume that if you had reason to charge her for that homicide as well as the two you did charge her for, you would have done so?"

"Your Honor?"

"You don't have enough evidence to charge her for the other murder?"

"Not at this time."

"At this time? Do you expect additional charges will be filed?"

"No, Your Honor."

"Okay. Clear enough. Miss Mize-Jones, is there any other reason to believe Mizz Lyle is such a danger to society the court must restrict her liberty?"

"No, Your Honor."

"Does the defense have anything to add?"

Mitchell Lucas extended his right hand and opened his mouth.

Jesús Garcia spoke first. "Your Honor, Mizz Lyle was not attempting to flee Arizona. She was driving to the Grand Canyon. Further, the deaths for which she is charged were not murders, they were justifiable homicide. The defense will demonstrate through witness accounts both by retired police, active police and another person who was the kidnap victim of the deceased, that Shirley Lyle is a hero and this prosecution a short-sighted scam unsupported by evidence. In light of this, the defense motions for dismissal."

"We are not there yet, Mister Garcia."

"In that case, Your Honor, the defense requests Mizz Lyle be released on her own recognizance."

Judge Bly frowned. "I am not convinced Mizz Lyle represents either a flight risk or poses a threat to the citizens of Arizona. However, we have bodies, and the state doesn't make accusations lightly. None of the qualifications for the death penalty are present, are they Miss Mize-Jones?"

"They are not, Your Honor."

"This court sets bail at one million dollars."

When it all ended, Jesús sat in his chair with his arms over the sides. His hands were frail and veiny. He seemed drained.

Shirley took his hand in hers. "Why didn't you go to the Canyon? I coulda handled this nonsense."

His thin lips lifted at the edges. "I think you're going to have to take it from here. Reach out to the ACLU in Phoenix and mention what happened. Will you do that for her, Mitchell?"

"I, uh, okay."

"Good. I'm curious." Jesús leaned to his side and Shirley closed the distance so their heads were inches apart.

"I've never seen a judge quite so helpful, while maintaining an air of impartiality."

"Is that a question?" Shirley said.

He raised his eyebrows.

Shirley shrugged.

28

*E*lvita woke with a fire in her spirit. Someone brought a battle to her doorstep and it was time to wage war back.

The police had promised to give her report their full attention. They took copies of the transaction histories she printed out from the websites, but didn't care to take the names or contact information of anyone she thought might be involved. Upon her mentioning her separated husband might be the perpetrator, the officer's eyes dimmed as if he turned off the lights and left the house. He warned her that in domestic matters, the police would always defer to the courts. Plus, of course, as long as the credit card company wrote it off, who was harmed?

She used to run in the mornings. Getting her heart pumping and her blood flowing made her feel good. Nothing like sweat and endorphins to reset the body from a bad day and start the new one feeling strong.

She'd fallen out of the habit since marrying Chico. They

spent so much time at the office, she'd needed to step back and make decisions about her priorities. For a short while, she told herself, she was willing to sacrifice her fitness to have more time for work. The short time turned into a long time. Instead of being able to run like an antelope, she felt more like a waddling pig. Time to buy new exercise clothes.

Instead of going for a run, she set her watch and walked 3 miles at a fast pace. Other than her arches feeling like they needed more support, the walk made her feel alive. She looked at the nearby Thunderbird Park mountains and remembered how she felt running full speed up the steep trail, bouncing rock to rock.

Why was business so important anyway?

She'd always felt that with just a little more work she'd finally get ahead. But all the extra work time had to come from somewhere. Fissures formed in the rest of her life.

She stretched on the rocks in her backyard after her walk and noticed a prickly pear cactus near the block wall with one of its broad, thick pads knocked off.

The block wall protected the cactus from storms and there had been no wind recently. Elvita studied it from a few yards away. She noticed the concentric circles of a partial footprint in the rocky dirt near the break.

The hair stood on her arms.

Chico still had a key. He wouldn't need to climb the wall and break-in through the back.

Tom? From the tire place?

Why?

She turned toward the back of her house. The window seemed intact and unmoved. The door was closed with no signs of tampering. She glanced to the corner where a two foot alley ran the length of the house before meeting a wood fence. Anyone trapped in that space would have to scale the fence.

Her gun was inside the house, upstairs in the bedroom in her purse.

She glanced about the ground and grabbed the first fist-sized rock she saw, then removed her house key from the pocket at the small of her back. She tried the door handle and found it locked.

Elvita inserted the key.

The house was quiet inside. Nothing seemed touched. She closed the door behind her and locked it. Still clutching the rock, she crept across the kitchen tile, kicked off her shoes at the carpet and ascended the stairs. She checked each room, returned downstairs and exited the front door. There were no strange cars or persons in the area.

Maybe the cactus pad was so heavy it broke by itself.

But that didn't explain the footprint.

Back inside the house, Elvita finished stretching and then made her morning breakfast juice. From the refrigerator she grabbed parsley, kale, two Red Delicious apples and ginger root.

Parsley gave her mental acuity better than the drugs she tried as a teen. She added kale because it was green, apples because the sweetness helped cover the taste of kale and parsley, and a little ginger root for the kick.

First she ground the apples in her juicer. Next the kale. She stopped at the parsley. She always bought the regular kind with the small leaves, but somehow sprigs of Italian parsley were all through the three bunches in her bag.

Elvita shrugged. She'd thought about substituting Italian parsley a couple times at the grocery store, since the leaves were so much bigger.

She ran the leaves through the juice maker and finished with a one-inch section of ginger root. She dumped the pitcher of green juice into her blender, set the machine on low for a minute to break up the green gobs of parsley chlorophyll, then filled her travel mug.

The rest she poured into a 12 ounce glass. She gulped it down and tried to discern exactly how the taste was different.

*S*hirley stared at her prison cell wall trying to spot a repeated pattern in the paint. Breakfast wasn't bad. It was nice to wake up — as opposed to not waking — but after food and fifteen seconds of a new stretching workout she invented, she grew bored. The paint on the wall was as perfectly dull as the floor and ceiling.

Having bail set at a mere million dollars the day before was a staggering triumph while sitting beside her crack legal team in the courtroom.

That victory was somewhat reduced as she perched alone on the edge of a concrete bed.

What do you do when you are deprived of sights, smells and sounds?

Remember.

Shirley saw the carnality in Jesús' eyes when she stood before him fresh from the shower. Nothing obscene about two people reveling in their essences: him a man and her, Venus.

One million dollars. She'd seen enough Law and Order to

know no one ever ponied up the full amount. There were these suckers out there called bail bondsmen who put up most of the money, so when you ran from the law, they took the hit. At least, that's the way it was supposed to work. She'd never been in jail long enough to have the experience. Regardless, she preferred her money in the safe deposit box.

Even if she did want to talk to the bail bondsman, the deputy took her deposit box key. Supposing she could get it back, she had no one trustworthy enough to fetch the cash. Jesús was — she hoped — driving to the Grand Canyon. Be a shame to miss seeing it, after his good fortune in Shirley finding him, feeding him, clothing him and at least starting north with him.

"Yay Shirley. Yeah. Woo-Hoo."

What? You're allowed to realize you're wonderful when it's a fair statement.

"Yay Shirley! YEAH! Woo-Hoo!"

The concrete didn't echo so much as contain and amplify her shrillness.

She waited for footsteps outside. The mechanical sound of the slot in the door.

Anything.

kay, time to ponder the bigger questions. She'd be released after the next hearing, she was sure.

Absolutely sure.

The questions:

Why were the police on the scene such a long time before they did anything? The two cops looking for her money said as much: they saw her when she noticed Lester and hid the money duffel. That meant they saw the whole exchange with Lester and possibly much more of what happened earlier.

Did they see Roddy pressing a gun to Donal's head?

The official story was that after the police and Shirley first left the Memmelsdorfs', the two officers went back for support. Nothing made sense. If they had suspicions about the Memmelsdorfs, as the deputy who questioned her at the scene said, how could they now be telling the prosecutor they determined Ulyana was not kidnapped? If that was true, they would have never come back and found the driveway to the house where it all went down.

Were they setting her up from the beginning? Did some unseen enemy pull the strings? Who hated her enough to do that?

A hundred thousand wives.

An even bigger question: Why didn't the wonderful State of Arizona charge her with murdering Maddix Heregger? With him, it was her word against his. With Ruth and Roddy, Donal had seen everything: Ulyana was kidnapped, Ruth had a gun on her and Roddy held a gun to Donal's head. The shooting mapped out right, with everyone seeing everything. There was no other way to spin it — unless Donal and Ulyana flat-out lied. Whereas with Maddix, no one but Shirley saw what happened. The prosecutor could make up anything she wanted.

Sure was nice to have a card to play.

The hooker card.

Her public defender Doofus Mitchell Lucas, Esquire, LTD... said that during the next hearing all the facts would come out and the judge could pitch the case out the window.

If that was true, screw bail. She'd make them feed her. Catch up on her sleep because she could rest easy after drawing Judge T. Howard Hang 'em Bly.

She'd met him... once.

Her memory of where the event fell on the calendar was sketchy. It was winter, not this past but the one before. She hadn't known he was an actual judge. A lot of guys like to pretend they're law enforcement; sex and power got tangled up in their minds like they were aspects of the same thing. Hence some men wanted to pretend they were cops and she was a very bad girl. The exercise of power was as important as the sex. Sometimes others who actually held power enjoyed pretending they didn't. Thus her black leather cheerleader outfit replete with pompoms mounted on dildos.

Judge T. Howard Bly introduced himself only as Tom and said he wanted to pretend he was a Superior Court Judge. Awful specific, but sure, Shirley thought, make believe is fun!

She knew half the lawyer terms he did. He probably watched Boston Legal before driving over and had the mumbo jumbo fresh in mind. Terminus analus in your briefs. He was a poser with a black gown bought from a Halloween shop, wanting her to role-play with him. Punish him for being important, call him Your Honor while working the pompom under the robe.

She met his needs and he never returned. Shirley assumed he didn't actually care for feeling powerless after all.

Too bad, because in the courtroom when he stared at her face, his gaze said he knew she could ruin him with a single outcry. One look and they were on the same page.

Mental note: make a list of every client you've ever had. Track them down. Find out what they do for a living.

You own them.

Shirley stood away from the bench, bigger than the room that contained her.

She held out her arms and did small circles, rotating

through the lingering pain in her shoulders. The joints worked again, now that the deputies were handcuffing her in front and only when moving her from one location to another.

Hours passed.

Squeaky footsteps on polished floors. The door opened. The deputy's mouth was narrow and flat. He didn't have lips, just a horizontal slit. It opened.

"You made bail. You are being released."

"No I didn't."

"Someone posted bail. Let's go."

"No."

"Excuse me?"

"There's a mistake. I'm not leaving."

"No mistake. Your lawyer posted bail. Time to go."

Shirley stood. It was a trick. Where did Jesús come up with enough money to secure a million dollar bond? Didn't the bondsmen take ten percent down or something like that? Where did Jesús have a hundred large?

She waited for the deputy to point and burst into laughter. Instead, he allowed his face to resume its resting mean asshole look.

"Okay, but if this is a trick I'm gonna own Arizona. I'm not putting up with you people's nonsense. I'm a citizen, you gestapo-looking thug."

"Ma'am. This way."

She shook her head. Didn't make sense but she'd play along. Just one more thing to mention to Judge Hang 'em Bly the next time she saw him.

"Do I get my things back? The stuff y'all took?"

"Yes, Ma'am."

Shirley followed into the main room and then through a

secured door that led to the same room where she gave up her only belonging: the safe deposit box key.

Great.

No cash. No purse. No cell phone. She'd left it all in the Durango and there was no telling where Jesús took it. Maybe she'd find her way to Walmart and see if he returned there, like a home base to meet up.

Wait — wouldn't it make sense for him to meet her at the jail, since he posted bail?

He's probably outside.

The deputy led her through double doors she didn't recall having come through on her journey into the jail. Down a hallway and through another set of locked doors. Enough walking to make her want to sit. Her new outfit didn't agree with her thighs. The seams didn't sit right and they rubbed. She'd dealt with it all yesterday and today without zeroing in on it. Her other troubles seemed greater.

Something to be thankful for: her giant problems were far enough away that the little problems could take over irritating her.

She followed the deputy into the lobby area. The plants were plastic. Too shiny. A man stood looking out the window.

That ain't Jesús.

He turned.

Mitchell Lucas, her public defender. He smiled.

"What's going on?" Shirley said.

Mitchell waited for the deputy to leave. When the door clicked he said, "Let's step outside. You're free, for now."

"How?"

"You have a benefactor who arranged bail. He insisted he remain anonymous, for the moment. He's waiting to speak to you at the courthouse."

"So why are you here? You do his bidding?"

"He, uh. He retained my service."

"He paid you? Like, to be a taxi? How much?"

"I'll take you to see him."

"The hell you will."

Mitchell strode toward the parking lot. Shirley saw cop cars and civilian cars. She'd been incarcerated less than two days, yet being outside the cage, smelling free air, with no one between her and... anywhere... left her feeling disoriented. Like she was born anew to limitless possibilities.

I need a gun.

She followed Mitchell. Stopped and took in her surroundings. Stared at the police headquarters, which apparently had a prison in back.

"What are you doing?"

She turned from facing the building. Mitchell stood with arms out, hands up.

"Who paid for my bail?"

"I can't say. You'll see in a minute."

"No. I'm not going."

"What else are you going to do?"

"I don't know."

"I don't understand."

"The way I been treated, I don't trust nobody right now. Not people who want everything to be a mystery. That's crap. Play it straight."

"I don't know his name. He's older. He's at the courthouse right now. That's a safe place to meet someone."

Shirley took one step.

"Unless you're a serial killer or something. Nah. I'm going to find Jesús. Find my Durango."

"It's at the courthouse. At least it was when I left. Jesús was inside. I saw him."

Something's waaaay off about this guy.

"What color is my Durango?"

"Black."

Oh. Maybe he's okay. You should go with him to the courthouse. He's tiny. You can always stomp him if you need to.

Shirley resumed walking. Mitchell led to a Toyota Corolla.

"I'll just sit on the trunk while you drive?"

"I don't understand."

All skinny people saw was fat this and fat that. Giggle. Look away quick. But make one inference. Huh? Duh? I don't understand.

"Your car is small. I'm not."

"Oh. Oh. There's plenty of room inside. You'll see."

She entered. Not too bad. Only took slamming the door four times against her thigh to get it to latch.

"Hot in here." She rolled down a window. Bigshot lawyer didn't have power windows.

Mitchell drove. His mouth twitched at the edge and the way his lower lip hung way out and down, she was afraid to see drool spill out. And his suit — she hadn't noticed earlier but the stain on his pantleg was a little crusty.

"They don't pay you lawyers much do they?"

"Oh, I'm just a public defender to get my foot in the door. There's a process. A ladder."

"And you're at the bottom. How long you been out of law school?

"Six months."

"And the state trusts you to defend someone charged with murder one. Wowsers."

"There's also a test. After passing the bar there's another test. Sixty questions."

"Sixty questions. What a relief."

Mitchell turned. He parked. "You should sit on that bench by the tree."

Shirley rubbed her jaw. Wasn't much harm that could come from sitting on a bench outside a courthouse.

"So what's next with my case? I figured I'd sit in jail and they'd come when they wanted. Now I got no way to know when they want me back."

"You — I don't understand. I thought the other guy was your lawyer. By the way, he's over there." Mitchell nodded.

Jesús was skooched down in the driver seat, sleeping. Seeing him there, she felt more secure. Though he was frail, he could wake up and honk the horn or something. Get some attention if something happened to her. It was just better knowing he was near.

"So how do I know what happens next?"

"Am I your attorney?"

"I don't know. Don't you? I didn't choose any of this and you people talk like I'm one of you. I ain't. No wonder half the country's in prison."

"I was never appointed to be your public defender. The prosecutor's office let me know after you were arrested to come in. It should have come up at your initial appearance, whether you qualify for a public defender, but I think your other lawyer threw off the judge. He sure seemed distracted. Anyway, your lawyer is in your Durango over there. I took money from an old guy to post your bail and bring you here because I'm broke and can't pay my loans. Anything else you need to know?"

Shirley opened the door and climbed out. She stepped toward the bench and whirled as Mitchell gassed his Corolla.

"Stop!"

He braked. She jiggled to the window. Ducked. "You said the prosecutor's office gave you a heads up?"

"Uh-huh."

"Is that normal?"

"I don't know. I'm new."

"Is there anyone newer than you?"

Headshake. Negative.

"Are there other public defenders?"

"Oh yeah. A few dozen."

Shirley tapped the door twice and stood. She walked to the bench and sat on it.

That prosecutor has a thing for you.

"Yeah, but why?"

Shirley placed her hands on her lap and wondered who made bail for her. She should run over and get Jesús.

"Shirley Lyle."

She jumped. Craned about to the left. He was going to kill her.

Lester Toungate stepped around the bench and sat beside her. "Easy, Shirley. Trust me. We're on the same team."

"How you figure?" She studied him up and down. "You carrying that pistol?"

"No. They took it. Crime scene and all."

"Yet here you sit."

"Here we sit.

"So what puts us on the same team?"

"The same woman is trying to put both of us away for the rest of our lives."

"And so you want a truce or something?"

"Ulyana gave me the thumb drive. You know where she is. I appreciate her relieving me of it, back there at the house. And I saw what you did, shielding her. Anyway, I need that memory stick. After that, we go back to the arrangement: Bygones."

"Okay, but doesn't this break the bad guy rules or something?"

Lester nodded. Stopped. "I was thinking about something earlier. I was a young man. Married at the time — though not for long. I saw I was pissing with the toilet seat down. I didn't dribble, nothing like that. I broke the spirit of the law but there was no real harm. I was a young man. I'd never taken a leak with the seat down in my life. Maybe as a kid and then it was spanked out of me. It was incomprehensible. A fixed star moved to another part of the sky...and here's the thing: The world didn't end. No cosmic flashes. No explosions. I broke the rule and there was no rule. See? That's the way with all of them. You're breaking a dead man's promise. Who cares, right?"

"I know what you mean," Shirley said. "I feel like that when I kill a man."

"About our mutual problem... I'm a known entity. I can't go anywhere near Kristin Mize-Jones. I'd have to get somebody from out of town."

"Wait a minute. You were ready to kill me in broad daylight six different times but you're scared of her?"

"She's somebody. They protect their own. Nobody else, but they do protect their own."

"And I'm nobody."

"Exactly."

"So you want me to go out and — "

"Hush. I notice you're skilled at putting your nose where it doesn't belong and rooting around until you get what you want. That's what I need. There's something not right about the prosecutor coming after you. Me — I understand. The deputy who handcuffed me — his son died last year of an overdose. Wasn't my stuff but he doesn't know that. I've been on their radar for years and this was always coming. But your situation is nonsense. They know it, I heard them. They know the prosecutor has a thing for you."

"So you think if I find out my deal, it helps you."

"It won't hurt me."

"That's it? You bailed me for that?"

"The other thing, too. The thumb drive. Where's Ulyana?"

"Don't know. Wouldn't say if I did."

"If I don't get that thumb drive, we go back to the way things were."

"I'll get back to you."

"That's all I wanted. Here." He reached.

She took paper from his hand, unfolded and read a phone number.

"I'll holler at you. If I want to." Shirley stood. Time to get Jesús.

"One more thing, Shirley. That FBI guy. You know him, right? Had relations?"

"FBI guy?"

"Skinny. Face like a parrot."

"Oh, Joe. Yeah, I know him."

"He wants you dead. He's the one who told me about you and Ulyana, doing El Jay. You're a problem and he thought I was a solution. I guess with a nose like that it's hard not to telegraph yourself. Anyway, you might see if he's tangled up with our prosecutor."

Shirley nodded. "Joe wanted you to kill me. Beautiful."

"Nuts. One more thing, I assume you know this. You seem one step ahead most of the time. Vanko Demyan wants you dead too."

"What? Really? We seemed to really hit it off."

He studied her face. "That Russian I shot — I came up behind him. He was gearing up to attack the house. That means Ulyana or you."

"Okay. What's one more?"

She held Lester's gaze a long moment as she turned, then walked without a backward glance. If it was all a ploy so he could shoot her in the back, so be it, but something told her Lester Toungate was one of the most honest people she'd ever meet. At least in that particular moment.

What happened to Lester?

At the Durango she peered inside and almost felt bad waking Jesús. So sweet with his head tilted forward, like the seat was too big or he slumped way down in it. Sometimes sitting that way took pressure off the back, but too much and he'd likely be sore when he woke.

Shirley tapped the window, light. Didn't want to startle him but she had a plan in mind. Things to set in motion.

Jesús was deep asleep.

She rapped the door.

She pounded.

Shirley grabbed the handle and pulled. The door opened.

Jesús was dead. She knew from the smell of the air.

30

*R*eleased in the morning, Shirley met Lester at a quarter after nine a.m. She discovered Jesús dead ten minutes later. An ambulance arrived, a coroner, stretcher, questions and nonsense. She took her purse out of the Durango, her keys from Jesús' pocket and ducked out to the shaded bench to wait it out.

It was a little ridiculous to grow attached to another person in the space of hours. She'd only met him. But he cared for her deeply—from the very beginning. He appreciated her glorious faults without an iota of judgment. He really appreciated her.

Naturally, he died.

She wondered how a man so wholesome and good could find a world so bitterly unaroused that it left him to die alone in a parking lot. She couldn't fathom it, so she wept.

The woman with the foghorn voice asked a couple bystanders if they knew who owned the Durango and reported the body... No one thought to look over to Shirley, sputtering tears under the shade.

The woman stood at the back of the Durango and spoke to someone on her walkie talkie. Then, forever charged with writing tickets, she walked the line of parking meters.

Shirley approached the Durango perpendicular then cut left ninety degrees and arrived unseen. She opened the door and checked the seat...

Unsoiled.

But the vehicle smelled. She hadn't thought to put the windows down before she hid on the shaded bench. Jesús probably died yesterday and cooked all afternoon, chilled overnight, then warmed up in the morning.

Is it even safe to be where a dead person was?

Shirley placed her purse on the passenger seat. Everything seemed normal. She fired the engine, backed out. On the road she glanced across. Foghorn hadn't noticed she stole back her Durango.

In fifteen minutes Shirley cut the wheel and grabbed a space in front of the Motel 6 where she'd left Ulyana. With luck, Ulyana would be inside.

"I dropped off my friend here a couple days ago. Little blonde thing, you know. Perfect."

The man smiled.

"What room is she in?"

"I can't — it's our policy not to — I mean if this person was here — "

Shirley slid a five-spot across the counter, held his eyes and grinned.

"What is this?"

"Buy yourself some chocolate chip mint and tell me how you like it."

He pushed away the bill.

"Look, I dropped her off. I'm her friend. I need to talk to her."

"You're her friend."

"Think! It makes sense."

He shook his head. Clamped his jaw. But then his eyes widened. He tilted his head. Frowned. "You're right. Pretty girls always — "

"Tell you what. I'm going outside. You call her and say Shirley's out front and really, really needs to talk to her."

Shirley smiled like to make her eyes twinkle... because her next step was to strangle him and check the computer herself.

"Okay. Without confirming the guest is here, I will agree inasmuch as I can."

"What the hell does that mean? Those aren't even words when you say them like that."

"Just go outside. I'll see what I can do." He grabbed the five spot.

"Thanks, Sugar."

Shirley exited, leaned on the wall outside, looking toward Subway.

Subway was next on her to-do list. She imagined the smell of bread fresh from the oven—except Subway never slathered their bread in butter. Could you imagine? Better yet, a Subway footlong split down the side, melted butter, then almond butter and apple butter and honey and marshmallows. Sprinkle a little cinnamon and twice as much cocoa powder. A touch of salt.

Wash it down with chocolate milk or melted ice cream, whatever's handy.

The door clicked and whooshed behind her.

"Psst!"

Shirley turned.

"Quick! Come inside." Ulyana disappeared and the door closed.

Shirley looked to Subway like a departing lover, then hurried inside, followed Ulyana down the hall, up the steps, down the hall and into room 219. Ulyana waited in the bathroom while Shirley entered. Ulyana popped out and locked the dead bolt. Swung the bar guard and pressed her eye to the fisheye lens.

She rushed to Shirley and hugged her. Released. "You're out!"

"Made bail."

Ulyana stood with her hands on Shirley's arms while she bounced on her toes like they were old time best friends. "Super awesome. I've been at work. I have some serious crap to show you. What? How? You made bail with your money?"

"With Lester's, but not mine. Slow down. Quit bouncing. You're making me sick. Not my Lester-money. Lester bailed me out with his Lester-money. I need to get the memory stick and give it to him. So if you're still all sunshine and love, I need it."

"Yes. I'm totally sunshine and love. Totally. Was that the deal? He didn't need to do that. Yes, he can have it. And you can have sunshine and love too."

"No, not that. Just the drive."

Ulyana released Shirley's forearms and sat beside the desk with a laptop computer open and on.

"When'd you get that?"

"Yesterday. There's a pawn shop across the street."

"Sit on the corner of your bed?" Shirley said.

"Sure."

Shirley dropped. Sat leaning back with her arms spread for support. Felt good to extend the shoulders. "The memory stick is only part of the reason Lester paid my bail."

"What's the rest?"

"He wants me to kill the prosecutor. She charged both of us, I guess."

"Lester killed one of Burian's guys."

"How — ?"

"I made a phone call."

"Aren't you in hiding or something?"

"No.... I just don't want anyone to know where I'm at."

"Oh. Right."

"Did he say that? He wants you to kill her?"

"Not in so many words; we were outside the court. But he said I need to look into the prosecutor."

Ulyana nodded with a squinty look. "He said that?"

"Uh-huh."

"Because I thought the same thing. I called Naomi at the trailer court. You know Naomi? She was one of Clyde's girls."

"Oh — yeah! Naomi."

"So we caught up. I'm thinking I might buy the place from Clyde's estate. Naomi's been there forever and I wanted some background. Anyhow, the police were already there and gone since you shot Maddix at my place. She said I could come back and I might go get some things."

"Where's this going?"

"Maddix. You killed Maddix. No one saw it."

"I know. That's the preferred method."

"So if Kristin Mize-Jones wants to prosecute you, why choose the one where there are two witnesses to say she's wrong instead of the one where there was no witness?"

"I didn't get that either."

"I have friends, you know? I told you that."

"Right."

"One's a cop. I had him check Maddix Heregger.

"And?"

"His ex wife had a restraining order. He served thirty days on a battery charge."

"So?"

"What do you mean, so? There's no way a jury would believe he didn't deserve it when you shot him. He broke the door in."

"Actually, that was Ruth Memmelsdorf, stealing my money."

"They don't know that."

Shirley shrugged. "I guess not."

"No, the jury would say he got what he deserved."

"But the kidnappers who had guns on us and threatened to bury me with a backhoe — they didn't deserve it?"

"Not the way I bet Mrs. Mize-Jones is going to spin it."

"Miss. The judge called her miss."

"Exactly."

"You're not making sense."

"She's going to charge me as an accomplice and say the whole kidnapping was part of a hoax."

"That makes zero sense."

"Aside from you, who knows I was kidnapped?"

"Donal."

"Does he?"

"He was there when you were in the root cellar."

"Ladies and gentlemen of the jury. Consider, we have a stripper known to consort with the lowest kinds, who fires a pistol into her car and leaves it beside the road. She disappears all right — hiding in an unoccupied house she knows belongs to Roderick Memmelsdorf, who she repeatedly had thrown out of her strip club. After the killing, she climbs out of the root cellar without so much as a rope burn on her wrist. She later refuses a rape test. Ladies and Gentlemen, we also have a former prostitute who bought a gun, stalked Roderick Memmelsdorf, then the day after feeling empowered by killing a man who attacked her, sought revenge on the man who tried to steal her lover."

"Yeah. Wait. What? Lover? That sounds like total bullshit."

"Real life sounds like total bullshit. I mean, everything we've done... who'd believe any of it?"

"Good point."

"Maybe she's made other connections that — what are you looking at?"

"That man, on your computer," Shirley said. "That photo."

"You recognize him, don't you?"

Shirley nodded as she stood and came closer.

"His name is Gary Mayer," Ulyana said. "He's one of your johns."

"How did you know?"

"It's the only thing that makes sense. I wondered why Kristin Mize-Jones might want to go after you."

"I'm not getting this."

"Mrs Kristin Mize-Jones's mother was Nancy Mize. Her father was Larry Jones."

"Talk to me like I'm five years old."

"Her hyphenated name is from her parents, not from keeping her maiden name when she married. That's why you never connected Kristin to her husband Gary Mayer."

Awe splashed through Shirley. She giggled. "That's so funny because I screwed the judge too! I love it!"

"It's like your past is your secret weapon."

"Yeah. Invisible Man is invisible. Superman can fly. And Shirley F'N Lyle has a photographic memory of half the gigglesticks in Arizona."

"You just have to make sure you never go anywhere you don't have former clients."

"What time is it?"

Ulyana read the clock on her laptop.

"Almost three."

"Oooh! I have time!"

"Where you going?"

31

Slow down! You're going to kill us!

Shirley wiggled in the seat. A forty-five speed limit sign approached at — she glanced at the speedometer — sixty-eight miles per hour.

Ulyana preferred to stay in hiding but Shirley had a town to upend.

She felt inside her purse and grabbed her cell phone. Opened to Google and thumbed "tipEye witnesd News."

A page came up with a number. She pressed it.

"Eyewitness News tip line. Whatcha got?"

"Yeah, this is Shirley F'N Lyle. I was charged with murder yesterday and I'm about to make a big announcement on the Superior Court steps. You got a camera crew handy?"

"Uh — "

"The action's going down in five minutes."

"Wait a minute! We have a van ten minutes away. You sound kinda... Are you okay? You're not going to shoot the place up are you?"

"What's the right answer?"

Shirley ended the call.

At ten minutes after three p.m., Shirley squealed tires into a parking space that by divine intervention was vacated as she approached. She popped out of the Durango and stood on the sidewalk taking it all in.

The courthouse was small-town quaint, constructed of reddish brown cut stone with a five-story tower on a two-story building. The lawn was small and flat and there were only six steps to the main entrance. It was approachable — built by people who thought court was a place for regular folks to get a fair listen.

Shirley left her purse inside and slammed the Durango door. The sun was out and the temperature in the sixties. Bright and clean.

Her heart pattered.

Shirley F'N Lyle you are muy loco! Let's do this!

"Muy indeed, Viva Shirley."

She crossed Birch Avenue and approached the courthouse on the sidewalk. A hippy with a guitar sat on the steps, strumming. His case held a few coins.

"You're about to be in the news," Shirley said.

He studied her face a moment, then gathered his coins, packed his guitar and left.

A man and woman in gray suits and shiny shoes exited the courthouse. They veered around her and the man looked back from the sidewalk.

"Just waiting on my news van," Shirley said.

The man withdrew a cell phone from his suit jacket pocket.

This is fun!

A news van raced up Birch Avenue and screeched to a halt. Four-ways flashed. A woman in a pink blazer and skirt tumbled out with a microphone already in hand. She stood on the road, head swiveling.

Shirley waved.

A man opened the back of the van. He emerged from behind the door with a camera on his shoulder.

You're gonna be famous.

The pink suit jogged across the lawn and the cameraman fumbled with his device and ran at the same time.

A police car with revolving red and blues screeched onto Birch and parked at an angle. A man in uniform burst from each door.

"Are you the one who called in the tip?" Pink said.

"Yes I am," Shirley said. "You got the camera on, Sugar?"

The man signaled thumbs up.

"You recording?"

"Recording. Not broadcasting," he said.

"Where's your gun?" Pink said. "Did you already shoot people? Where are they?"

"No, hell no. That ain't what this is about."

"You said you were a murderer at the courthouse."

"I said I was charged with murder and I'm about to drop a major bomb on this perversion of justice here in the fine heartland. And shit."

"FREEZE!"

"Not this again."

"PUT YOUR HANDS IN THE AIR!"

Shirley raised her hands. "Talking to a reporter's against the law?"

"WHAT'S GOING ON HERE?"

"Stop shouting. You're three feet away. And why are you pointing a gun at me?"

The deputy on the left said, "You the one who called in the tip?"

"I called a tip to the news line. I'm about to make news."

"What kind of news?"

"Jessica Pink, EyeWitness One live at Coconino County Superior Court with breaking news."

Jessica Pink shoved her microphone in front of Shirley's mouth.

"I'm Shirley F'N Lyle. That stands for Shirley Fed Up N Lyle."

"Jessica Pink here at Superior Court with Shirley Lyle, who was charged with murder yesterday."

"Stop interrupting. Lemme say my piece. My friend was kidnapped and I hunted her down just three days ago. I found her in a locked root cellar and got her out. Then the police came in like stormtroopers and next thing, I'm in jail. I saved that girl! But since I shot the man and woman who took her, this little stinker of a prosecutor wants me to get the death penalty. Now I thought that's weird, 'cause I killed another man a couple days before and let me tell you, that one looks a whole lot sketchier than these two Memmelsdorfs. I mean, it was on the up and up, but it looks pretty bad. So I got to wondering — "

The policemen lowered their weapons. Glanced at each other.

"If I could just interrupt, you killed three people in the last how many days?"

"I kinda lost track of time, what with being in jail. Call it a week."

"Jessica Pink with serial murderer Shirley Lyle. Eyewitness News. Go ahead, Shirley."

"Yeah, like I was saying. I got to wondering why that twunt

prosecutor would charge me for murder when I rescued a kidnapped girl and shot a woman who had a gun on me."

"What did you find out?"

"I screwed her husband a hundred and twenty three times in the last six years."

"Excuse me?"

"Oh hell yeah. Musta blew him twice as much. I didn't put it together because his wife is a modern woman who kept both her parents' names and didn't take his. She had good instincts on that."

"And are you prepared to name your lover?"

"Lover — right. We was lovers all right. Old Gary Mayer and me was madly in love."

"And do you have proof of this alleged multi-year affair?"

"Proof? What, like did I steal his underwear?"

"Do you have any evidence at all, so viewers know this isn't some wild attempt to smear a prosecutor?"

"Well, I guess I got some proof. Yeah. He's only got one nut. And he has a freckle the size of a nickel on the base of his — "

"Jessica Pink here at the Coconino County Courthouse with cold hearted killer Shirley Lyle."

"Hey, we ain't done. I got more to say."

The police officer on the left waved his arm and turned. The other followed.

The cameraman kept the lens pointed at Shirley.

"So the big question," Jessica Pink said, "who's the prosecutor? What's her name?"

"She's a hyphen. I don't remember all of it. Mize-Jones. That's it. Kristin Mize-Jones."

Jessica Pink lowered the microphone. Drew a slash across her neck and the cameraman pointed away, lowered the camera.

"I wish you would have said that earlier."

"What are you talking about? I got lots more." Shirley faced the cameraman. "Pick that up. Turn it on. I have it on good authority — "

"Look, we're done here."

"What the freakin' hell?"

"You don't know who Kristin Mize-Jones is, do you?"

"Uh, I know her husband better."

"Her mother owns Channel One."

Shirley took in a lungful of air. Kept inhaling until it hurt because the only other thing she could think to do was grab the microphone out of Jessica Pink's hand and shove it down her throat. Shirley released. She lowered herself to the six-inch steps, put her elbows on her knees and her head in her hands.

"Have a nice day," Pink said.

Shirley locked her fingers on top of her head and squeezed her cranium with her palms.

That was just one idea. We'll come up with more.

The news team left.

Shirley sniffled.

"Power. That's all it boils down to. The people who have it never give a royal damn about anybody but themselves. And the people who don't have it learn to kiss ass or die. Well screw everybody but the little people. VIVA the REVOLUTION."

An ant hesitated before attempting to scale her shoe. Shirley wiped snot from her nose. Tried to push the ant away with her shoe. Crushed it.

"That's the way of it, little man. Tried to help you out."

"That was totally righteous."

Shirley turned. A man held a cell phone camera on her. It was the guitarist... but he'd originally been on the other side of the steps.

"You circle behind the building or something?"

"Yeah."

"What are you doing with your phone?"

"I'm taking video. You have anything else you want the world to know, Miss Shirley F'N Lyle? 'Cause in ten minutes this video's going up on YouTube."

Shirley blinked.

"You got anything else to say to the world?"

"Well, an apology would be nice."

"And does that go the other way? I mean, didn't you say you screwed the woman's husband?"

"Well, I didn't think of it like that. You must be a hippy or something. Another sunshine person. Well yes, I apologize for everything I did with Gary Mayer. I just don't understand why everyone who has power thinks they have to use it to screw people over instead of help them. Police, prosecutor. Even the news?"

"Where's the love, yeah?"

"Right. Where's the damn love? That's what I want to know. All that I said... that's why Mize-Jones brought me up on murder one. They should knock her out of the lawyer's club for that."

"Are you calling for the prosecutor to be disbarred?"

"I'm not trying to ruin her life. She can go to the bars and clubs and whatnot. Just not as a lawyer. I'm done. Shirley Lyle. Out. Turn that thing off."

Shirley gained her feet and retreated to the Durango.

32

*F*irst thing after Elvita arrived at the office, Mendi played her a voicemail. The Ramirez accounts were in jeopardy.

José Ramirez was the patriarch. He had four million under Elvita's management. His sons Jorge and Esteban each had another million with her and his extended family, another two.

If there was such a thing as a gold client, José Ramirez was platinum. With all the other accounts she'd lost, José's defection meant she wouldn't earn enough fees to pay her staff, rent and keep the lights on. It meant losing her business.

"Play it again."

Mendi pressed the button.

"Elvita this is José, up at Flag. Need to talk. I made some deci-sions and it's time for a change in direction."

Elvita closed her eyes. Her stomach cinched, stealing her breath. She looked about her desk for a bottle of water. Finding none she grabbed her travel mug of juice and gulped. Wrinkled her brow; it tasted much worse now that it was getting warmer.

Done gulping, she dry swallowed. The back of her tongue felt thick.

"Grab José's file. In fact get all of them, Jorge and the bunch, I'm going up there."

"I'll need a box..."

"There's one in the copy room. I need to visit the restroom. Excuse me."

"You look sick. Are you coming down with something?"

"No, the entire world is coming down with something, right on top of me. Just get the files ready so I can go."

*T*he drive from her office to the Ramirez residence in Flagstaff usually took Elvita just under two hours. Between stabs of stomach pain and cramps in her feet, she thought about the chaos ready to engulf her.

One of her newest reps quit that morning — Claude McFadden — the one Chico insisted she hire. Another firm recruited him away. The loss wasn't consequential in terms of money — in fact it would probably improve her bottom line because new reps seldom became successful and usually wasted office resources. But a departure always felt like a personal failure to her.

It was unlike Chico to take an interest in newbies but when Claude submitted his resume, he requested Chico interview him because he'd heard of his reputation. It was off putting. Chico was the mouth, she the brain. Bewildered into curiosity, Elvita consented to the request and Chico, with an accommo- dating smile, agreed to the interview. Afterward he said Claude had the makings of success and urged Elvita to offer him a position. Her business plan didn't call for rapid growth: adding recruits during a recession felt aggressive. Elvita decided to give him a shot, but to let him go quickly if he didn't find success.

A loose strand of hair fell into Elvita's face. She brushed it away. Her hand shook.

Something weird was going on. Her stomach burned and she was salivating.

Just thinking about Chico turned her into a mess.

How did everything fall apart? They had something amazing, for a while. But it seemed like almost anything could cause a fight in the last few months. Their last happened in the office.

She was at her desk preparing for a client review, in a hurry because her investment company had recently launched a new double verification login protocol and the website wasn't accepting the text code she'd received.

John — her most successful money manager — raised his voice loud enough that she closed the file on her desk and went to the door. John stood at the window, looking down on the parking lot.

Elvita got close to the glass. John pointed.

Chico spoke to a man next to a car on the pavement. His posture indicated jocularity and fun.

"That's my client," John said. "What? Chico thinks no one sees what he's trying to do?"

Elvita shook her head. "Your client is your client, but he also has a relationship with the firm. I'm sure Chico is just being friendly."

She needed to get back to work.

The next day, John knocked on her door while it was closed. "Yes?"

The door pushed open.

"You got a minute? Thanks. Listen. I asked my client about Chico talking to him in the parking lot yesterday. He said it felt uncomfortable, like he was being too friendly. People in the same office shouldn't be stealing each others' clients."

"Come in. Have a seat."

"No thanks. I have to run to a meeting and I wanted to put the problem with you so I don't have to deal with it. You'll say something to him?"

John studied her as if she stood in a lineup behind glass.

Elvita saw the Sedona exit coming up. She knew it from memory, but couldn't focus on the sign well enough to read the numbers. What was going on? Her stomach had been rotten and achy all morning. Her heart was thumping. She read the Sedona sign again, imagined Bell Rock welcoming her to Oak Creek, the red rocks and canyons.

She needed a get away. A severe getaway. Grab her cash from the safe, buy a tent, sleeping bag, cook-stove... and disappear.

As the highway began to ascend she pressed the gas and felt a slight cramp in her thigh.

She shook her leg: she was dehydrated. She'd stop at a gas station and get a bottle of water before driving out to see José Ramirez.

Though the money managers in her organization competed with her in a broad sense, they also relied on her to protect their interests. Her instinct, from years of being the underling before she started her own company, told her to always be suspicious of other reps' motives. Her view was particularly informed by, as a rookie, watching a registered representative steal a client from his colleague over the space of a few weeks.

At the time she had been dating the client-thief. She smiled at him with naïve disbelief and he took her grin as a signal she would be suitably gobsmacked by the truth.

"I'm playing 3-D chess and they don't even know they're in a game."

"How do you do it?"

"You wait for your mark to arrive for an appointment. He's a big fish so he's used to having people kiss his ass. So you go out and kiss it before his rep gets there. Offer to get some coffee. Schmooze a little. The only real goal is to get him to know your face. He'll assume you want his business. You don't have to say it.

"Next, you have a random encounter at the ball game. You shake hands and when he asks how business is, you tell him you're not looking for new clients because the ones you have keep you running twenty-four, seven. You look around to make sure nobody's watching, and lean in. It's none of your business, but it feels like the right thing to do. You tell him he needs to go on the Internet and check out his advisor's U4. Or if he has a perfect record, ask if the rep tried to borrow money from him. A couple people were suspicious, is all.

"Last, you run into him at lunch. He wants to know what you would do with an equity portfolio, with the economy such as it is, yada yada. You're in the front door and the only thing between you and signing those papers is whether you have the skill to close any deal at all."

Elvita knew Chico's friendliness seemed egregious. The industry was cutthroat and only the suspicious reps survived. But stealing clients wasn't Chico's way. He put in the same long hours as she did and they worked cases together. He couldn't steal a client without involving her, and there was no way that was happening.

"I understand how sometimes in this industry you have to be suspicious, John. I've seen it firsthand. But Chico works every case with me. If he was trying to steal your client, then that would mean I am too. I hope you know me better than that."

John frowned. "This doesn't look right." He left.

"I'll talk to Chico about it," she said to the door.

She mentioned it that night before she and Chico sat down to dinner at nine. She was tired and didn't think to use kid gloves.

"I'm friendly by nature. I like people and I'm not going to stop being who I am because other people have thin skin and lack self-confidence."

She blinked. He spoke to her like the man of the house, not a registered representative in her company. She'd made a mistake in addressing a business matter in their home. The office was the seat of her authority and pressing her interests from home was waging battle from low ground.

The air between them was cold. Things were already tense with the markets, and they'd recently seen the first of the gold-client defections.

Knowing she should redirect the subject and resume their discussion from the office, another part of her thought, this is your house. You bought it. It's your company. You founded it. This is your husband. You're the brain in the relationship, and your clients know it.

She said, "Chico, I'm tired and I'm only going to say this once. You are married to the boss. I expect you to uphold the same standards I do."

Chico nodded while holding her stare. He closed his eyes a moment, opened them and backed away. "I'm going out for a beer."

The next day, John gave his notice. He'd already cleaned out his desk before she arrived that morning. Within two weeks, $15 million of assets under management disappeared.

What would have happened if Chico would have apologized to John for creating the wrong impression, and given him his word that nothing fishy was going on?

They would never know, because with Chico it was always about Chico. His plans, his goals, his ego, the whole thing.

Slightly lightheaded from the elevation change, but more woozy than she would ordinarily feel, Elvita rested her head against the seat. The final climb on Interstate 17 was behind her. The highway before her sloped gently and branched off to the right to join Interstate 40 eastbound. She stayed on 17 and curved to the left.

Speed limits fell until the highway morphed into a boulevard.

Moving her foot from the gas to the brake, her leg seemed to ignore her will. She lifted her thigh, but the muscles in her foot, ankle, and calf didn't move. Her toe dropped when she slid her leg to the left.

She looked up.

The stop light flashed from yellow to red. Her speedometer read fifty-five. Her foot wouldn't move. Her brain spun. She lifted her leg and slammed it back down but hit the gas.

Elvita charged into the intersection and t-boned a black Dodge Durango.

33

*C*hico Marín woke shivering and rolled his face from a patch of leaves soaked in vodka and hot dog vomit. His neck vertebrae cracked and the muscles on the right side felt like they were attached to a horse galloping downhill. He blinked until the blur cleared. His tent entrance flap was open and his subzero sleeping bag was inside. As was his backpack, cook stove, water bladder and dehydrated meals. Everything was snug in the tent except him. He stretched his neck the other direction and it hurt more.

Why am I such an asshole?

Chico lay on his back until the shivering returned. His fire was dead.

He'd climbed half of Kendrick Mountain, west of Flagstaff, and set up camp a short distance off the logging trail that zigzagged to the top, just above the farthest burned trees of the Pumpkin fire from year 2000. The mountain terrain jutted and rolled and all the trees were vertical black needles. Looking downhill, then over to one of the mini mountains nearby, he felt vertigo.

Chico threw up again — little vomit, lots of sinus gunk.

He shivered. Probably had hypothermia and didn't feel it through the intoxication.

He wiped his face. His throat burned.

Below, the trees were dead. Above, they were pristine and surrounded by reluctantly melting snow.

He'd been in the woods for days, wandering up the mountain, wandering back down. Yesterday was day three. He'd left the tent and everything but his empty pack, returned to his Grand Cherokee, drove to a service station and bought five gallons of water, then rolled into Flagstaff and stopped at Peace Surplus for enough dehydrated backpacker meals to last a month. Next, a couple liters of Gray Goose.

Why not?

He stopped at a gas station and bought an orange juice and a half dozen hot dogs sans buns from the roller grill. Dropped them in condom-looking plastic bags intended for the taquitos.

Chico returned to the woods, parked in the same place, refilled his water bladder from the plastic jugs and wondered if the estrogens in the plastic would make him grow boobs. That's what Elvita used to say, teasing him into being more healthy.

"Why not?" he said. "I like tits."

He dumped vodka from the Goose bottle into one of the plastic water jugs and tucked it into the top of his backpack.

At the bottom of Kendrick Mountain, Chico shouldered his pack and humped everything past the ice age boulders, back and forth across the tedious foothills, then when the climb became difficult, slowed his pace and stopped to soak in the stillness.

When nothing in life makes you feel glad to be alive, get out

of your life. Go where you're connected to nothing and absolutely everything at the same time and ask the wind:

Where did I go wrong?

At his tent he unpacked. Ate hotdogs and washed them
down with Grey Goose until he blacked out still waiting for an
answer.

34

*E*lvita's airbags deployed. Her jaw felt like when she took a softball in the face as a kid. Nothing was broken but she knew she would soon die.

The front of her Mercedes crumpled. Smoke lifted from the engine compartment and a hissing sound swirled in her mind with the others noises she had just experienced: squealing tires, metal smashing, glass shattering, her voice screaming.

Is my car going to blow up?

She moved her arm to the seatbelt buckle but her hand fell. The top part of the window and the roof of the car, which had been clear in her vision a moment ago, blurred. She closed her eyes and relaxed into a soothing whiteness.

Rapping on the window. Shouts. Someone was pulling but the door wasn't opening. She twisted her head. A woman with fury on her face and beefy shoulders yanked the handle and the door popped. The woman was a giant, tall and huge and strong. She dropped to one knee and took Elvita's hand in hers.

"You're okay, Baby. Is anything broken? Can you tell? You're going to be fine. I got you now."

Elvita's vision moved in and out of focus. She opened her mouth but no words issued.

The woman at her door pressed Elvita's legs, then her arms. "Nothing broke there?" The woman placed her hands on either side of Elvita's neck and said, "Does anything feel strange in there? Is your neck moving okay?"

"I'm fine. I'm just going to drive home now."

The woman laughed. "Neither one of us is driving anywhere, Sugar."

The woman reached across her lap and unfastened Elvita's seatbelt.

Elvita noticed others standing outside the door. A woman with a baby in her arms. A teenager lurking a few yards back. A man on a cell phone speaking while his eyes studied the car, as if he was giving details.

She was alive.

But the numbness that had begun in her feet was now at her hips.

35

*P*oor woman. Still young and beautiful. She was lucky, though it would probably take distance to see herself being almost dead as a bout of good fortune. Sometimes you need to have your face pressed into a pile of crap to fully appreciate a rain shower.

Much as Shirley wanted to go to the hospital and make sure the woman wasn't alone when she came out of surgery or whatever they were going to do to her, Shirley had work to do. She called her insurance company and braced herself for the inevitable argument, the rigmarole, the wasted time and breath. A woman answered. She spoke with a clear Midwest accent. She spoke English and Shirley didn't have to Press One. The woman summoned a tow truck. Then she called Enterprise and said, "Stay put a few minutes and you'll have a ride to your rental car. We'll pay twenty-five dollars a day toward the cost."

"But the other driver caused the accident. Shouldn't her insurance pay? Now my rates are going to go up."

"We'll coordinate with her insurance for reimbursement. Your rates won't change."

"But... this is too easy. Don't you want to shake me down for cash or something?"

"Thanks for calling! Try to have a super day!"

"Okay. Yeah. Super."

A half hour later she was signing forms at Enterprise. "Just give me whatever twenty-five dollars a day will cover."

The man passed her the car key. "It's the shiny white one at the end of the row."

She took the key, folded the papers she'd just signed and stepped out to the lot.

"Oh, hell no." Back inside at the counter. "You didn't think when you was looking at me, hey, this bitch won't fit in that tiny car?"

"Uh."

"Yeah, 'Uh'. Gimme a truck or something. I'm a woman in motion, no time for games. Let's get this done."

"Hey!"

"What?"

"No offense — but was that you on Youtube?"

"Sure. You got a truck or something?"

"They cost more. Did you really do all that?"

"I'll pay the difference."

More forms. He kept looking at her face.

Next time she exited, the man led her to a cobalt blue Dodge Ram with an extended cab.

"Hey, did you really do all that — what you said on the video?"

She held his hungry look. "Oh, Sugar... I *loved* that man."

Shirley closed the door. Fired the engine and let it run. She fished out the paper Lester gave her and pressed the numbers into the phone. The Enterprise man was still standing outside her door. She powered down the window.

"What? You need something?"

"Have a good day."

She powered up the window. Lester answered his phone.

"I got that thing you wanted."

"Meet me same place."

"Yep."

"Hey."

"What?"

"Saw you on channel five."

"Cool."

"Maybe. We'll talk."

Shirley tossed her phone into her purse. The dashboard clock read five minutes of six. The sun was already approaching the horizon and the air was getting chilly. She put the RAM in reverse. Exiting the lot she chirped a tire and fishtailed.

The truck made her sit way up high, like she was looking down on the little people. Shirley braked. The car in front signaled, slowed and turned right.

Okay, road's clear. See what it'll do! Step on it!

Shirley crushed the gas pedal to the floor. The Hemi roared. Her boobs and belly flattened as the truck surged forward.

Sideways gravity!

Shirley braked, came to a turn.

Okay, another straight stretch. Do it again!

"Actually, I think I'd best mind the speed limits."

Shirley kept the speedometer at thirty-six until she turned at the courthouse. Lester was already on the bench. She parked and joined him.

Shirley fished the thumb drive from her pocket and slid it across the wood seat. Lester covered her hand.

"Shirley. Let's savor this moment. You've vexed me. Now it's over. We in agreement?"

"I don't like your hand on mine."

Shirley placed her hand on top of Lester's. "That's better. So yes, we're in agreement. But you ever do something like that to me again — come in my place and tear it up, I'll be ready for you."

Lester nodded. "Reasonable."

Shirley lifted her hand.

"I don't understand," Lester said. "Ulyana — she's always been a little scattered. Her giving up the memory stick after those crackpots took her, I can see that. But you've been both the brains and the brawn. Why'd you change your mind?"

"Oh, that's easy. Though it only made sense just now."

He waited.

"I tried being good: playing by the rules as much as I could while being a hooker and keeping my head down and hoping nobody bothered me. But what I found is there's no help. All my life, every single place I turned to there was only broken people and other people preying on them. Victims and predators. I don't want to be either. Just leave me alone or I'll kick your ass. I'm sick of it. Not you — society in general. Well you too. I'll kick your ass if you do that crap again."

Lester smiled. "If you're not a victim and you're not a predator, what are you?"

"I take that back. I am a predator for the good team."

A bird flew onto the sidewalk in front of them, close enough Lester could nudge it with his boot. They watched as it flew away.

"I was thinking. You said I was on channel five. That girl who interviewed me was from Channel One. She said that skiznit prosecutor's mother owned the station, so the video wouldn't get on the air. She packed up, soon as I said her name."

"Well it did the trick. She's already resigned."

"Who? The pink reporter?"

"No. Our prosecutor. It's all over channel five. Your charges are going to be reviewed and they won't stand up. The rest of Mize-Jones' cases are being transferred to a fella named Travis Noake."

"You're shitting me."

"Nope. You're free."

"Yeah, I get that. You said Travis Noake?"

"You know him?"

"Let me handle this for you."

"Well..."

"I got this, I understand the game. I'm gonna play — and after it's all done, you and me have separate paths. If we happen to meet, we're old friends. Fair?"

"Why?"

"Look, Lester. You're a criminal. You're a bad ass dude. Even a hundred and forty years old, you're a bad dude. No one thinks you're wholesome and trusts you to be righteous. No one puts a badge on your chest and says, we expect you to use this power on our behalf. I mean, kudos and all. You got away with some trouble. But the people I'm gunning for — they're the ones who betray us. We give them power so they can point the power out and instead, the bastards point the power in."

"I guess the system roughed you up."

"No — not the system; the system's fine. Just some of the people in it, I got a problem with. I'm sick of it. The cops and reporters and money people, the politicians. The whole bunch are crooks. They'll shove your face in the wall just 'cuz they can. Those are the people I'm going after, and having Travis Noake in my pocket... I can see how a prosecutor scared for his life is a good thing.

They shook hands.

"You're a big woman, Shirley Lyle."

"Damn right I am. Now I got a favor to ask. A mutually beneficial favor."

36

*C*lutching her purse at her chest, Mendi Garza entered Elvita's room at the Flagstaff Medical Center. Her mouth fell.

Elvita wore a clear mask with a giant hose connected to a breathing machine. The skin around her eyes was bruised. A bandage circled her head. She had a fat lip under the plastic mask, like she'd been punched. Tubes and cables everywhere, while another machine beeped.

A fifty-something woman smothered a chair against the wall. "You know her?" the woman said.

"I'm Mendi."

The woman nodded. "I guess that means something."

"I am Elvita's assistant. I work for her. What happened?"

"She's resting now. The respirator is just to make it easier for her to breathe."

"Who are you?"

"She hit me, plowed straight in. Didn't brake or nothing,

like she was on dope. So they did a blood test and found no drugs at all. So they did another."

"And?"

"Touch and go. Somebody poisoned her."

"Poison? People do that?"

"Doctor says it's the same stuff Socrates drank."

"Hemlock?"

"Wow, first try." The woman regarded her with suspicion.

"I minored in philosophy."

"Is that where they teach poison?"

"Socrates was a philosopher."

"Sure. Of course he was. Anyway, the doctor said that stuff grows all over the place. Like a weed."

"That doesn't make any sense. Why would — ?"

"Yeah?"

"Never mind. Is Elvita going to be okay?"

The woman met her stare with squinty, disbelieving eyes. "The doctor said he doesn't know how long the poison's been in her system. If she improves from here, then she'll be fine in no time. She goes downhill, there's no guessing how far."

Mendi glanced away.

"How's that make you feel?"

"Horrible. There was a car accident and she hit you?"

The woman nodded.

"So... why are you hanging out here? She's unconscious."

"Because hitting me was the luckiest damn thing that ever happened to her. Ambulance driver knew something else was wrong with her, besides from the car accident. Without the wreck, she probably would have driven off into a ditch some-where with no one to hook up all these tubes and wires."

Mendi nodded. "But why are you here? Because I might be able to help you. I work very closely — "

"I came to check on her and found she was poisoned and had no one else in the world to look after her. That made it me. So how did you know to come here? You come up from Phoenix?"

"Our office is in Phoenix. Elvita drove here for an appointment; a very important appointment. When she didn't return my calls all afternoon, I reached out to the police and the hospital."

"Did they reach back?"

"What?"

"Sounds mighty convenient to me. Don't mess with me. You try to kill this woman?"

"No! She's my boss! She's my friend! Oh my God!"

"Okay — don't get your panties bunched up. She's going to be fine. I've been listening to her for three hours. She's not getting worse."

Mendi pulled a chair from the wall to the bed. She took Elvita's right hand and studied her face. Tears welled.

"I'm Shirley Lyle. I help women who need helped and can't take it to the cops. A minute ago you were about to ask why somebody would want to poison Elvita. Then you stopped."

"Uh-huh."

"Because you knew."

"She just split up with her husband a week ago. He hasn't been to the office. He hasn't answered her calls. It looks like he's trying to undermine her business or even steal it from her somehow. He never seemed like a bad guy until all of a sudden."

"That would be Chico, right?"

"Yes. How did you know?"

"I got it out of Nurse Wretched over there." She nodded

toward outside of the room, at the nurse's station. "They tried to call him but there was no answer."

"So what do we do?"

"We wait."

*T*he doctor appeared in the room entrance. He appeared abundantly satisfied with himself.

"Oh, a new face. Are you family?"

"No, doctor. I work with Elvita."

"Will any family members be coming?"

"Just us girls who care."

Mendi said, "How did you figure out it was Hemlock?"

"A paramedic who was on his toes noticed she had symptoms incongruent with a car accident. He brought in her travel mug. She had some kind of green juice — she juiced the Hemlock. There is no antidote. People usually ingest hemlock accidentally because it can be confused with parsley or carrot greens. Years ago, it used to be used as a muscle relaxant, but ingesting more than a few leaves from the plant can be fatal. The poison works like nicotine. Do either of you know, was she feeling depressed or talking suicidal?"

Mendi shook her head. "She's going through some rough times, being a financial planner in the Great Recession. But she's strong-willed. She's never acted depressed around me, not like that."

"Why don't you pump her stomach or something?" Shirley Lyle said. "Hook her up on an iron lung?"

The doctor nodded. "From how far the paralysis advanced — it starts at the extremities and moves toward the core — we could tell the poisoning was fairly advanced. Most if not all of the toxicity already left her stomach. There's nothing left but for her body to process it. If the paralysis goes much farther, we'll intubate her to keep her breathing — but so far she doesn't need it. Our only achievable goal is to keep her alive and buy her the time she needs."

"How long will she be like this?" Mendi said.

"Her symptoms will likely alleviate in two or three days."

"Shouldn't we call the police or something? If she was poisoned?"

The doctor shook his head and winced. "Honestly, it seems more like an accident. She could have picked that stuff in her back yard."

Mendi nodded.

"Please excuse me." The doctor breezed out of the office.

"So what do you think?" Shirley Lyle asked Mendi. "Is Elvita suicidal? Does she go around eating weeds all the time?"

Mendi shook her head. "No. There's no way she did this to herself."

"Then you and me pulled guard duty. You got first shift. I'll be back in an hour."

37

*S*hirley Lyle steered her rented Dodge RAM with its 5.7 liter HEMI engine while stroking a sweet .38 revolver with wood grips that rested on her thigh. Back at the courthouse, Lester had hesitated before placing the weapon in her hand. He glanced around for cops, then looked straight ahead. "I got another on me, just so you know."

"Well it's a favor to me and it'll spare you the considerable inconvenience of a murder trial."

He'd loaned her the piece.

What are you doing teaming up with him?

"A truce isn't a team. And I have a use for him. VIVA the REVOLUTION has a use for him."

He's still going to try to kill you.

"No he won't."

You hope.

"Why would he give me a gun if he wanted to kill me?"

I'll let you figure that one out.

Shirley checked her side views and wondered if she'd recognize a Russian if she didn't already know he was Russian. Sure would be helpful if the bad guys wore a uniform.

Her cell phone rested on the tray in front of her speedometer and tach. It slid when she turned, but remained upright. She watched the map application and followed turn for turn.

Had to love the Internet. Got both Travis Noake's address and the directions in forty-five seconds. Shirley pulled the RAM onto his driveway. The eastern sky was dark and the west glowed gray. The outside light was on, for some reason.

Travis sat on a porch swing, cigarette in one hand and a snifter of booze in the other.

Unless that's how he likes his iced tea.

"You always see the best in people, Viva Shirley."

She killed the motor and stepped around the hood.

Travis jumped. "You can't be here!" He pushed out his rear end. Shoved the cigarette to his mouth and moved his drink from one hand to the other.

"We can't talk. You can't be here. I'm responsible for your case. You have to leave!"

"Soon as you and me come to an agreement."

"That is precisely what we cannot do!"

He opened the screen door. Paused.

"Shirley F'N Lyle begs to differ." She pointed the .38 at him. He raised his hands. Held the screen open with his butt.

"Travis, I don't want this to turn ugly. You can jump inside the house if you think that scrawny door will stop me. But I'll be inside chatting up your wife before you cross the living room. She and me can get on the same page talking about that curvy scoliosis wiener of yours."

He pressed both hands down — the *shush* signal. Mouthed words without sound. Spilled some of his drink.

"Out back?" Shirley said. "Or inside?"

He placed his drink on the porch rail and flicked his cigarette to the lawn. Strode past her in his slippers and she followed him on the sidewalk to the deck at the back of his house. He stood out from the wall and peered up at the windows.

"They closed?"

"Shhh."

"You said you're responsible for my case. I heard the charges was dropped already."

"Not yet. But they will be. So you can go. Now!"

"Hold on. We got something else to agree on."

He clamped his jaw.

"Lester Toungate. You don't have enough evidence to prosecute."

"What? Yes I do. Kristin brought me in as co-council on day one. We have everything. Murder weapon, casings, striations match. Motive, all of it. Slam dunk."

"You're not hearing me, Bentboy."

"Shhh."

"Yeah — no. Lester shot that man in self defense. I was there. And if you want Lester's lawyer to call me up on the stand and explain how the Russian assassin was shooting at him and risk me also explaining how much you like to snort Viagra and go down on thick white girls, so be it."

"You wouldn't."

"Where's your wife? I'll make her jealous in two seconds."

Travis stared. "This is beyond the pale. You're blackmailing me."

"Beyond the pale. Listen to yourself. I'm forcing you to do the right thing instead of the career-move thing. You're supposed to go after the people who use power to screw regular people. Instead you kiss their asses and hope for a promotion."

He shook his head and kicked an imaginary rock like a frustrated ten year old boy.

"I'd like us to have a professional relationship," Shirley said. "You come to me for advice sometimes. Now and then, I'll bend your ear on something important to me."

"So you can blackmail me into letting criminals walk free."

"Not exactly. Well, yes, with Lester. That's a long story I'm not telling at the moment. But here's what I have in mind. I'm going to bring you some seriously corrupt pieces of human trash. Big fish. Powerful people. And you're going to be the man who takes on city hall."

"I'd rather go after drug dealers."

"Yeah, don't ever go after the evil in your ranks. Well, Travis, I'm gonna be the steel in your spine."

"You're going to cost me my career."

"I'm going to make you famous."

He shook his head back and forth, slower and slower.

"That's right Travis. Start thinking of the good stuff. You play this right, people will think you actually have balls."

"I'll be out there alone. No one does this."

Shirley turned away, stopped. "Wrong. I've bedded you and every man like you in this town. I'll destroy as many as it takes — and that means in the end, the only people standing will be the ones who fight for the little guy. Pick your team."

"That does sound better than it did."

"Drop the charges on Lester tomorrow, first thing."

He nodded.

$\mathcal{E}$lvita awoke slowly from dreaming she was bounding in a field of purple and pink flowers with sunshine glowing from every direction. Gravity felt lighter — but maybe that was from the brightness of her spirit..

She dreamt that Chico came pounding down the steps in nothing but a bath towel, running up behind her in the kitchen and shaking shower water from his hair on her and kissing her.

She realized she was in heaven and it was the same as being on earth, except the evil was gone.

As she roused, nausea overcame her. She opened her eyes. A mask was clamped to her face. Tubes came and went. Something beeped. She felt a pinch in her arm: a needle was taped to her skin. She moved her eyes left and saw an empty chair. To her right, a mean looking woman just roused from sleep.

Elvita's heart jumped. She'd seen the woman's face before her Mercedes smashed into the woman's black SUV.

The woman had knelt beside Elvita while she was dazed, and attempted to calm her before the paramedics arrived.

Now sitting next to her bed the woman said, "Hey, don't worry, Sugar, you're going to be fine. You're through the rough patch."

The oxygen mask over Elvita's nose and mouth prevented her from responding. She swallowed cool air and remembered not being able to move her feet; panicking, she pushed out with her leg and pointed her toes toward the wall and then straight up. She exhaled. Some of her fear receded.

The woman looked at the clock on the wall. "You want me to get a nurse? Or you want to collect your thoughts for a minute?"

Elvita blinked twice and twisted her wrist a little and extended her thumb. She closed her eyes.

*A*n amount of time passed but Elvita couldn't gauge it. While her eyes remained closed, she heard the woman's voice again.

"She was awake a few minutes ago."

"Why didn't you get a nurse?"

"She wanted a minute."

The empty chair to her left slid on the floor signaling Mendi had returned. Elvita kept her eyes closed. As soon as she opened them she would be back in charge. There was no escape. Mendi might try to protect her from physical activity, but underlings were not people of action, accustomed to making decisions and reaping results. They didn't know the burden of constant awareness — of constant responsibility.

Elvita needed rest before she would be able to stoop to one knee, throw her life's troubles over her shoulder and hoist their weight again.

· · ·

"*I*s she awake?" *(A man's voice.)*

"She was snoring until you came in. Why don't you punch her arm?" *(The big woman.)*

Elvita snorted in her mask.

"No, she was sleeping a moment ago." *(Mendi.)*

Elvita opened her eyes. Mendi was on her left and her guardian angel on her right. The doctor stood in the doorway, a man of great importance and limited time.

The doctor entered and directed his gaze at his clipboard. "Elvita. I heard you laugh a moment ago. Having a sense of humor is a good sign." He looked at her.

Elvita's voice wilted in her throat.

"You don't have to say anything. I want to bring you up to speed. Do you feel okay? Can you give me a thumbs up to let me know you understand what I'm saying?"

Thumbs up.

"Good. So there are two things going on. You sustained injuries in a car accident: bruising around your face, arms and chest, a couple of bumps on your legs. A little burn on your forearm from the airbag. You may find other injuries to your back or neck once you're able to move around, but the accident didn't cause any broken bones and you should be on your feet in no time. This all make sense?"

Thumbs up.

"The other thing you're dealing with... We analyzed the contents of your travel mug and found Hemlock — a deadly poison. Any reason you're juicing poison?"

He laughed.

She winced: Ha Ha. Dumb me.

"It takes only a few leaves to be fatal to a human. You're probably the luckiest person I'll ever see. You should play the

lottery today. I had to look it up to refresh my memory —
because we don't usually see Hemlock poisoning. It begins by
causing weakness in your extremities, which becomes paralysis.
It moves from your feet and hands to your core. The way you're
moving now, I expect within another twenty-four to forty-eight
hours you should be feeling quite a bit better. You'll want to
have your primary doctor run some liver and kidney function
tests after you recover, but you should be fine."

39

"You should tell him," Claude said. "He's going to find out anyway."

"What are we doing? Having this conversation right here, right now?" Bubbles turned right and looked down the sidewalk. She looked left, then back at Claude. "Let me in! Did anybody see you?"

"No."

"Move." She pushed into the motel room. "You can be so rude sometimes." She strode to a battered desk and tossed her purse on it.

Claude moved to her with his arms outstretched, head back with a big smile. "What, you don't like teasing anymore?"

He shoved his face between her namesakes and shook his head back and forth. "Let's play windshield wipers."

"Stop! You are in the doghouse, mister."

He grabbed her waist and pulled her hips to his belly, then climbed on the bed. Towering above her, Claude stooped and clamped his mouth to hers.

She giggled.

He unzipped.

"I can't help but notice your mouth and Napoleon are at the same elevation."

"Napoleon?"

"Yeah. Bonerparte."

Claude packed his lip with a wad of snuff from his Copenhagen can. He spat loose grains and pulled the window curtain away from the wall. He looked outside, then repeated the act from the other side of the window.

"There's no one out there. There never is," Bubbles said.

He pushed the blinds aside and let in a beam of sunlight.

She pulled sheets over her body. "You should put some clothes on if you're going to stand at the window."

"Feels good to be in my birthday suit." He spat into the garbage can.

"I wish you wouldn't do that; you need to quit. Nobody wants to vote for a man who chews tobacco. It shows you don't care about yourself."

"That's a long way off. Years."

"But still, you should be looking forward. You have to think about everything this time."

He studied her. "You should be satisfied that you have nice tits."

She pulled the bed sheet to her neck. "What's that mean? That's horrible. How could you say that?"

"Sweetheart. Bubbles. I didn't mean anything by it. Oh, Sweetie." He snorted. Laughed. "Really. You should try to not have opinions. And when you have them anyway, despite your best efforts, you should keep them to yourself."

"You're always so mean after we do it. What did I say that was so bad?"

"Voters."

"What? Voters? People vote. And they won't if they see you spitting all the time and your lip sticking out. Your breath stinks and it looks like you have rotten food between your teeth."

"I will be elected from city council to the White House because donors will put me there. Voters don't matter. They don't vote anyway."

"What does that mean?"

"Nothing exists but money. Every form of government is a mask used by the people who have money. Every form: democracy, socialism, fascism, communism... all they do is pander to different sets of fictions. In the end, money runs everything."

"Yeah, but voters still vote."

With a dip of Copenhagen snuff in his lip, Claude opened his brief case on the round table by the entrance and withdrew a red deck of Marlboros. He lit one, inhaled. "I guess we better start the paperwork." He slid the blinds all the way to the right, turned on the light at the entry and the other by the bed.

He sat naked on the motel chair.

"That's disgusting," she said. "How many other men had their balls on that seat?"

"The old man said to the warrior, there's a storm coming."

"What?"

"The warrior said — "

"The old man told the warrior, don't put your balls on the seat. It's gross."

"*I am the storm.*"

"You're a dork. Just because you're in your manic phase doesn't make everything funny."

"I am not manic. I am invincible."

"Not to be the voice of reason or anything, but you're thirty-eight, you lost the state rep election five months ago and you're making ends meet by selling insurance."

"Exactly. That's why it's different this time. I cracked the code." Claude stooped, grabbed and shook his underwear, stepped into each leg and lifted. He snapped the band then pulled on his pants. "Anyway, we have forms to complete."

"You closed deal with Ramirez?"

Claude withdrew three folders from his brief case. "Two out of three: the old man and one son. Have to go back for the other. Long story."

Inside each folder, Claude had organized stacks of forms into sets. Each brokerage account application packet contained fourteen separate form groups, each separated by a paper clip. There were nine folders.

"Did you sign all those?" Bubbles said.

"Just getting started."

"Okay, I'm going to take a nap. Wake me."

"No, get up. Look these over while I sign. I don't know this company's forms yet."

"I'm new there too."

"Yeah, but you have a brain built for mediocrity and I have one more account I want to grab."

40

They removed the breathing mask and by afternoon Elvita was able to move her body as she lay on her bed. She felt as if someone had clubbed her with metal while she slept, but she could press her toes against the footboard — that was an improvement.

Mendi was away again, but Elvita's guardian angel sat in the chair against the wall. She looked up from a copy of Popular Mechanics.

"Did you know people in other countries can look at you through the camera in your cell phone? Like, when you're peeing?"

Elvita enjoyed the unreality of the moment. She smiled and raised her hand to her throat. "Where is Mendi?"

"Oh, wow! You sound good! She was here all night and half the morning but she had to go back to Phoenix. I guess she's running your business. Speaking of which, I have some cash I need to invest, when the time is right."

Elvita closed her eyes.

"Anyhow she said she'd be back this afternoon. Since you're off the machine she was going to stop at your place and get some clothes and stuff for you."

"Thank you."

"So who tried to kill you?"

"I don't know. Did somebody try to kill me?"

"Did you put weeds in your juice on purpose?"

"I don't remember doing that. I've never done that before."

"Yeah, that means somebody else picked a peck of pickled poison. You got a beef with anybody? Who'd want to do something like that?"

"Wait a minute, who are you? I mean, I know I drove into your Suburban but — "

"Dodge Durango. My brand-used Dodge Durango. But go ahead. You was saying?"

"I crashed into you. I remember you helping me at the accident. And every time I've woken up you've been here. Do you want my insurance information?"

The woman smiled. "My name is Shirley Lyle. I stopped by to check on you because I had a bug up my ass. No other reason 'cept girls gotta stick together. The hospital couldn't track down your old man, and then I found out about the poison. You had an enemy that wanted you dead and no one to stand guard. What's a girl gonna do?"

Elvita knew her face was blank.

While the woman spoke Elvita remembered pieces of the last few days. She saw the broken cactus at the back of her yard. She remembered the parsley that looked like the Italian variety. She remembered the clients she was losing, and that she drove to Flagstaff hoping to save her last big client because losing him would mean losing her company. She remembered her husband, Chico, missing for the last week since they had separated.

"I'm sorry, I just remembered how terrible my life is."

"Don't you remember what the doctor said?"

"What? Yes."

"He said you're the luckiest woman alive. That's better than being dead. For most people."

"I'm going to throw up. My husband is behind all this."

From the hallway came Mendi's rapid footsteps and then her voice. "Elvita, this is important!"

Mendi rushed into the hospital room. "I'm sorry, Shirley, but I have to steal Elvita for a minute."

Elvita drew a breath and nodded.

"I got an email from the brokerage back office. They got an ACATS transfer request for Ramirez."

The Automated Customer Account Transfer Service request meant that as soon as her brokerage verified the new company's account information matched theirs, the securities in José Ramirez's accounts would reduce to electrons and reappear in new accounts at some other company.

It was a deathblow.

Elvita closed her eyes. Opened them. "José, or his family too?"

"So far only José."

"The rest will follow. José runs everything."

"We have to fight this," Mendi said. "You can't go see him, but I can."

"What can you say? He's made his decision."

"He doesn't know you were in a car accident on your way to see him. He doesn't know someone's trying to kill you."

"Probably be better if he doesn't learn that."

"But he might have a little sympathy for you being in a car accident — enough to pause the transfer for a few days."

"I don't want his sympathy." Elvita rested her head against the pillow. "Maybe it's time for me to flip burgers."

"You know anything about textiles?" Shirley said. "Bras and denim jeans and shorts. See I got this idea — "

Elvita frowned.

Mendi paced.

"Let him go. We'll find a new location as soon as our lease is up. And I'll have to let some people go. And sell my house. The worst-case scenario is that we get smaller, so I don't want to think about it anymore."

"I'm going to go see José."

Elvita shook her head, flicked her hand. "Don't tell him about me. Just see what he's doing. And why."

Mendi left as quickly as she entered.

"I don't care anymore," Elvita said.

"You can't give up."

"Turning a new direction isn't giving up."

"You seem ripe for the revolution, Babe."

"I'm ripe for sleep."

"You can't do that yet. We need to figure out who's trying to kill you."

Elvita didn't know why, but she trusted this woman. No one else — none of the people paid to care for her — was at her side every minute like Shirley. She had a bare knuckle integrity about her. No nonsense, no frills, blunt force kindness. She looked like a woman who decided to stop caring about the stuff that doesn't matter, and only paid attention to what does. Elvita could learn something from Shirley — but that would mean letting her in.

"So this is why I'm pretty sure my husband is trying to murder me."

Elvita explained a torrent of facts to Shirley.

He still had access to the house. He had a key.

If she died, he would receive two million tax free dollars in two weeks, from a policy that would have lapsed had he not suddenly reinstated and caught up the premiums.

The cash advances from her credit cards totaled one hundred and sixty thousand dollars, a little more than the amount Chico said he would need to start his hedge fund and operate it for one year.

She told Shirley about a time when Chico explained to her how they could peel away client assets from their financial planning company into his hedge fund. He would have to move his licenses to another company, and ultimately leave retail financial planning... meaning they would have to work the plan together.

Elvita told Shirley about all of her largest clients disappearing in the space of weeks. It started right before she separated with Chico. He was probably smooth talking them away to another company, possibly even saying that she was part of the move. His ultimate goal was to "talk the money loose," as he put it.

"Wait a minute," Shirley said. "If you're dead, why would he need to go to another company? Wouldn't he take over your business and have them all anyway?"

"I thought about that. Two things. First, moving his licenses to a new firm would give him the ability to steal clients. If he stayed at our existing broker-dealer, our compliance department would question so many big accounts moving from rep to rep. He wouldn't have been able to hide it right under my nose. He needed space to operate. Second, he wouldn't have been able to go after my other reps' clients. Not out in the open. I lost a rep who caught him trying to do that."

Shirley Lyle stood from her chair. She stretched her back and twisted side to side. "These little chairs, I tell you."

Elvita stared at the whiteboard on the wall where nurses left notes for each other.

"Is there any way to know if he actually did get set up with another company?" Shirley said.

"I don't know."

"Someone does."

"You're right. My compliance department would be able to find out."

"I could never do what you do. I quit complying."

"Wish I could. Is my cell phone around here somewhere?"

"I don't know." Shirley stood and walked to a cabinet. She opened it and withdrew a plastic bag. "Looks like your things." She brought the bag to Elvita.

She found her clothes in seemingly the reverse order that they came off: blazer, blouse, skirt, bra, panties. "Oh, wow. Wonder who saw me naked."

"Oh, that was everybody. We called in patients from the other rooms and held off until the nurses on the next shift could come see too."

Shirley grinned.

Elvita smiled but her eyes didn't feel convinced.

"No phone?"

"No."

"Here, use mine." Shirley bent over, grabbed her purse from beside the chair and pulled out a cell phone. She pressed the button on the side. "Almost dead. But you can talk a few minutes."

Elvita accepted the phone. She pressed digits from memory.

"Lou, Elvita. My cell phone is about to die. Quick question, and I know this is from left field, but did Chico register with another broker-dealer recently?"

"Not likely, Elvita. We run checks every month because we're not a dual registration company. Almost no one is. So we would have known if he'd been doing it very long. Why do you ask?"

"It's probably my mind running. How long until the next time you scan?"

"Well now that you got me curious, about twenty seconds. Let me log into the system and I'll call you back. This a good number for you?"

Shirley nodded.

"Yes, call me back on this phone," Elvita said.

"Are you okay? I mean what we talked about yesterday?"

"Listen, Lou. My battery is about to die and I need to go."

Elvita pressed END.

"Hang onto it a minute," Shirley said. "If it wasn't your ex, who would be second on your list?"

"If it's not Chico, I have no idea. Until four days ago I had no idea I had any enemies at all. It seemed like the same random chaos everybody else is dealing with in the markets."

"You know," Shirley said, "something similar happened to me and it seemed like all hell was breaking loose in every direction. Actually, it was. So that doesn't help you at all. Never mind."

The cell phone rang in Elvita's hand.

"Lou?"

"Nope. Chico is not dual registered."

Elvita shook her head. "I'm at a loss."

41

*C*hico heated water on his propane cook stove. When little bubbles formed at the bottom, he added two packets of instant coffee and two of white powder.

His head throbbed: he'd slept most of the night with his face in vomit, then without cleaning himself he dozed most of the day with his face pressed against his sleeping bag. Waking, his right eye burned and his throat and mouth were sticky. His tongue felt hairy.

He dug a metal spoon from a side pocket on his pack and stirred his coffee until the creamer dissolved. Chico sipped.

Horrible.

He reached for the plastic jug containing Grey Goose vodka, dumped half the coffee and refilled with vodka.

Standing with the metal cup in his hand, Chico wandered from his campsite to the trail and stood overlooking the charred forest below. Maybe he'd spot a bear or elk. Maybe if he'd go without food for a week he could have a vision and finally learn who he was and what he believed — because so far, the things he held dear only seemed to lead him to contradictions.

He grew up poor and wanted money more than anything. He learned young that he had a gift for communicating and convincing. His enthusiasm almost tricked people into following wherever he led. And he learned that if you study numbers long enough — not numbers in a test tube, pure math — but numbers in real life, fractions of profit applied to gargantuan numbers — you discover there really is a secret, you know it and it's going to change everything.

Chico lifted the steaming metal mug to his mouth. When the liquid hit his tongue, he spat. He closed his eyes and wished tears would come so he could empty his soul, kick the earth and know where it was.

But his eyes were dry.

Chico dumped his metal cup and pitched it toward camp. Without coat or gloves he turned up the mountain and walked.

42

_S_hirley said, "Didn't you say somebody's trying to steal your clients? And that's why you came up here, to try to save one?"

Elvita nodded. "Mendi went there to see him."

"So listen. If all these people leaving at the same time is unusual, and there's only one person behind it, they all know who he is. This client of yours... he big? Could I kick his ass?"

Elvita wrinkled her nose. "He is not big. Question for you — where'd your attitude come from?"

"That's the REVOLUTION, Baby. You're almost ready for it — just as soon as you can unplug all those tubes. Meantime, I have a knack for remembering names, faces and a fella's credentials — if you know what I mean."

Elvita frumple-smiled. "I understand. I think."

"Okay, good. Mendi said your client was José Ramirez. I'm going to visit him, or his sons. What were their names?"

"Jorge and Esteban. But I can't have you threatening people on my behalf. I'd be fined out of existence."

"I've been doing business a lot longer than you girl, and let me learn you something: the bad guys know the good guys don't want to break the rules. The bad guys also know the cops aren't our body guards — and a couple of 'em don't even like us. So when the bad guys ruin your life, you have to get in the mud and break some bones. Either that or you're done."

"I can't be a criminal, that's all there is to it. I can't discuss it. I can't think about it."

"Of course not, Sugar. I didn't mean *you*. I'm already been there, done that."

*S*hirley sat in her RAM truck. The more she used it the better she liked it.

You need a break. Take your money to the beach or something. Eat, drink and be merry. You've worked enough. Saltwater is good for sore feet. You can drink margaritas all day...

Shirley yawned. "BORING."

Oh hey! Look around for Russians again. They're out there somewhere.

"I don't know if I believe all that. I mean I believe Lester thought that guy he shot was there for us, but I don't know if he's right. Why would Vanko want to kill me? He said Ulyana was super important to him, and he could have had me whacked ten times already if he wanted."

You're right. Don't think about the Russians at all.

"Now you're being smart. All I'm saying is Russians aren't my primary concern."

Sure, I get it. We should wait until one jumps out with a bazooka.

Shirley scanned three hundred and sixty degrees.

"No Russians. No bazookas."

She keyed the ignition and powered down the windows. Keep things cool and fast.

"Think."

Mendi already went to see José Ramirez. Maybe it'd be better to visit the sons, Jorge and Esteban. Catch one of them by surprise.

When you find him, you need to be prepared. You need a way to get information out of him.

"Broccoli."

What?

"Watch and learn, Viva Shirley. You're gonna dig this."

Shirley stopped at a grocery store and filled a thin plastic bag with four bunches of broccoli, each held together by a thick blue rubber band.

"Yes, a diet," she said to the woman at the register. "I hate broccoli. I figure, if that's all I have in the fridge, I'll lose weight."

The woman nodded.

"You look skeptical but you should try this stuff. It's truly, deeply disgusting."

Back in the RAM she looked up Jorge Ramirez in her cell phone. No go. Name, no address. She thumbed in Esteban and hit pay dirt: phone, address. She pressed a couple links and found his picture.

"Oh, Esteban..." She squirmed in her seat. "Goodness."

It's going to be hard to convince him you're serious if you're drooling.

"Maybe there's a way to use it. Waterboard? Spitboard!"

She pressed Esteban Ramirez' address into Google Maps and rested the phone on her dash in front of the speedometer.

Approaching his driveway Shirley slowed. A short, Josef Stalin-looking man who was definitely not Esteban opened the back door of a Volvo and placed his briefcase on the floor. He removed his drab olive suit jacket and whipped it across the seat.

Punctilious.

"Ooh — where'd you get that?"

Mister Dullock, Elementary school.

"I'm keeping that word!"

I bet his briefcase has a bunch of financial documents. That's the guy stealing clients from Elvita!

Shirley misaligned her jaw and wrinkled her brow. It was easier to think sometimes with teeth that didn't mesh. She slowed and took in Stalin-boy. His hair was dark and slicked back. He was slightly taller than his vehicle — the size man Shirley could hoist on her shoulder and pitch in a car trunk... hypothetically. His trousers were triple-pleated and his tan shoes gleamed.

The man lifted his head and connected gazes with her. His expression didn't change. She hated people like that, who could look at you and hide their thoughts. People like that were always up to no good.

Shirley smiled huge and waved.

She braked and pulled to the side of the road and leaned halfway out of the window. The nearby houses were all worth millions but her truck was shiny and new, so even if it wasn't a Mercedes or Cadillac, at least she could pretend she worked for someone who belonged.

Ask him for directions!

Shirley thought fast; had a much better idea.

"Hey, Sugarloaf. Yeah, you. Hey, listen. I wouldn't have stopped but you have such a cheerful demeanor I thought you might help me. I came into some big, big ass money. There was supposed to be a seminar up here somewhere. The library. You know where that is?"

"A seminar?"

"Yeah, you know. For rich people like me. Never mind the truck. I borrowed it from my grounds keeper 'cuz my Coon-tash is in the shop."

"You own a Lamborghini?"

"Oh hell, yeah. First thing I bought. So where's the library? Ooh. I'm gonna be late and I have so much money to invest. Winning the lottery's a burden, I tell you. A curse."

The man finger-combed his hair and wiggled his tie knot. "I don't know where your library is, but I can tell you, being a wealth manager for the high net worth and ultra-high net worth demographic, the people who run those workshops are con men."

"Say it ain't so!"

"That's right. They are mere salesmen."

"Oh no! What'll I do? Wait a minute. Did you say you invest money for people?"

"Well, yes — but like I said. My clients are affluent."

"Get them to the doctor! Ha! So how much does a person have to invest?"

"My minimum account is five hundred thousand — but I only take on accounts of that size when the relationship has room to grow."

"Five hundred large? Pfff. Walk around money."

"If you don't mind me asking, where do you invest now? Why are you unhappy with your current team of advisors?"

"Oh, the usual: bounced check fees, ATM fees. These people worry me. Say, I'm parked on the road but I like your style. Why don't I put all my money with you and I won't have to find that stinking library?"

"We could discuss the matter."

"How do I find you? Better yet, I'm in a hurry. Money's in cash and I saw this feller on CNBC — so why not let's get together tonight?"

"Tonight?"

"Sure. Gimme your card. I'll call you with the address."

"I'm based in Phoenix and have to drive home. I just had my final appointment of the day. Why don't I follow to your place?"

"Because, well, uh. The mansion is a mess. You know I got these contractors putting in marble."

"Countertops?"

"No, dummy. Columns. Floors. Stairs. I like marble. But there's dust everywhere. I saw a motel at the bottom of the hill. Thought we'd grab a room and sit at the table."

He nodded. Placed his hands on the car roof. "I suppose that could work. But why don't we go to a coffee house?"

"Air my business all over the place? Thank you, no. Look. I need my money invested like yesterday, so if not you, someone else will get those fat commissions."

"I'll follow you to the hotel."

"Motel."

"Okay."

*S*hirley parked at a motel she knew would accept hourly rates. She secured a room while tiny Stalin waited, then backed the RAM into the space in front of the door. He parked beside her.

"You know, Sugar, it's going to be better if you park at the gas station over there. Here's why: if we're both here, it looks unseemly. I'll explain when you get back. Okay?"

"Wait, I'm not liking this."

"What?"

"I don't know. You don't sound like a person who has the kind of money you're talking about."

"I lived in a trailer park thirty years and won the lottery. I didn't grow up with money and to tell the truth, I don't own a Coon-tash. I only said that. But I have five hundred large at the bank and if you handle money for Esteban Ramirez and his daddy, José, you're the one I want."

"You know them?"

"I know every swinging dick in Coconino County. Now let's stop talking business in the parking lot. Leave your car at the gas station — not the Circle K beside us. Go to the BP across the street and park by the trees. Come back here and I'll bring you up to speed. Bottom line, there's a mysterious force at work and we didn't meet by accident. Chop chop."

Shirley exited the RAM holding her plastic grocery bag.

"What's that?"

She opened it and showed him. "I don't like vegetables sitting in the afternoon sun. It bakes the vitamins and they're no good."

"Oh."

Shirley swiped the motel key and entered.

Don't look back! He's watching for that!

Shirley sat on the edge of the bed with her broccoli.

You overplayed your hand. He's gone for sure.

She waited.

No way he's coming. He saw right through. He knows.

Shirley spread her arms and leaned back. Almost couldn't tell her shoulders were nearly ripped out of their sockets a couple days before.

*He's long gone. It's been forever. Look out the window or
something.*

Shirley remained seated on the bed.

A knock sounded at the door.

Shirley hurried to the bathroom and flushed the commode.
She slow walked to the door and undid the chain and deadbolt.
Opened the door and when Stalin entered, popped her head
outside for a quick look left and right.

Stalin crossed the room to the desk and stood beside it.

Shirley locked the deadbolt and swung the latch bar.
Turned.

"What's your name, Sugar?"

"Claude McFadden."

"Anyone ever say you look like Stalin?"

"No."

"He was from Germany: killed people. Is that what you do?
Are you a killer, Claude McFadden?"

"What? Excuse me? You have the wrong idea. What's going
on here?"

Shirley approached. He shifted toward the sink — ducked
into the bathroom and tried to slam the door.

Shirley wedged her foot and leaned.

Claude McFadden couldn't overcome her heavier weight
pressing on the door. She reached in, grabbed him by his
necktie and dragged him out. She jerked the tie. He stumbled
forward. She yanked again. He fell to his knees and his hands
went to his neck. She lifted, felt her shoulders bulk up like she
was Arnold in the gym. She felt the burn in her muscles and
the pain made her even stronger. Claude's cheeks flushed red
then purple and at last his arms fell limp.

Shirley stretched him across the floor.

"Okay, Claude McFadden, if you was conscious I'd tell you

to be very afraid. But you're a bright guy, and you'll figure it out. I don't want to risk being patronizing."

*H*er preparations complete, Shirley loosened Claude's tie so blood could seep back into his brain. Not enough to let him run a marathon or anything, but the bare amount to revive him. One of the many tricks she learned satisfying men's most intimate and freakish fancies.

"How do I put those skills on a resume?"

Claude opened his eyes.

"Not you. I was talking to myself. You remember when that singer from the Aussie rock band died jerking off with a noose around his neck? You wouldn't believe how many guys were asking me to suffocate them after that."

He looked up at her with dancing eyeballs and a mouth too contorted to form words.

Claude McFadden lay naked on a shower curtain, stretched flat beside the bed. His belt secured his hands over his head at the desk. She'd moved lamps from each side of the headboard and placed them on the floor beside Claude's wide-spread ankles. Using their power cords and the bed frame, she'd immobilized Claude's legs.

The only light in the room came from the fluorescents above the sink. Shirley sat on the edge of the bed with her feet between Claude's knees.

"You notice anything funny yet? Anything not seem right?"

"What did you do? Organ thief? My liver! What? You ate my liver? What'd you do?"

"No, I didn't steal your organs. Relax. You're still in good shape, and if you tell me what I need to know, you'll be right as rain. No lasting damage. But the clock is ticking."

"What do you want."

"Shut up. I'll tell you when it's your turn. I didn't cut you open or anything, but here's what I did do. That pressure you feel building up... Look at this." She lifted a piece of broccoli. Tore off a floret and chucked it at his face. Another. "This is broccoli. When you buy it, these thick ass rubber bands hold them together. Guess where I put four of them."

"AAAAAHHHHH!"

"That's right. Back in the day that's how they castrated bulls, except they didn't have rubber bands. They used leather straps or rope or something, but the concept applies. See what's going to happen is eventually your nuts rot off."

"You bitch!"

"Come on Claude, you're playing games. Get it all out!"

"AHHGH!"

"You pussy."

"AGGGGGGGGHHHHHH!"

"Okay, good. See I know this motel — I used to be a hooker. Ain't proud, just saying. Anyhow, I told the guy at the desk you're a screamer. In prostitution parlance, that's a guy who makes a lot of noise when he's feeling good. Long story short, there's no one beside us for four rooms on either side. So feel free to get all that yelling out of your system, then we'll get back to business. Tell me what I want to know fast enough, you might save the family jewels."

"What do you want to know?"

"First, the rules. I've been with a hundred thousand men and I have a photographic memory. I've seen every lie told. So when you say something that doesn't sound right, I'm gonna do this."

Shirley lowered herself from the bed, reached out, and

thumped his puffy purple rubber-banded scrotum with her middle finger.

Claude screamed and bucked. The bed moved. "Easy, Claude. Tell me the truth."

"AHHGGHGH. I'll tell you the truth! AHGHGH! Don't do that! Please, I'll tell you the truth!"

"Ok, let's see how this goes. I want you to be calm, cool and collected. Talk like we're old friends. You're stealing clients from Elvita. Why?"

43

Claude's stones felt like they'd been ground to powder. The pain was excruciating. He imagined a giant needle piercing them each time the fat woman thumped. The pain had a stomach-churning intensity and each time her middle finger thwacked his puffy privates, vomit came up his throat and he swallowed it back down. The corners of his eyes stung from tears and the back of his head ached because he slammed it to the floor each time she thought he lied.

"Talk to me," she said. "I'll let you go if you behave and tell me what I need to know."

"Why should I trust you?"

"You have no choice. The clock is ticking and those teeny nuts of yours are not long for this world. By the way, I've seen kittens with bigger man-sacks than you. Tell me about the poison."

She thumped him.

"AGGGHHH."

"Oh, bull. That didn't hurt. I'm about to grab a fork from my purse."

"No! No!"

"Tell me about the poison."

"It's a weed. It's everywhere."

"How did it get in Elvita's refrigerator?"

"I put it there."

"How?"

"I came up on the house from behind. She's in a gated community so I came in from the back. Other side of her wall there's a canal."

"How'd you know which house was hers from the back of the wall?"

"Google maps."

"Don't you love Google Maps? I use that app all the time! Crazy that it's free, right?"

"Yeah. Uh."

"So anyway, what? You climbed the wall."

"I climbed the wall."

"Bull. You're too short."

"That side of the wall is a wash. A lot of brush. I climbed a cottonwood next to the wall."

"Then what?"

"Cut my leg on her cactus."

"Then."

"Pulled on gloves and unlocked her door."

"You remembered the gloves. See, I never remember gloves. This is good. Then what?"

Claude closed his eyes. "I drank water."

"You brought water?"

"I was disguised in running shorts. I had a Camelbak — that's where I kept the hemlock."

"How did you know no one was inside?"

"I called the office and asked for Elvita. I told her I was looking for Chico. Asked if he was at home."

"Ah. You knew where she was 'cuz she answered. You tricky little devil."

Claude smiled. Attempted to shrug. Coughed with pain.

"I got a question. You work at being evil, or does it come natural?"

"Am I still doing cocaine? Am I still beating my wife?"

"I'd say probably, and if a girl was dumb enough to marry you I'd say yes, you'd still be beating her. What's that have to do with anything?"

"You asked an impossible question."

"No it's not. Does evil come easy to you?"

"No, not really."

"So you work at it? See, that's no good. That's a problem."

"I mean, no! Uh, yes! Yes it comes easy."

"Well damn, Claude, that's even worse."

44

The mountain rose so steep on his left Chico could almost reach out and touch the ground. A slip to the right, he'd pinball a thousand yards off trees before reaching a draw that would sluice him into the next. But the path was wide and bermed with dirt and logs where the down slope was steepest. Chico thought more about suffocating on thin air, or freezing, than toppling to his death.

As the sun fell and he gained elevation the wind picked up. His nose and ears stung. He stuffed his hands into his pockets and kept his shoulders curved inward. He leaned and the trail bent to his feet. The harder he worked, the more his brain throbbed but the pain was relief from his thoughts: a storm front of madness rolling from the edges, attacking from each and every angle.

His chest constricted as if from fear. His lungs wilted.

Everything he ever did was for himself.

His wedding.

His job.

His cases.

His appetite.

His dreams.

His *dreams.*

Nowhere in his soul resided a sacrificial concern. Nowhere could he point and say here is the evidence I gave a single damn about another person.

The moon rose before the sun disappeared.

Chico climbed. His camp was at eight thousand feet and the mountain reached ten thousand three hundred.

The thin air weakened his thoughts.

He couldn't give up his ambition. The system was alchemy: magic. It allowed him to conjure dollars from keystrokes and electrons. The premise worked no matter how he back-tested: a ten basis point move — either direction — signaled momentum. Get into the trade. A three basis point reversal signaled end of the run. Most runs that lasted ten basis points—a tenth of a percent—continued several more before pulling back. Since more than half of all pullbacks over three basis points resulted in giving up the gains, he built his system to execute a sell on a three basis point pullback. Ninety percent of his initial back-tests produced a profit.

So why wasn't everybody doing it?

They were. At least, the insiders were: money made money. Everybody else waited tables.

Thinking his numbers looked too good, Chico tested every conceivable time frame and market condition. He ran hundreds of iterations on backward looking data and still found seventy three percent of his hypothetical trades produced a profit.

It meant markets were not random.

They were predictable — and that meant someday soon Chico would enter a profoundly different world of investing.

The premise behind modern retail investment advice was built on the argument that since markets were ultimately random but sometimes moved in non-correlating sequences, the best way to create profit was to allocate dollars across a spectrum of assets. Retail advisors told a good story and made money.

But the players with real jack didn't screw around with Modern Portfolio Theory. They ensured their money advanced in value all the time. They didn't park their wealth in dollars because dollars didn't hold value. It was like relativity. You're in a spaceship moving near the speed of light while the government sucks the bang out of your bucks — and all the other big currencies, the euro and yen are in other spaceships — every central bank is racing to debase before everyone else — and your job is to figure out where in all the chaos the value will retain.

But here's the thing.

You know.

You think of money in principles, not math. You understand politics in every developed nation. You know which candidate in the upcoming election is about to be busted for being stupid in his teens.

Everywhere.

Your game is global. You hitch your wealth to the ascending... but only until the moment it crests. How do you know when it will break and roll?

Because you get people elected. You tell them who to appoint to their bureaucracies. You inform the views of the appointees and — things get fuzzy here — somehow, miraculously, the policies shat out the other side are always to your benefit.

Power becomes magical when you hit ten digits.

Chico stopped walking. He was dizzy and realized another forward step would begin his descent. His face was numb and his mind in a flurry.

He wanted money more than anything because not having it was like being nothing.

Except the universe was ordered so that for the final get, he owed the final give.

Elvita.

45

*C*laude confessed his sins — some Shirley didn't even ask about. Confession was good for the soul.

Shirley activated the voice recording app on her cell phone.

"Thank you for explaining yourself, Claude. Here's the deal. I want you to move away from Phoenix. With everything you've told me, you'll never work in the money business again. But that's not good enough; I want you to move away so Elvita and me never have to think we're going to run into you shopping at Walmart."

"You're letting me go?"

"Of course I'm letting you go. I just wanted the truth. So you agree to leave?"

"I agree."

"And all those clients you stole... You'll have no more contact with them. As far as they're concerned, you fell off the face of the earth. Got it?"

"I got it! Thank you! I see the error of my ways! I'm a disaster! I'll go to — "

"Shut up! Don't tell me. I don't want to know. All right." Shirley woke her cell phone and readied her finger at the red dot that would stop the recording. "That concludes our conversation. You're free to go." She pressed the button.

"Thank you. Please take off the rubber bands! Please! The pain is unbearable."

Shirley stared into Claude's eyes.

Every hero is a judge.

Shirley nodded because she made perfect sense.

She lowered herself from the bed, straddled Claude and placed her knees on either side of his shoulders.

"HEY! What? Don't!"

He bucked.

She leaned hard and threw out her right leg. Rested her rump on his chest and kicked out her left leg. Claude thrashed but his limbs were tied and he couldn't bounce her a centimeter. His eyes screamed fury. In a moment he stopped squirming.

"Claude, you're evil. I wasn't going to do this. My plan was to let you go — even keeping your balls. But some of the stuff you told me, I guess it's my duty to make sure you don't get to ruin anybody else's life. You stole, over and over. You tried to kill a woman with poison and set up her husband to look responsible. You cosmic turd. I'm making the call. You don't get to live no more."

Claude's eyes were still.

46

Shirley untied Claude's ankles, placed the lamps in their dust circles on the stands where she found them, stuck their plugs back in the outlets and turned them on.

Killing Claude on a shower curtain wasn't quite up to Dexter standards, but for thinking on her feet, it was pretty darned close. No blood spatter. No hair. No crime scene. No murder weapon.

Which introduced an interesting concept. Of course there was a murder weapon: her ass — or rather — her excess ass. If she could drop two hundred pounds overnight, it would be the most interesting way to dispose of a murder weapon, ever.

Alas... she was keeping her ass.

The real problem was not the murder weapon, since it was disguised as part of her body. The challenge would be getting rid of the corpse.

Shirley folded Claude in half and tied his arms and feet together with one of his pant legs, then cinched him in the shower curtain like a giant sack of Christmas presents, tied off with his belt at the top.

Outside, she moved the Dodge RAM so the side door faced the motel. She lifted the back seat, making the back half of the crew cab into cargo space, and though there were no other cars or activity, she hurriedly carried her Christmas sack and, struggling a bit, pitched it behind the driver seat. So much evil in a tiny bundle — except it was no longer evil.

In the form of a corpse, Claude McFadden was good.

Bad people aren't bad forever.

"Wow. A powerful insight."

If you think about it, killing bad guys is kind of like recycling.

"So you're saying it's a type of conservation?"

Exactly.

"Who am I to argue with saving the environment?"

She closed the motel door and leaned against it for a minute, catching her breath and letting her gaze roam the room seeking any clue that might hint what had happened there. She stood at the door and examined the space Claude had occupied walking to the corner where she trapped him.

He hid from you in the bathroom too.

Shirley turned on the bathroom light and looked inside the tub. She turned and nearly stepped in pee dribbled on the floor in front of the toilet. Maid must have missed it.

You should pay them for the shower curtain.

"If I do that, someone will know something weird happened here."

Tell them you slipped and grabbed the curtain. You owe them another. Simple.

"Everybody knows you use a shower curtain to get rid of the body when you kill somebody in a motel room. This is kindergarten stuff. Everybody knows that."

Okay, fine. Steal the shower curtain.

"Damn."

Shirley dug her fingers into her pocket and pulled out a wad of bills. She peeled a twenty and placed it on the dresser.

"I'm not a thief. I only steal from drug lords. So I entrust these dollars to the universe, to get them to the right place."

Too bad Ulyana's not here. She could burn candles or something.

Back in the bathroom, Shirley grabbed a towel and wiped the bathroom door handles, lamp stands, the dresser top, bed frame, sink area and the front door handle on both sides.

She left the key on the dresser next to the money, placed her finger on the edge of the brass deadbolt and swung the door closed.

Inside her Dodge Ram, she sat with the engine off watching the sun dip into the San Francisco peaks.

Did she dare go back to the warehouse with another dead man?

"I can't leave him with the shower curtain. There, or anyplace else. Somebody could trace that to a motel — and then find this one."

Dahmer ate his victims.

"No way. Though I could do with six or eight cheeseburgers."

John Wayne Gacy buried them in his house.

"I don't have a house. Or a trailer."

The Green River killer dumped bodies in the river.

"I don't exactly have a river either."

Ted Bundy left them in the woods.

"I have woods. I like that."

The zodiac killer left them where they lay.

"Except it's too easy to connect me to the truck and the motel."

On the Sopranos they buried bodies in the woods. Dexter got rid of them in the ocean. Everyone else dissolves them in acid.

"How you know all this?"

When you zone out in front of the television, I'm actually watching.

"So help. What do I do?"

Why not dump him on the street?

"Cops would question who he worked with. That's Elvita. I've been at her hospital room nonstop. I'm connected."

Yeah, right. Wait a minute.

"What?"

Wait a minute....

"WHAT!"

Lester owes you.

"I can't do that. It's bad enough I helped him avoid getting locked up."

No. He's a tool. He's a hammer. A shovel. A backhoe. He gets things done. You need someone who can get rid of a body so it never comes back. You're not helping him, you're using him. And since you have a high moral purpose, his doesn't matter.

"I'll bet the real Stalin said something like that."

Except he was Stalin and you're Shirley F'N Lyle, champion of the little people.

"I bet he said that too. Champion of the little people."

Yeah. Hmmm. That is ironic.

"I can't ask for Lester's help. He's a bad dude. He's a drug dealer."

If this country was actually free, every little tiny drug wouldn't be illegal.

"That's true. And VIVA The REVOLUTION is all about freedom."

"ester, Dear."

    "No."

    "What?"

"Woman says *dear*..."

"Lester, Honey."

"That's no better."

"I have a present for you."

"I don't want it."

Lester stood in the doorway. Behind him, the chair where he sat when Shirley thought he was dead. Next to it, the sofa where she sat.

Be nice to crash on that couch a few minutes.

"Okay, that's fair. It's not really a present so much as a job. You need to take it. For me. And then get rid of it."

"Why?"

"Because I have a vision, Lester. I can see the whole state of Arizona suddenly giving a damn for the people who live here.

All the politicians working for the little people. All the cops being courteous. All the judges giving fair sentences like in Amsterdam. I saw a documentary. Did you see it?"

"You been stealing my product too?"

"I've had a revelation. Every time I go to the courthouse I see a dozen men I... let's say I have a photographic memory — for sex. I remember every scruffy detail — and so long as I'm alive and not in jail, I can use all those memories to make powerful men do good things."

"By blackmailing them."

"Isn't it beautiful? I mean, blackmail's wrong and horrible and all of that but dammit, we have a real chance to change the world."

"Shirley, have you given any thought to who I am? We just brokered some peace, but damn. What're you doing on my doorstep?"

"You have your faults, I won't take that away. But even if you're full of every kind of sin and wickedness, you have a skill I need. And since I don't want to go to jail, I need you to take this present off my hands. Since you know how to get rid of presents."

Lester stepped onto his porch. He got close to Shirley.

She moved back.

He shifted forward again and dipped his hand into her top. Felt around back and forth, up and down.

"I'm not wearing a wire."

"Too much terrain in there; I'd never find it. Show me."

Shirley shook her head. Exhaled. "One time." She unbuttoned her blouse and opened the front.

"Everything."

"Really? This is par for the baseball diamond." She removed her top. "Well at least be a gentleman and help me with the clasp."

Lester moved behind her and she felt the elastic go slack. He stepped back in front.

"You never seen a rack like this in your life. I guarantee."

She held her bra in her right hand. Waited for him to adjust his crotch or otherwise signal appreciation.

"Lift 'em."

"Oh, for shit's sake."

"Pick 'em up."

She hefted and he looked underneath each boob. Shook his head and turned away.

"No, that's crap. You help me clasp this thing — or I'll charge admission to the show."

Shirley bounced herself into her bra and turned her back to Lester. He cinched her up.

"Okay. No wire. What's the deal, Shirley? And remember, I'm one of the people who wanted you dead three days ago."

He's trying to scare you off because he's lazy. See the best in him. That's leadership!

Shirley shook her head. "That's before you realized my worth. And same with me for you. We don't have to like each other to use each other. At least tell me that makes sense."

Lester nodded.

"Okay, progress. I have a body in the truck. I don't have a way to deal with it right now, so you need to."

Lester looked into the night.

Shirley turned around and stared with him. Then faced him. "Heard on the radio they dropped the murder charges on you today."

Lester nodded.

"Sure must be nice for you to have a friend who can — "

"One time. I'll help one time. But you need to think about

that nonsense you spouted. You dick with a prosecutor, you'll maybe get away with it once. But the rest you're talking about... How long you think it'll take before it's your body someone's getting rid of?"

"I mixed with you and stayed alive."

Lester chuckled. "I'm nobody. Well, not exactly nobody, but my misdeeds are nothing compared to the people you're crossing swords with. You don't even know who they are."

"Sure I do. I remember every one. Every detail."

"You're not hearing me. You're not pushing around your johns. You're dicking with the people who own them. Every politician is bought. You know that."

"I... guess so."

"I own a handful. Other people own others. Every politician carries water for somebody — that's the job. So when you start pushing around a politician you didn't buy, you're pushing the man who did."

"Or woman. Don't be a pig."

"Sure, women are rotten too."

"So at least we're on the same page there. I get that. But I'm talking about — "

"Shirley. Here's where you need to shut up and listen."

She stood with her mouth open.

"These people will kill you. Not like me. Seems I need a bit of luck to make anything happen, these days. No. These people operate in a different world. They see a shadow and call it by name."

"How's that different from you?"

"If I break rules and get caught, I go down. Same with you. But not them. They write the rules."

"Lester, I hear you. I'm swimming in deep waters. They

might sink me but I'm betting I float. So right now I need your help getting rid of a body wrapped in a shower curtain."

"From a hotel?"

"Uh-huh. Well, a motel."

"Mistake. Everyone knows a missing shower curtain means a body."

48

*V*anko Demyan was visiting his father in Phoenix. His name was Nikita but Vanko had heard his father referred to by nothing other than Old Man Demyan for at least twenty years.

They'd arrived in the United States, Nikita, Vanko and his brother Pavlik, in the late eighties. Old Man took over a failing organization in Phoenix and installed Vanko in Flagstaff and Pavlik in Tucson.

Vanko stood with his arms in the air at the entrance to his father's basement. Old Man wanded him, searching for a wire. The first hundred times he said, "You understand."

No longer.

Vanko understood. He didn't have to turn state's evidence for their conversation to be a threat. With the right warrant, the FBI could break in and plant a listening device. They could also plant one on a person likely to carry the microphone inside.

Finding him clear, Old Man placed his hand on Vanko's elbow, squeezed and smiled.

He led downstairs to a plain room with a polished cement floor, bare plaster walls and a drywall ceiling. The roof had a single light in the center: a yellow bulb with no cover.

Old Man sat on a wooden kitchen chair and Vanko took the one beside it.

"How often do you sweep down here?"

"Any time I leave house. When I kome back, I sveep."

Vanko knew he would someday have to take the same precautions. That day had always seemed far away, but with Ulyana turning on him and Shirley Lyle in cahoots with Lester Toungate, if he judged his success by the size of his problems, it was probably time to take steps toward better security.

"I need a room like this."

"Zat why you kome? Is virrred to block transmitterrrs — in valls. I send you my kontractorrr."

"Send him."

Old Man waited.

"A woman vexes me."

"Ahh."

"The key to controlling her is here."

49

*C*hico descended Kendrick on the same trail he'd climbed. At ten thousand feet a tiny cabin sat off to the left. It contained a bed and a stove that looked to have been fired within the last few days. Chico placed his hand in the ash and smelled, not knowing why he cared. Wind was constant on the false summit. The cabin walls calmed the air and made him feel warmer but without a way to start a fire, he'd freeze nonetheless.

Thin air made it hard to think. Chico sat on a rusted wire and spring bed and observed his breath freeze in a bolt of moonlight.

He could stretch out for a few minutes. The cold wasn't so bad.

Upon leaning to his side he shook from his core — a surprise muscular revolt that bounced him to his feet. Quivering, he rushed from the cabin toward the trail that led down Kendrick Mountain. He scampered with his arms tight to his body, not seeing the trail but sensing it. He kept his footsteps short and close to the ground with his body hunched, ready to catch himself should he stumble.

Between thoughts that told him his situation was serious and could easily kill him, Chico thought of how Elvita was when they met: the flirting, their mutual desire to please the other, forgiving every tiny offense. She never wiped the water off the counter top between the faucet and the splash guard after doing dishes. They behaved as if forging their relationship for the long haul. Getting the foundation right mattered.

They took their time and developed an appreciation for one another's talents before imagining they were in love.

Maybe that was a tiny indication of giving a damn about one person other than himself.

They joined their lives together at the home and shortly after the office. He moved his securities licenses to Elvita's broker dealer and began splitting cases with her. Business boomed.

But it stopped booming, leaving them with all the pressure and none of the success. Clients with good relationships started to disappear because someone was making a better pitch.

Chico and Elvita spent every minute of the waking day in a fighting stance — it was no surprise they eventually fought each other.

But why were so many accounts disappearing? Clients who seemed like pals when the markets were climbing suddenly couldn't find time to take his phone call when the markets were down? That was usually exactly when people *wanted* a phone call.

Maybe he would have seen it coming if he hadn't been spending so much time working on his trading system and trying to figure out how to gather a few million in seed capital.

It was hard to think of anything else. With a system that

would allow him to pull cash out of his computer monitor, it was difficult to think of anything but logistics and tactics. The premise was proven, now he needed capital.

The problem: his system only worked with large numbers. Trades had to be huge because the profit averaged a third of a percent per trade. With a few million for seed money, he'd be printing cash and in no time be managing billions.

Chico was finally at the cusp of having it all.

But...

With money comes worry. The more you have, the more you fear losing. The more energy it takes to manage. The more responsibility to others — if you dare to think you're part of something, rather than aloft. You don't just rule the world and everyone gets along because you've got billions.

Other people have billions, and more experience throwing elbows.

Did he really want to give up the one person who at least used to understand him, to swim with snakes who would as soon destroy him as say hello?

There was no way to put his toe in the water. No way to part-time a hedge fund. If he was in, it would be all in. Not just heart, but soul too.

Chico stumbled on a rock and lurched to his left. The log edging the trail caught his foot and he sprawled over the side, arms flailing as he accelerated into a jagged black and gray chasm. His arm hit a tree — bark scraped his bicep. He folded his elbow and after a jolt the tree swung his body and legs. He dropped to the tree's trunk still clutching it, trembling at the seeming infinite blackness below him.

Standing at the tree and shaking, he listened to rocks crash through brush and leaves below him.

Instinct — throwing out his arms — had saved him.

Chico clawed up fifteen feet of crumbling slope and resumed the trail. Trembling with cold, he walked as close to the right and upward sloping side as possible.

How much of life was stumbling along in darkness, preoccupied, enamored with dreams but only alive because instinct remained grounded?

Chico arrived at a bend he recognized and cut off the trail. Twenty yards back he unzipped his tent and squirmed into his sleeping bag. He squeezed himself fetal and locked his arms around his knees while his body rippled and shook.

50

"*hank you for explaining yourself, Claude. Here's the deal. I want you to move away from Phoenix. With everything you've told me, you'll never work in the money business again. But that's not good enough; I want you to move away so Elvita and me never have to think we're going to run into you shopping at Walmart.*"

"*You're letting me go?*"

"*Of course I'm letting you go. I just wanted the truth. So you agree to leave?*"

"*I agree.*"

"*And all those clients you stole... You'll have no more contact with them. As far as they're concerned, you fell off the face of the earth. Got it?*"

"*I got it! Thank you! I see the error of my ways! I'm a disaster! I'll go to —* "

"*Shut up! Don't tell me. I don't want to know. All right.... That concludes our conversation. You're free to go.*"

. . .

*S*hirley allowed the silence to linger.

Elvita's jaw hung.

"It was never Chico?"

Shirley shook her head.

"But my credit cards. That was Chico, right? How else — "

"No. Claude stole Chico's house key and made a copy. He knew when you were at the office."

"But — "

"He had a girl working with him. Air-Bubbles. She kept an eye on you and Chico at work so he could spend hours going through your finances. He said you were ultra-up tight and super-organized. Separate files for everything, all in alphabetical order, by groups. He took photos of your credit card statements and had Bubbles pretend she was you on the telephone to set up the wires."

"But my pin number? And my passwords? And the other stuff."

"You must not be one hundred percent yet. You keep all that in a book he found in your desk."

"But if he received the money from the wire, how does that frame Chico?

"That's where it gets interesting. Chico and Claude have a joint account."

Elvita's eyes flashed alarm.

"Claude said he opened the account then added Chico to it afterward. Then he deposited the money from the credit card advances, so a prosecutor who thought Chico killed you would see an account with Chico's name and a hundred and sixty grand. After that, he probably wouldn't look into whether the signature that added Chico to the account was a forgery."

"Is the money still there?"

"He said so."

"I can't believe it. Why would somebody do all this?"

"His whole plan was to set up Chico to either catch the blame or become his first big donor when he got back into politics. Chico would readily enough see all the evidence designed to point at him. All Claude would have to do is threaten to tell the police."

Elvita shook her head.

"No... the life insurance. That had to be Chico. How would Claude know I canceled our policies? And how would he pay the premium?"

"Elvita, Dear. Listen. Claude set it up so no matter what happened, it was good for him. He wanted to recruit Chico after you died. Starting the hedge fund was Chico's dream, not Claude's. Claude's ambition was to be in politics."

"But how would he take the two million from the life insurance if Chico used it to start a hedge fund?"

"Claude said Chico really has a gift. He figured out some trading process that would change everything. He called it a black box. You know what that means?"

"In the real world, it's a system where you don't know what happens inside. You judge it by the output. In securities slang, it's a trading system that actually works, so nobody knows how it was designed except the person who made it."

"Oh, I see commercials for those all the time. Trading stocks and options and stuff."

"Those are scams. If they worked, the people who made them would hole up somewhere and make a trillion dollars. They wouldn't sell it on television. Nothing works when everyone does it."

"Oh. Well that's exciting. I mean, if you're into money. I like money."

"So Claude was going to kill me, then show Chico all the evidence against him? Then set him up in his hedge fund and force Chico to cut him in on the profit? What if the police figured out it was poison? Then they'd be looking at Chico anyway and all the big money disappears. No life insurance money and no hedge fund money."

"Maybe, but you were supposed to die on the drive to Flagstaff in a car accident. And the bottom line for Claude was that if Chico went away for murder, he still stole a hundred and sixty thousand plus all your best clients. If Chico didn't go to jail forever, even better, Claude taps into the hedge fund profits too. Either way, you're dead, the clients are his, and Chico's either rotting in jail or paying dividends the rest of his life. Claude set it so he'd either win big or win bigger."

"Except you."

"What do you mean?"

"He didn't count on Shirley Little."

"Shirley Lyle."

"Oh. That sounds better. But wait. How could anyone trust Claude? Chico's the charmer. Claude's a wannabe politician trying to figure out how to get to the next level."

"He said he cut the account fees in half, figuring he'd increase them later when no one was looking. He told them you and Chico were charging too much money, and that he got all his clients out at the top of the market."

"He what? No he didn't." Elvita chewed ice from a Styrofoam cup. "I can't get my head around this. Can I use your phone? I need to call my compliance office. I have to turn in Claude to FINRA. The SEC."

"If I was you, I'd forget about him. Your clients will come back to you."

"Why?"

"Get your man Chico to give them a call."

"I don't even know where he is." Elvita's eyes narrowed. "Wait a minute... What did you do?"

"Me? Nothing at all. Now if you'll excuse me, I'm going to start a business."

"What?"

"Oh yeah! Bras — with gun holsters sewn in. Pants that zip front to back. And baseball caps that pop up like a hood scoop on a hot rod. They're gonna sell like hotcakes."

"You're changing the subject. What did you do to Claude?"

You can't tell her the truth!

Shirley looked at the ceiling. "You heard the recording. I. Let. Him. Go."

She dropped her gaze to Elvita and dragged her chair next to the hospital bed.

"I have a friend I call Sunshine. She turned. Used to be cool as all get-out. Stripper liked to sing in Russian. Then a couple people stuck her in a root cellar for a week and she came out thinking rotten people need love."

"She sounds remarkable."

"Oh, crap. Not you too?"

Elvita stared at the wall. She closed her hand around a clear tube that happened to be next to her fingers.

"I take that back," Shirley said.

"I want away from my life. I want to live where there's no rat race. I want a garden."

"So you can...?"

"I've been stuck in this bed for days and all I keep thinking is that I wouldn't be in this situation if I didn't want so much.

You know, success and money. If I didn't want to be seen in a nice car and living in a perfect house. All that chasing put me next to everybody else chasing the same stuff — and some are willing to kill to get it. I don't want it that much. I don't want to be near people chasing the same stuff I am."

"Let me give you the other side of that."

"What's that?"

"There's nowhere for your garden and everybody has to make a buck. There's no escaping. You got to play — and I'm not talking about you, I'm talking big picture. Us little people have nowhere to go but the regular world."

"Sure. Of course."

"So what I'm saying is there's people out there who make the regular world hell. They lie and cheat. They use their power to hurt people instead of help them."

"That's why I want to get away."

"But everybody can't get away. We have to fix the world we live in. Some people are defective. Flat out broken — they don't want to be good. They're wired wrong. You go to the grocery and buy a can of health food, crack it open and inside it looks like rotten snot and smells like last week's fish. You think, golly, the company that makes these cans wants them all to be good, so now I have to treat this turd dripped out a cadaver like it's snow peas. It doesn't matter if God wanted Claude to be good, he wasn't. I'm not gonna eat a can of snot. I'm gonna kill it. I mean, throw it away."

"We're supposed to love our neighbor."

"Sure, but not your killer."

"Well, yeah, your killer too."

"There's a difference between a person who tries to be good but does a rotten job of it, and a person happy being evil."

"I know. It's just... You can't fight everyone."

"The hell I can't."

Elvita swallowed. She reached for her Styrofoam cup.

"You want more ice, Sweetheart?"

"I think I still have some."

Elvita crunched. "So... about Claude."

Shirley placed her hand on Elvita's wrist. She leaned across the hospital bed and whispered in her ear: "I'll answer for him."

51
<hr>

*C*hico Marín stood at Elvita's door, listening to her tiny sounds: feet on linoleum, whispers as she talked to herself. A cabinet door clicked. He looked down the hallway and a nurse caught his eye. Made him feel like a weirdo, standing outside a woman's room. Like a perv or something.

He cleared his throat and stepped inside. She was on her knees in front of a wardrobe with her back partly exposed by her baby blue hospital gown.

Elvita Marín had a beautiful back.

She stopped and lowered her head..

He heard a sniffle.

His throat was thick. He'd thought of a hundred words on the drive to the hospital. After leaving the woods and getting back to the highway and cell phone reception, he tried calling Elvita's cell. No answer, so he tried the home phone. The office. At last he called Mendi. After receiving a good ass chewing he learned Elvita was about to be released from the hospital.

His foot smashed the accelerator to the floor and in fifteen minutes he squealed tires into the parking lot. He passed a mirrored surface and saw flecks of dried vomit in his hair but if she could forgive — or at least be open to thinking things through and putting their marriage back on the tracks — she ought to be able to get over his camp fire stink and wild man appearance.

"I needed you so much this week, but I thought it was you."

"It is."

"No, that's not what I mean. It wasn't. How did you find me?"

"Mendi."

"Did she tell you everything?"

"You were poisoned."

"Anything else?"

"That's all she said."

"I figured out where all our accounts have been going. I thought you were moving to another company and taking them behind my back."

"What?"

"For your hedge fund."

"That's not how it works."

"I know that. But with some sales talk... Anyway, it wasn't you. That's what I meant."

He stepped closer.

She stood. "You disappeared, and everything happened all at once. Where were you?"

He frowned and lowered his head. "Kendrick."

"And you couldn't tell me?"

"As rough as things have been I didn't think you'd care."

"Did you have any grand revelations up on the mountain? While I was here on the ventilator?"

"I can leave." He coughed. Half-turned. "If you'd rather not have me here."

"No, let's have it out. I want to know."

"Actually I did. It's why I'm here. I don't want it any more. The hedge fund. That life. I've chased it so long I've been blind to everything else, and now that I'm right on the edge I want to quit everything."

"Everything?"

"Everything but you. I don't know how we get there, but if we could go back a few years and start over..."

Elvita sat on the corner of her bed. "Guess I'm not ready to be up very much."

"Can I get something for you?"

"I need a ride. I don't have a car anymore."

"But does that make sense? Everything I've been chasing. Climbing Kendrick made me realize everything I've been working on nonstop — it was all the wrong mountain. I want to be with you. Make a living somewhere simple and be with you."

"When I was at my worst I kept wishing for one more chance — and at the same time I almost hoped I would die so I didn't have to go back to the securities world. I don't want to go back to that business."

"I don't either."

"Want to start over?"

He sat beside her and placed his arm against her lower back.

She leaned to him.

"I want to start over."

52

Shirley drove her rented Dodge RAM without a clear direction in mind. The San Francisco Peaks outside of Flagstaff rose gorgeous and snowy and all the trees had leaves. Maybe she'd go out somewhere in nature and sit with the windows down and enjoy the birds. See some elk.

She wondered about the dog everyone was hunting a couple weeks back — the dog that started everything. Someone probably caught it by now; maybe the killer from North Carolina.

She slowed going into a curve.

"I don't know who I am anymore. Or what I'm doing."

Yes you do. For the first time you do.

Shirley nodded.

Up ahead, a bunch of taillights flashed and she braked. Someone making a left turn — no — it was a cop. She saw revolving lights. A Camaro had been pulled over.

"I can't go around killing people all the time, don't get me wrong, some folks are made for it. But I'm too old to start a new game. I want to find a new trailer and get healthy. You know what?"

What?

"I don't even necessarily want to lose weight. I just want to stop gaining all the time."

You need rest, that's all.

Hearing it made her want to cry. "I know. I'm so tired."

Shirley F'N Lyle, you've earned a nap.

"It's been a whirlwind."

Her phone buzzed and she reached to the passenger seat. Her son Brass's picture came on the screen.

She answered.

"Hey, Baby! I'm glad it's you. What's going on?"

"Mom?"

"What's wrong?"

"Mom, I'm okay."

"BRASS?"

A click came through the speaker, then another male voice. "Shirley Lyle. Zis is Demyan."

"Vanko?"

"Nyet. His father."

"Why is my son with you?"

"Bekause I about to kill him forrr sins of mother of him. You must kome see me. Da?"

A WORD FROM CLAYTON

Thank you for reading Shirley F'N Lyle: ONE at a TIME, BOYS. While I'm hard at work documenting Shirley's mad race to Phoenix and the ensuing destruction in book 3, TOTALLY SUNSHINE AND LOVE, may I suggest another title to hold you over?

Shirley had a life before VIVA the REVOLUTION...

She first appeared, and the idea of VIVA was borne, in the fourth novel of the Baer Creighton series, The OUTLAW STINKY JOE. While it is part of a series, the book isn't difficult to read as a standalone.

Many of the folks who read the Baer Creighton Series tell me it is nothing like what they usually read, but they love it. If you're in the mood for something new while you wait on the next Shirley Lyle novel, consider it a prequel!

Baer Creighton Book 1: MY BROTHER'S DESTROYER.

Ever since his brother electrocuted him as a boy, Baer Creighton feels an electric tingle when people lie to him. He lives in the woods, stills unrivaled moonshine, and limits human contact to regular buyers, his niece Mae, and her three kids. It's a good life, sharing humor and philosophy with his sole companion Fred, a back-sassin pit bull getting on in years.

Until Fred goes missing, then arrives dumped in a ditch, a victim of a local dog fighting ring.

Armed with a Smith & Wesson, audacity, and a moonshiner's know-how, Baer hunts the dog thief.

Was it Cory Smylie, pothead son of the Gleason police chief —who resented Baer for making him treat Mae right?

Or Baer's brother Larry, whose real feud with Baer started not with the prank electrocution, but back thirty years, to when Baer stole Ruth and Larry stole her back?

Maybe it was Joe Stipe, or one of those lugnuts he kept at his side like a private Secret Service? Stipe ran the dogfights, exerted a heavy influence on every form of backwoods commerce, and a couple years ago tried to muscle Baer out of his stillin operation.

Convinced justice must be proportional, Baer seeks the truth. But he tips his hand and begins a war of attrition against a cabal steeped in blood sport and thirsty for violence...

With his niece in danger, the ex-love of his life Ruth missing —either dead or plotting against him—and all the town's finest trying to burn him down or shoot him on sight, Baer vows to bring a reckoning to every man present at the fight ring.

Though vengeance doesn't come easy for Baer Creighton...

It comes.

And when you discover who stole Fred, you'll know you've found a new master of the dark surreal.

Buy My Brother's Destroyer

Book 2: *THE MUNDANE WORK OF VENGEANCE.*

Six days before Baer Creighton cut down a cabal of dogfighters, a sixteen-year-old girl disappeared while walking home from school in Asheville, North Carolina. Witnesses later claimed they saw her in the back of a police car.

Twenty-five years before that, an illegal fireworks plant blew up in Benton Tennessee, killing eleven, and raining M100 fire-crackers over half a county. A few days later, a thirteen-year-old boy learned his highest calling was murder.

The Mundane Work of Vengeance begins where My Brother's Destroyer ends: Baer Creighton taking buckets of gold to Mae, dreaming of driving west.

But Baer has no idea the treachery, blood, and misery in store. At his lowest with no one to trust, he'll have to decide whether to save a family who betrays him—or a kidnapped girl buried in a basement, a half state away.

If he can save anyone at all.

Buy THE MUNDANE WORK OF VENGEANCE

Book 3: *PRETTY LIKE AN UGLY GIRL*

Luke Graves turned the family butcher business into an empire by cutting fat off the ledger as well as he cut meat off the bone.

He also learned many men sold beef, but few sold girls and

boys. Demand was high—especially for the ones with brown skin—and supply, small.

Ten years later the family business included three sons and a distribution chain that delivered kids for any purpose throughout the western United States.

One evening, returning to Williams, Arizona from a pickup in Sierra Vista, the tire blows out. A chavo bolts the truck and runs for the plain. Cephus Graves takes him down with a deer rifle, then fires at a stray pit bull that catches his eye.

In the woods two hundred yards away, Baer Creighton looks up from his fire. He has a nose for evil men and he's found a clan of them. But he's met his match in Luke Graves.

Baer bleeds in Pretty Like an Ugly Girl.

Everyone bleeds.

Buy PRETTY LIKE AN UGLY GIRL

Book 4: THE OUTLAW STINKY JOE (April 2019)

Stinky Joe survives the wild Flagstaff winter alone.

But with first melt, he succumbs to warm broth and sleeping pills, placed at the doorstep of a scheming prostitute at the vortex of a politician looking for an issue, a money-launderer wielding leverage, and his 83-year-old meth-dealing target.

Stinky Joe learned as a pup: don't ever bite a man. He'll beat you near death. But cornered in a bath tub by a pothead with a gun, Joe goes outlaw.

Within hours the best and worst of Flagstaff are mobile. Sheriff's deputies, the meth dealer and his tracking dog, news crews, and Baer Creighton—with the FBI after him, seeking vengeance for yet another agent down.

Joe has survived the wild, but civilized man is a different kind of devil.

Wounded, hunted, and holed up, there's no way out for The Outlaw Stinky Joe.

Buy THE OUTLAW STINKY JOE

GRAB A FREE EBOOK FOR YOUR GRIT LIT LIBRARY

Building a relationship with my readers is the very best thing about writing. If you enjoyed this book and would like to know about upcoming releases of Baer Creighton, Solomon Bull, or Shirley Lyle books, join my email list. You'll get maybe two or three emails a year. I hate spam. Won't ever do it. If you get an email from me, it'll be worth reading.

Join the email list and you'll get a free download of SOME-TIMES BONE.

If you like to jaw with other grit lit readers, get book recommendations for awesome authors, ask me questions, or get an occasional advance review copy of a new release, join my Facebook group, the RED MEAT LIT STREET TEAM.

There you have it. Grab a free book, stay up to speed, and connect with some awesome like-minded readers.

CLICK HERE for SOMETIMES BONE

CLICK HERE for THE RED MEAT LIT STREET TEAM

ADDITIONAL NOVELS BY CLAYTON LINDEMUTH

Tread

Hunted by the FBI and a recently released death row inmate, secessionist Nat Cinder brings down the governor of Arizona.

Buy Tread

Sometimes Bone

Set in 1917, Grace Hardgrave leaves the streets of New York to face the predator who made her life go wrong, and learns everyone has a secret, an angle, and a reason to kill.

Buy Sometimes Bone or Grab it Free Here!

Nothing Save the Bones Inside Her

Grace Hardgrave's nephew Angus Hardgrave has grown up, leaving three dead wives buried under the walnut on Devil's Elbow. The fourth won't be as easy.

Buy Nothing Save the Bones Inside Her

Strong at the Broken Places

Nick Fister is the winningest ultra-distance runner in history. He runs the last race of his career, the brutal Badwater

135, while fending off a murder investigation and an upstart rival trying to take down the champion.

Buy Strong at the Broken Places

Solomon Bull

SOLOMON BULL is the son of a rebel who died in the eighties fighting for the American Indian Movement. He trains for an Arizona race called Desert Dog, designed to shred a man, while using monkey wrench tactics to unseat a corrupt senator.

Buy Solomon Bull

Cold Quiet Country

Gale G'Wain is alone and close to dead. He's holed up in an empty farmhouse, half-dressed and nearly dead after falling through lake ice. Innocent, but unlikely to ever stand trial in a town as corrupt as Bittersmith, he loads his gun and prepares to defend himself against a dead man's bloodthirsty sons and the Sheriff's Department.

ABOUT THE AUTHOR

Howdy. I appreciate you reading my books—more than you can know. If you've read this far, (not only the third book in the series, but the stuff at the back of the book as well), you and I are fellow travelers. I suspect you sense something is not quite right with the world. It's not as good as it's supposed to be. We human beings aren't as good as our ideals. Yet, we prize and want to fight for them.

I do my absolute best to write stories that portray the human situation with brutal transparency, but also I strive to tell stories that are not as bleak as the human condition sometimes seems. There's no limit to the darkness. Light is rare. But it exists, and I hope when you complete one of my novels, you find your values validated. I hope I encourage you to fight the good fight, just as you encourage me when you buy my books, review them, and join my Facebook group, the Red Meat Lit Street Team. Y'all are an awesome community. It's good that we're in this fight together, and I'm grateful you're out there. Thank you.

Remember, light wins in the end.